WARRIOR'S VEIL

W.L. BACH

ENDURE ALL PUBLISHING

ISBN Print 979-8-9879630-6-7

ISBN ebook 979-8-9879630-7-4

Book cover design by Getcovers at https://getcovers.com/

Printed in the United States of America

DEDICATION

Dedicated to those veterans who carry the invisible wounds of war.
May we all share in making their load lighter

1

April 2004, Iraq

Jake looked to the east and saw dozens of helicopters heading his way, like a flock of black locusts ready to devour anything in their path. He had been deployed to Iraq now for a little over a month and it was his first combat tour after training with the Marines at Camp Pendleton for over a year. He was now a fully trained Fleet Marine Force Navy Corpsman assigned to a Marine infantry company that was part of the 1st battalion, 5th Marines. Shortly after their arrival in Iraq, Jake and his fellow Marines had witnessed the brutal killing of four American military contractors from the private security firm Blackwater, and their subsequent hanging, like pieces of meat, in the town square. The US contractors had been killed in March 2004 and now the US military was out for revenge. Several thousand US Army soldiers and Marines were on the cusp of executing Operation Vigilant Resolve, a large-scale military operation to root out insurgents in Fallujah, the hotbed of the Sunni insurgency, as well as punish the perpetrators of the death and torture of the Americans. Fallujah was also the home turf for former Bath party members loyal to Sadam Hussein. Jake and his platoon knew that they were in for some hot action.

In early April, Jake and his squadmates rolled out of Baghdad in armored Humvees on the way to the village of Fallujah, just west of Baghdad. They moved in a large column surrounded by their company, and the rest of the 1st battalion. Jake's squad of thirteen was led by Staff Sergeant Crawford. Jake was the sole Navy corpsman in the squad. The battalion had been assigned a sector of Fallujah to attack and Crawford's squad had been assigned two buildings in the sector on the eastern side of Fallujah. The small, dense city was tightly packed with narrow, twisty streets and firing positions for the enemy on virtually every avenue of approach. The ISIS and Al Qaeda insurgents holed up in Fallujah were among the most deadly and ruthless terrorists faced by the US-led coalition forces in Iraq. It was the enemy's home, and they wouldn't give it up easily.

As they approached the city, Jake's squad broke off from the large column, and drove slightly north on the approach to their target buildings. Staff Sergeant Crawford directed his four Humvees to circle up behind a knoll about fifty yards from the outskirts of Fallujah, close to their intended target buildings. Crawford passed his orders over the radio and the thirteen men dismounted together as a squad, and patrolled into the eerily quiet city. The insurgents allowed the invaders to enter the city so they could trap them in the convoluted and narrow streets of Fallujah, which favored the home team.

Jake and the other twelve members of his squad entered into the first floor of the building that was their initial objective. It was a three-story brick structure with a flat roof, and they cleared the first floor and found it empty. Crawford then broke his squad into three fire teams. He ordered Jake's fire team, led by Corporal Martinez to clear the 2nd and 3rd stories of the building they were in. Crawford would take the second fire team and clear the building next door, their second objective, while the 3rd fire team would stand by as a quick reaction force if either of the other two teams needed help.

Sergeant Martinez was the leader for Jake's squad of four. He'd grown up in El Paso, was on his second tour to Iraq and was known as a tough, no-nonsense Marine. The other two in the fire team with Martinez and Jake were Davis and Tony Luongo, Jake's best friend. Luongo had grown up in Hawaii, and like Jake, had been a surfer before joining the military. The two became instant friends when they were assigned to the same company in 1st Battalion. They'd even rented an apartment together outside Camp Pendleton near the beach, where they surfed when they weren't training. Luongo was part Hawaiian, and he was bigger than Jake, just north of six-foot-two with big shoulders, a broad back and large legs with calves like melons. He had that easy-going way of many Hawaiians, and made friends with everybody.

Davis was a skinny black kid from Atlanta who was a natural leader. He organized the best poker games in the platoon and also the best parties. He was known as the comedian in the squad, keeping everything light for the guys, no matter how hard things got.

Martinez organized his fire team into a stack and together they moved quietly up the stairwell to the second floor of the target building. As usual, Davis led the way as point man, followed by Martinez, Jake and finally Tony. They heard footsteps above them and knew there was someone on the second floor likely to give them a less than pleasant welcome. Just as Davis reached the top of the stairs, a hail of bullets ripped through the door above him and the three Marines and Jake jumped down to their knees on the stairs.

Davis looked back at his teammates with a smile, "Hey, these motherfuckers are serious, I almost got another ear piercing!"

"Use a grenade," whispered Martinez.

Davis nodded, pulled a fragmentation grenade off his vest, and while laying down at the bottom of the door, pulled the pin, pushed the door open slightly and tossed the grenade into the back of the room. A loud explosion was followed by a scream. The Marines and Jake were quickly up on their feet, rushing into the room, which was full of dust and smoke. Davis and Martinez took the left side and Jake and Luongo moved down the right wall to the back corner. The two teams cleared every piece of furniture, entry point, window or potential hiding place they came across. At the back of the room, Luongo found one fighter who looked to be about 25 years old with an AK-47 at his feet. He was leaning against the wall with his hands across his stomach. The grenade shrapnel had sliced him open, and his intestines were spilling out the front of his shirt. Jake kicked the weapon out of the way, then did what he could for the poor man, giving him some painkillers and wrapping his stomach in a large bandage.

Now that the dust had settled, the men could see that the room, or what was left of it after the blast, contained several beds, a bookcase, a teapot, and several boxes of ammunition in the corner. It looked like it had once been a bedroom, but had been taken over by fighters and used as ammunition storage.

"Guys, we gotta take the third floor, too," said Martinez to his men, as Jake worked the bandage around the dying militant.

Davis and Luongo were both drinking out of their canteens as Jake finished helping the wounded man. "Alright, we got one more room to hit," ordered Martinez, "Let's finish the job." The three Marines and one corpsman moved to the next flight of stairs and lined up against the wall as they prepared to assault the third floor.

Davis walked to the bottom of the stairs and the other three got ready behind him, checking their weapons. "Hey, lemme go in front of you," said Tony, tapping Jake on the shoulder. "We can't afford to have the corpsman injured." He smiled and winked at his buddy. Jake always took the third place in the line of four because Tony was so big, Jake had a hard time seeing around him. Jake acquiesced and let Luongo move in front of him, leaving Jake last in the line.

"Alright, move out," Martinez ordered, and the four started walking carefully up the stairs to the third floor entrance, rifles at the ready. They all knew that the element of surprise was lost now. Whoever was on the third floor knew they were coming and would be prepared.

At the top of the stairs, Davis knelt down, looked back at the team and Martinez gave him a nod. Davis took a big breath, crossed himself, then kicked in the door and rushed into the room. Martinez followed on his heels while Luongo and Jake brought up the rear. After a few tense moments, the men realized the room was empty. There was a dirty rug in the middle of the floor, battered furniture along the walls and to their surprise, a baby lying on a pile of rags in the far corner of the room.

"What the hell?!" exclaimed Davis, kneeling over the baby. "Who leaves a kid in a place like this?" As the other three finished clearing the room, they moved to the corner where Davis was reaching down to pick up the baby. As he lifted the child off the floor, a thin wire attached to the back of the baby's diaper unleashed the detonator on an improvised explosive device hidden below.

The blast of the half pound block of SEMTEX explosive was thunderous, sending splinters and shrapnel across the room like a thousand knives shot out of a cannon. Davis was killed instantly as he took the brunt of the blast, which tore his torso nearly in half. Martinez, standing beside him, had a large piece of shrapnel lodged in his throat and was lying on the ground, gurgling, blood pouring from his throat. Luongo had taken a piece of shrapnel in his waist, just below his body armor. He was knocked against the back wall, blood pooling between his legs.

Jake had been behind Tony when the blast occurred and took the least damage. Thrown to his back, he felt several small pieces of shrapnel in his legs, but nothing too deep. There was a large piece of metal sticking out of his chest, but he quickly realized it was embedded in his body armor and hadn't penetrated his skin.

He stood up and surveyed the ghastly scene before him. There was a huge hole in the floor where the baby had once been. The room was filled with the acrid smoke of explosives, dust clogged the air and the two windows in the room were blown out.

Jake's job was to save Marines, but he quickly assessed he could only save one. Davis was dead, and blood was spurting out of Martinez so fast that he would be gone in a few seconds. Luongo, leaning against the wall with a wound near his groin, was the only one Jake could possibly save. He jumped into action.

He pulled off his small backpack containing his medical kit and tossed it on the dusty floor next to Luongo. He bent down and slipped Luongo's body armor off, tossing it to the side. He fished a pair of medical scissors from his backpack and was starting to cut away portions of Tony's pants when he heard footsteps to his right. He grabbed his M4 off the floor and flicked the selector switch to full automatic. Two insurgents stepped into the room from the stairway, but did not immediately see Jake in the corner behind an overturned table. Jake peered at the men from a crack in the table and saw that they were both carrying AK-47's and were starting to search the room. He gritted his teeth then stood up behind the table and sprayed both men with a hail of .556 automatic weapons' fire, dumping half his 30-round magazine into them. Both crumpled in place before even getting off a shot.

Jake turned back to Tony, who was still slumped against the wall. The sharp chemical smell of gunpowder and explosives filled the air. "Hey, buddy, I've got you," he said, trying to comfort his friend, who was breathing in and out rapidly. Jake was shocked at the amount of blood that was pooling next to Tony's leg, but his training kicked in and he grabbed a small clamp from his kit; somewhere the shrapnel had nicked an artery and Jake needed to stop the bleeding.

"This is gonna hurt, man!" Jake yelled, as if he was the one to feel the pain, sticking his fingers in the hole in Tony's waist and trying to find the source of the bleeding. Tony screamed and bit his lip, blood spilling from his mouth. The wound was jagged and slick with blood as Jake dug and twisted his fingers into the gash, trying to find the exact source of the blood loss. "Shit!'" he yelled, fear rising in his throat as if he'd just been bitten by a deadly snake.

He bore into the wound once again, but this time Tony was quiet. Jake thought he felt a vein pulsing blood deep in the hole and jammed the clamp into the wound with one hand while trying to find the leak with his other fingers.

Tony was sweating profusely and his head drooped forward. He lifted it and spoke to Jake in a hushed voice. "Tell.. my mother.. that

I love her." He struggled to get each word out, then nodded slowly to Jake, his eyes now reflecting his understanding that he was not going to make it.

Jake felt like he was skydiving without a parachute, his mind ready to explode. His best friend, his battle buddy, was slipping away, and he couldn't stop it. "NO! You're gonna make it, Tony!" he yelled. The big Hawaiian reached his hand over slowly and laid it on Jake's forearm. Jake looked his friend in the eye, tears streaming down both their faces. Tony nodded, knowing it was over now, closed his eyes and let his head fall back against the wall. He was gone. Jake sat there frozen, blood dripping off his arms, his hands still covering Tony's wound.

That's how the second fire team found Jake 20 minutes later when they moved up the stairs on Crawford's orders to check on Martinez's fire team. "Hey, we've gotta get you outta here," a big Marine said, slowly lifting Jake off of Luongo.

2

OCTOBER 2022, MONTROSE COLORADO

Jake sat under a tall pine tree in Cerise Park, to the west of the prosperous ranching and farming town of Montrose, Colorado. The large tree blocked out the sun on the warm fall day, where even the birds were too lazy to fly. He reached for the large bottle of Michelob next to his leg and took a drag of the tepid beer as he peered through the trees and watched a group of boys in the distance playing soccer on the field. A tattered military poncho on the ground next to him had made a suitable bed in the soft pine needles last night. He pulled up his pant leg and scratched at a red mark where a bug had chewed on his ankle. He was watching a squirrel in the tree above him jump from branch to branch chirping like a bird when a soccer ball came bouncing towards him from the treeline. A tall, skinny teenage boy who looked to be about seventeen came running through the trees and stopped in his tracks when he saw the ball laying 10 feet away from the homeless man under the tree.

The kid crept up on the ball, keeping an eye on Jake like he was trying to swipe an egg from a snake's nest. Jake said nothing as the young man snatched the ball and jumped back. "Why don't you get the hell outta here? We don't need bums in the park," the kid said in a high, nasal voice. Jake looked up. The boy was pale with dark wavy hair and purple acne scars pockmarking his face, and he was wearing expensive-looking white Nike shoes.

Jake said nothing and returned to watching the squirrel above him collect food for the winter. The kid picked up a pine cone and threw it at Jake, hitting him in the jaw, before he ran back to the soccer field with his ball in hand.

Jake reached up and felt the welt where the hard cone had popped him in the face, anger simmering under the surface. Below his scraggly beard he felt a small trickle of blood. He took another long pull on the bottle, drained it and tossed the bottle to the ground next to the tree. The afternoon sun broke through the branches above, shining a spotlight of warmth on Jake. He tried to fight off the sleepiness that hung behind his eyes like an anchor. For most people, sleep was rest, but for Jake, sleep brought nightmares, and the nightmares brought bloody visions of Iraq and a struggle with the past, with things he couldn't change, events that haunted him. Sometimes the alcohol let him sleep without the nightmares, but not always. His eyes felt like lead and eventually he fell asleep against the tree trunk.

Jake awoke to an intense pain in his thigh. He opened his eyes and saw two figures standing over him wielding long sticks. A blow bashed his ribs and he felt a crack in his chest. He tried to stand up but someone had lashed him to the tree with a rope while he'd been sleeping against it. He was fully awake now as the pain surged through his body and the blows rained down. He saw now that the kid with the soccer ball and another young man with tattoos on his neck were both swinging sticks as they cursed and laughed.

"Find some other place to hang out, you creep!" yelled the guy with the neck tattoos, swinging the stick over his head and landing it on Jake's shin, shooting a spike of pain up his leg. Jake wriggled and pulled his arms free of the rope, allowing him to block the blows with his hands. The soccer kid swung the stick like a baseball bat, aiming for Jake's head. Jake reached up and caught the stick mid-air, but the impact smashed his palm and bent his wrist back. That gave the other young man a chance to swing and hit Jake in the head. The whack across his skull was a blinding flash of pain, and made a gash that caused blood to pour down his face.

Jake tried to get to his knees, but the loose rope around his body wouldn't let him. Suddenly a voice yelled out of the trees behind him, "What's going on here? Get away from him. Get outta here!" A short man walking a three-legged Pit Bull came into Jake's view. The two assailants looked at the short man and his dog, dropped their sticks and ran off.

The man approached Jake and stooped down to look him over. He appeared to be in his forties and had dark eyes, a sharp chin and a small mouth. He wore a scally cap and big horn-rimmed glasses. "Hey buddy, you alright?" he asked in a Boston accent. Jake nodded, blood dripping down his face from the cut on his head. "Hang on, I'm gonna call 911." He pulled out a cell phone, punched in 911, and gave the operator the location. "Yeah, he's hurt pretty bad," he told the operator. The sky turned dark and Jake passed out.

Jake awoke to someone shaking his shoulder. "Wake up, we're gonna get you outta here." Jake opened one eye crusted with dried blood to see a female police officer kneeling next to him and unwrapping the rope from around his body. The man and his dog, who were standing behind her, watched Jake with curiosity. The officer had jet black hair pulled into a bun behind her head and she wore the uniform of the Montrose Police Department. Her skin was as white as Ivory soap and her deep blue eyes stared at him with concern. Jake tried to open his other eye but it was swollen shut. The officer kneeled beside him, checking his pulse. With his good eye, Jake read her name tag: *Officer Livingston*.

"EMTs are on the way. This gentleman called 911," she explained, pointing to the guy and his dog. "I was close by and responded. He said some men were attacking you with sticks?" she asked, looking over her shoulder at the man and his dog. "Can you tell me anything else about them?"

"The older one was late twenties, demon tats on his neck, a small mustache, sandy hair," Jake croaked slowly. "The younger one was maybe seventeen, black hair, pale skin, acne, tall, wearing expensive sneakers."

Officer Livingston took notes, stood up and looked around. Seeing the camouflage poncho on the ground and the olive drab backpack, she accurately pegged Jake for a homeless veteran. There was no tent or any trash strewn around except for one beer bottle beside the tree. "Is there anything else you can tell me about the attack?" she asked Jake.

"The kid was playing soccer earlier, came through the trees to get his ball, saw me and wasn't too happy," Jake said before coughing and groaning at the pain in his ribs.

"What do you mean he wasn't happy?" she asked, as the ambulance pulled into the parking lot, sirens filling the air like the wailing of a wounded animal.

"He told me to get the hell out of here, that I don't belong, then he threw a pine cone that hit me in the face," Jake said, reaching for the sore under his beard. "I guess he came back later with the other guy to finish the job."

"Jeez," said Officer Livingston, shaking her head as she looked at Jake's swollen eye, the gash on his head and the dried blood all over his face. "This is not how we treat people in Montrose. Are you a veteran?" she asked.

"Yeah," he replied, almost reluctantly. She looked like she was going to ask more, but saw him turn his face away like he didn't want to talk about it.

Just then the EMTs rushed out of the treeline carrying a stretcher. Officer Livingston stepped back as they started a triage on Jake, checking his vitals and helping him lay down on the stretcher. One of them was huge with a crew cut and muscles bulging from his EMT jumpsuit. The other guy was wiry, short and stocky.

"You need anything from me, Cummings?" Officer Livingston asked the big one. She'd worked with him on several crash scenes but didn't know the smaller man.

"No, we'll take it from here. Thanks, Officer Livingston," Cummings said. Hannah nodded, then returned to the man who had called 911. "Can I get your name and contact info, sir?" she asked, pulling out her small notebook.

"Why do you need that?" he asked, puffing up his chest.

"In case we need to follow up with any further questions," she lowered her voice, trying to calm him down.

"Ardon Donnelly," he said reluctantly, as his dog sniffed Hannah's shoes.

"Thanks for intervening, sir, your dog probably scared the attackers off."

"Yeah," he agreed, looking down at his dog. "So I guess it's a good thing they didn't know Daisy's sweet as puddin." The three-legged Pit Bull didn't seem bothered by her disability and moved around with grace. "These punks in the pawk," he said. "They got no respect."

Hannah nodded as she pulled a pen and pad from her belt. She too had noticed the uptick in crime the last few years, most of it related to drugs. Worst of all, there was more violent crime than when she had joined the force a few years ago. She wrote down Donnelly's name and cell number. He nodded respectfully to her, took one last look at Jake and he and Daisy walked back into the park.

The EMTs completed their initial assessment, lifted the stretcher together gently and carried Jake to the ambulance parked in the grass just outside the treeline, across from the soccer field. Hannah followed them to the ambulance, then sat in her car and typed out her draft report on a laptop. The EMTs helped Jake inside the back of the ambulance and strapped him down to one of the beds. One stayed with Jake while the other jumped in the cab and sped off to the Montrose Hospital, lights and sirens blazing. In a matter of minutes, Jake was delivered to the Montrose Hospital emergency room where two ER nurses helped unload and escort him inside to a curtained triage room.

"I'm OK, I just need to get my stuff from the park," Jake said to the young nurse who was starting an IV drip on his arm. Her blonde hair was tied in a loose ponytail and she wore a thin gold chain around her neck.

"We just need to make sure you don't have a concussion," she said soothingly. "We'll get you out of here as soon as possible."

While she placed a blood pressure monitor on his arm, Jake looked around at the array of medical equipment. Before he'd been trained to work with the Marines in the field as a corpsman in the Navy, he'd completed part of his initial training at the Balboa Naval Hospital in San Diego. He recognized all of the medical equipment, noting that it had become more high tech since he had seen it last.

"Your blood pressure is a little high, but that's to be expected," the nurse said, pointing to the digital screen next to his bed. A small sensor on his finger relayed his pulse and oxygen level to the screen. "Someone will be in to take your personal information," she said before stepping out of the room.

Alone now, the bruise on his head swelling, the white wall of curtains began to close in on Jake. All the medical equipment, the IV's and sensors attached to his body, the beeps and bongs, the smell of the hospital and the site of blood on his bandage triggered a flashback. Staff Sergeant Crawford had assigned Jake to a makeshift field hospital in Fallujah, which was set up to treat Marines injured in combat before their evacuation to a hospital. Crawford thought that Jake needed a short break from direct combat after the loss of his entire fire team and his friend, Luongo. Little did Crawford know at the time that he was exposing Jake to even worse stress—an endless parade of injured and dying Marines and civilians that Jake had to either try to save or watch die amid a cacophony of screams and the boom of rocket-propelled grenades landing nearby.

Now here in the ER, Jake's mind tripped off-line and took him back to that bloody triage tent. He was trying to save the life of a young Iraqi boy who had lost his leg when he stepped on a roadside bomb set by the insurgents in Fallujah. The boy's father had scooped him up and carried him to the impromptu medical ER in the basement of a nearby bombed out building. A Marine guarding the entrance had refused to let the man in, but Jake looked up from securing a sling on a young Marine who had been shot in the shoulder to see the father push past the guard into the room, the boy in his arms and blood spewing from the child where his lower leg was missing.

"Bring a tourniquet!" Jake yelled at the other young corpsman who was attending to a Marine who had lost an eye. Jake grabbed the boy from his father and laid him on the operating table. He reached to stop the bleeding by squeezing the wound with his hands while waiting for the tourniquet. He looked down, saw the blood streaming through his fingers, and thought instantly of Luongo. He squeezed the boy's leg with all his strength and let out a roar. The Marine guard and the other corpsman looked at each other, dropped what they were doing and rushed to Jake's side.

The blonde nurse from the Montrose ER heard a commotion and rushed into the triage room. She found Jake standing next to the hospital bed, his IV and sensors torn off, his eyes ablaze with panic. He turned and yelled at her, "Where's that tourniquet!" then turned back to work on some invisible patient on the bed, squeezing a pillow as if to stop a wound from bleeding. The nurse froze, unsure what to do. She stepped quickly outside the curtains, punched an emergency button on the wall then hurried back into the room.

In less than a minute, a doctor and another nurse came running into the room. To their surprise, the blonde nurse was helping the patient install a tourniquet on a corner of a pillow. The doctor put his hands on Jake's shoulders and spoke gently to him, "It's OK, we'll take it from here." Jake looked up, turned to the doctor, bowed his head and a stream of tears fell onto the pillow.

"Hey, it's gonna be OK," the blonde nurse said calmly, putting her hand on Jake's shoulder as the three of them gently laid him back on the bed and reattached his monitors and IV.

After settling Jake and reattaching his sensors, the trio stepped outside the curtain. "What the heck was that?" the nurse asked the other two. "Schizophrenia, flashbacks, drug-induced paranoia? I've never seen anything like that."

"Remember he took a whack to the head. That could have had something to do with it, too," the doctor said. "We need to do a full body CT scan. One of you add a light sedative to his IV drip. I'm going to set up the CT scan," the doctor directed, heading off. The nurses nodded and returned to Jake's bedside. The blonde nurse asked, "How're you doin', Mr. Hanlon?" while the other one attended to the IV drip. adding the sedative.

"I'm fine, I'm ready to get outta here," Jake said.

"I understand. But first we'd like to run a few tests on you, make sure nothing is broken, OK? Then we can talk about your release. How's that sound?"

"Sure, I understand," Jake nodded with a sigh as he let his head fall back on the pillow, closed his eyes and tried to hold off sleep again.

3

OCTOBER 2022, MONTROSE COLORADO

Later that evening, Jake awoke with a start in his hospital bed. Officer Livingston was standing in the doorway. He blinked and asked groggily, "What're you doing here?" as he sat up and rubbed his eyes. Something had knocked him out pretty good after the CT scan.

"I brought your backpack. The EMT's accidentally left it in the park, so I grabbed it for you. It's in the back of my cruiser in the parking lot."

"Thanks, Officer Livingston," Jake said. "I was wondering where my gear was."

"Call me Hannah," she said, noticing that he used the term 'gear' for his stuff, like so many military personnel.

"OK, thanks, Hannah." He attempted a smile.

"What's your plan after you get out of here?" Hannah asked, stepping into the room and sitting down in a chair along the wall. She'd already spoken with the doctor and found out he had two bruised ribs, a banged up shin, a sprained wrist, a gash on his head and a concussion. The doctor also told her that the CT scan revealed what looked like previous brain trauma. When the doctor added that Jake had experienced a type of realistic flashback, she'd shown no emotion.

The hospital couldn't keep him indefinitely, so the doctor planned to let him go at 6 p.m. Hannah figured he was homeless, but didn't want to assume anything.

She'd been a military police officer in the Army and had been stationed in Iraq for a year. She had a hunch Jake was an Iraq vet too, even though he hadn't spoken about it. She'd made some bad choices in her life that she wasn't proud of, and she was always looking for a way to make things right. This guy looked like he could use some help, so she decided to see what she could do, maybe add a small weight to counterbalance the scale, where one side was weighed down with the guilt and shame that seethed below the surface of her life.

"I don't really have a plan right now," Jake said, taking a sip of water from the cup on the table next to his bed.

"Well, they opened a new veteran's shelter in town. I stopped by on the way here and they have a bed for you tonight," Hannah said, sitting forward expectantly in her chair.

Jake wanted to say, "Wow! You did that for me?" but he remained silent. It had been so long since someone had done anything nice for him that he'd forgotten how to react. He certainly didn't expect kindness from this police officer. He figured she was here to ask more questions about the attack.

"Yeah, sure, I'd like that," he said haltingly.

"OK," Hannah said, standing up. "I'm gonna check on your discharge paperwork, so I'll be back."

Ten minutes later, Hannah returned with the blonde nurse, who had some papers on a clipboard. "Mr. Hanlon, we're going to let you go tonight. You're banged up pretty good, but the doctor said it's safe to release you." Jake nodded. The nurse handed him the clipboard and pointed out the places Jake needed to sign. He came to the question about his health insurance provider and looked up at the nurse, the pen hovering over the board.

"It's OK if you don't have insurance, Mr. Hanlon, just write *none* in the box." Jake scratched in the word and handed the clipboard back to the nurse.

"Don't you have a VA rating and insurance?" Hannah interjected. She knew that if he was a veteran, he would be covered by the VA for any service-connected disabilities. Jake shook his head and handed the pen back to the nurse.

The two women left the room so Jake could remove his hospital gown and dress in his own clothes. When he finished, he stepped gingerly outside the curtains. His bruised ribs made breathing painful so he walked like he was on eggshells. His head still rang like a bell.

Hannah led him out of the ER to the front entrance where her Ford SUV police cruiser sat parked against the curb. It was seven o'clock at night and she hadn't had anything to eat since lunch. "Are you hungry?" she asked, as he stood beside her car.

"Yeah, I could eat something."

"Good, because I'm starving," she said, remembering that the hospital had a cafe with decent food. "Let's see what's on the menu here," she said, leading Jake back into the hospital and to the cafe in the basement. The place was empty except for a young cashier who was admiring her long fingernails and an elderly matron behind the buffet line, stirring the food with a big metal spoon. Hannah led Jake to the start of the buffet line, where they picked up trays and slid down the line to where the woman served up large helpings of turkey, gravy, green beans and stuffing. They both got drinks and Hannah pointed with her chin to a table in the corner of the room, where they sat down to eat.

Hannah studied Jake as he gobbled up the turkey dinner. He was about 6 feet tall with golden brown eyes, tangled brown hair and a jagged scar on his cheek. Most of his face was hidden underneath a scraggly beard that looked like a couple of mice lived in it. He ate slowly, occasionally looking up at her as he shoveled forkfuls of turkey and dressing into his mouth. His shoulders were broad and his bare forearms were wiry and tough like oak tree branches.

"So, where are you from?" Hannah asked hesitantly, sipping her iced tea.

Jake paused and looked at her. "I grew up in San Diego."

She was almost afraid to ask the next question, because she didn't want to sound like an interrogator. "And what brings you to Montrose?"

Jake hesitated, then spoke softly, "I was trying to get out of California. I took a bus to Grand Junction and got a hitch to Montrose. Someone in Grand Junction told me Montrose was a veteran-friendly town," Jake replied. He wasn't going to tell her the real reason he was here.

"I'm a vet, too, and I'd say this town is pretty friendly to veterans. We even have a Warrior Resource Center that helps veterans find the services they need," Hannah told him.

Jake nodded without commenting.

"What did you do in the military?" Hannah asked, sipping her water.

Jake took a big gulp of water before answering. "I was a corpsman in the Navy. I worked with Marines."

Hannah knew that the Marine Corps used Navy corpsmen and doctors as their medical experts. She had met a few in Iraq. The corpsmen who were specially trained to work with Marines fought alongside their ground combat brothers and sisters.

Hannah took a gamble. "Did you serve in Iraq?"

Jake looked off into the distance like he was remembering something, then spoke, "Yeah, I was there in 2004 during the battle for Fallujah."

Hannah knew that the battle for Fallujah in November and December 2004 was the bloodiest campaign that the US military had faced in the Iraq war. Her tour to Iraq had come later in the war when there were fewer large battles and more small skirmishes with insurgents and roadside bombs.

"I was there in 2008," she said. "I was an MP and worked security in the Green Zone." In truth, her job was as dangerous as any ground combat unit. The insurgents were constantly trying to penetrate bases where American and allied troops were stationed in Iraq. They used innumerable methods to attack security at entry points to US bases, including suicide bombers, trucks laden with explosives and even women and children wearing explosive vests. At one checkpoint in Baghdad where she had been working, an insurgent blew through the vendor gate in a truck loaded with explosives. Hannah had stood her ground in the middle of the road, fired her rifle into the windshield of the truck and killed the driver before he could ram his truck into a building filled with soldiers. The truck had swerved at the last second, barely missing her as the driver slumped onto the seat and let go of the wheel.

It was hard to understand, but Hannah felt like she had more in common with those who served in Iraq than with anyone else she met. The sights, the smells of death, explosives and burn pits, the constant roar of mortar rounds, the helicopters buzzing overhead, the gruesome attacks by Al Qaeda, the Sunni-Shia divide, the crazy militias, the extravagant palaces of Saddam Hussein; the whole experience was seared into her psyche. She instantly felt a kinship with anyone who had experienced that shithole of a war. She felt closer to this damaged Navy corpsman, even though he was homeless, and probably a drunk, than she did with most other citizens she encountered in her job as a police officer. It was the knowing of what he'd been through, especially the Fallujah battle, the shared experiences, the terror and the constant threat of death that made her respect him, even if he was now homeless.

"We better get you down to that veteran's shelter before they close," she said, picking up her tray. The city of Montrose had allocated a couple of acres off of Niagara Street and donations had poured in from businesses and citizens to provide a shelter for the growing population of homeless veterans in Montrose. Hannah pulled her police cruiser into the shelter parking lot and waited for Jake to grab his backpack from the back seat. He stepped out of the car and stood looking at the shelter reluctantly.

"This is a nice place," Hannah said encouragingly. "I know some of the volunteers. You're gonna be OK here." Jake looked around one more time, shrugged and started for the entrance.

"There's one thing, though." Hannah looked worried. "They have a no drug or alcohol policy here." She didn't want to mention it earlier in case it scared him off, but he considered it a moment then nodded his assent.

They walked to the entrance and she pushed open the glass door. Inside, behind a counter, was an older woman with long gray hair and glasses attached to a thin silver chain around her neck. "I called earlier, spoke to Missy about a room for this veteran," Hannah explained, gesturing toward Jake, who was scanning the foyer with his dark eyes.

"Yes, of course," the woman said, looking down at the paper on her desk. "Right this way, please." She stood and led the way through a door near the foyer that led into a hallway. The shelter was similar in design to an indoor mall. There was a long open area in the middle with tables, couches, ping pong tables and a few fake trees. On either side of the hallway, were the rooms for the veterans. All the doors faced into the hallway and had windows on the opposite side of the room that faced out into the property grounds. Each room had a bed, a small desk, a sink, a toilet and a small shower. There was a kitchen at one end of the hallway where meals were served three times a day. At the other end was a social area where veterans could congregate, read, play games or just hang out. There were also two small rooms where counselors conducted one-on-one sessions with those who needed help and support. The whole place was designed around the concept of building a community where veterans could support one another in a healthy environment and enable them to move from homelessness into steady work and eventually a place of their own. The design had been modeled after cohabitation structures in Denmark that were very successful at facilitating a sense of close-knit community and family.

The woman led Jake and Hannah to a room at the end of the hallway near the kitchen. "This will be your room, dear," she said, handing Jake a key. "And here's a copy of our rules and schedule." Jake took both and nodded to the woman.

"Hey, I'll let you get settled here," Hannah said, not wanting to intrude any more on his privacy. "I'll swing by in a few days to check on you, if that's OK?" Jake turned to her and Hannah saw the sadness in his eyes, as if he knew he was at the end of his rope, being dropped off into some institution where he didn't know anyone. It was the same feeling she'd had on her first day in Iraq. He nodded to her and she walked down the hallway and back out into the dark, starry night.

4

OCTOBER 2022, MONTROSE COLORADO

Jake awoke and for a moment forgot who and where he was. The drugs he'd been given at the hospital had made his head foggy and his head was still throbbing. He sat up on the edge of the single bed and looked around. The sun was coming through the plastic blinds like so many thin razors of light. He reached up and felt the gash on his head; they had closed it with stitches and medical glue but it was still tender. His ribs were sore and he rubbed his shin where a big lump protruded above his socks. Those guys had done a real number on him. That was something he hated about humans, and one thing he couldn't stand after Iraq - people hurting each other for no good reason.

He showered, pulled a clean set of socks and underwear from his bag and got dressed. There was no coffeemaker in his room, so he walked down the hall to the kitchen where two older veterans sat at a table eating pancakes. Jake went up to the serving line, where a middle-aged Hispanic woman with high cheekbones, charcoal hair and dark eyes stood behind the counter facing him. She had no lines on her face, but her eyes and a few strands of silver in her hair suggested a story of pain and loss.

"You must be new here," she said in a melodic voice, one that sounded like it belonged in an opera.

"I came in last night," said Jake, noticing that USMC was tattooed on her hand.

"You'll do alright here, just don't get caught drinking."

"Yeah, that's what I hear," he said. "Were you a Marine?" he asked, pointing at the tattoo.

"Yep, 3381 Food Service Specialist. Did my four years, then got out," she said, reaching for a plate. "What can I get you?"

"I'll take eggs, bacon and toast, please," he said. She scooped up the food from metal trays behind the counter and handed him the plate.

"Were you in The Corps?" she asked.

"No, Navy corpsman; I worked with Marines."

"Tough job patching up all those leathernecks," she smirked. She paused. "I'm Lucia, by the way," she said, holding out her rubber-gloved hand.

"Jake Hanlon, nice to meet you." She nodded and Jake took a seat by himself in the corner of the dining room, digging into his breakfast.

Another veteran entered the kitchen and worked his way down the breakfast line, making small talk with Lucia. "Cayn't you make me an omelette?" the tall, lean veteran said in a deep southern accent.

"Only on Fridays, you know that Billy Bob."

"But it would only take a minute," he pleaded with a big smile.

Lucia reached for a bag of shredded cheese, sprinkled a handful on his scrambled eggs and handed him the plate. "Here you go, the best I can do today."

Billy Bob, looked at his plate like it was a coiled snake, "You got any Grey Poupon to go with that?" he joked.

"Sit your ass down Billy Bob. It's too early in the morning for me to take any more of your shit."

Billy Bob saw Jake eating alone at the corner table and said, "You must be new," as he pulled up a seat. "How long is your tour here?"

Jake was taken aback. *Was this guy off his rocker?* He looked across the table and sized up the man's gray eyes, cowboy hat and wiry arms.

"Whaddya mean by tour?" Jake asked, sipping his coffee.

"You know, how long is your deployment here?" Billy Bob said, waving his hands.

Now Jake was sure he was talking to a nutter. "I'm not deployed here, I'm just here for a hot and a cot."

"Listen Buddy," Billy Bob said, leaning in close like he was sharing a secret. "They only do omelets on Friday, but if you sweet talk that Mexican cook," he said, looking over his shoulder, "She'll hook you up."

Jake looked past Billy Bob to see Lucia shaking her head and trying to hold back a giggle.

"Were you in the big turkey shoot?" Billy Bob asked with a mouthful of cheesy eggs.

"Turkey shoot?"

"You know, DESERT STORM, the big left hook, Stormin Norman, Sodamn Insane, the whole fukin' turkey shoot."

"No buddy, that was before my time. Were you in that war?" Jake asked hesitantly, afraid that the guy might go off on an endless ramble.

"Damn straight, combat engineers, US Army, Ist Infantry Division. Have you seen that mile of death on TV?" Jake nodded. "I was there Buddy. It was way more than a mile—it was an endless line of destruction. Like the Devil halted traffic on the highway to hell and decided to shoot everyone in the head just for the fun of it, while they were driving."

"You ever seen pictures of the oil rigs burnin'?" Billy Bob asked.

"Yeah, it looked kinda dark," Jake said.

"Kinda dark! Are you kidding me! It was fukin' apocalyptic. In the middle of the day it was as dark as six inches up the Devil's asshole. I was drivin' a Humvee through Kuwait City at noon and could barely see my headlights. Some poor Kuwaiti woman standin' in the middle of the road waved me down and I stopped to try and help her. She hurried me into her apartment where her husband and son lay on the floor like two pieces of meat. Iraqi soldiers had tortured the shit out of them with power drills. She wanted me to help, but there was nothing I could do." Billy Bob wiped his eyes with his napkin. "Fukin' animals."

"Hey Billy Bob, are you alright?"

"Yeah, it's just been a long deployment," Billy Bob said, shaking his head.

"How long have you been here?" Jake asked slowly, afraid of the answer he might get.

Billy Bob poked at his eggs with the plastic fork, then looked at Jake, "I don't know man...they said I got some brain injury when my Humvee got blown up, then I was in the hospital for a long time, then homeless and now I'm deployed here. I'm waiting on orders for my next duty station. How about you soldier?"

Jake didn't know how to answer this poor guy, but his humanity bubbled up unexpectedly, "Yeah I'm deployed here for a while too Billy Bob. I'll see you around huh?"

But for the grace of God, thought Jake standing up from the table. His life had followed a similar pattern; military service, injuries, hospitalization, homelessness and now ending up in a shelter. He realized that the lives of many of the vets at the shelter and those still homeless probably followed a similar pattern with occasional detours through the dark forests of alcoholism and drug addiction.

After breakfast, Jake went back to his room, grabbed his backpack, and left the shelter to return to Cerise Park. There was something he needed to do there. He planned to scout out an area beyond the park but first he wanted to know the ways to travel in and around it.

Hannah strode into The Coffee Trader next to Montrose High School, ordered a tall Mocha and headed back to her cruiser. She walked with the fluid motion of a dancer, which caused people to stare at her, noticing her black hair, creamy skin and cat-like movements. Today she was working a swing shift and it was 5:30 p.m. She needed a little jolt to get her to midnight. Her beat was to the west of Montrose so she took a left on Chipeta Road and headed south, on the lookout for any mischief. It was mid-October and the aspen and cottonwood trees in the Montrose valley were beginning to show their fall colors. A bite in the air reminded her that winter would soon arrive.

At 5:47 p.m., dispatch came over the radio, "All units in the area, there are reports of an attack in Cerise Park."

"Roger, this is Officer 201, I'm close," responded Hannah. "Two minutes away. Any idea where in Cerise Park?"

"Caller said he was near the dog park, and heard screaming in the woods to the south."

"Copy all, on my way," responded Hannah, flipping on her lights and siren, spinning a U-turn on Chipeta and gunning the motor. She drove in the west entrance, sped down the hill and pulled up to the curb next to the covered picnic area.

"Officer 201 on site," she reported into her radio as she exited her car. "I'm going to clear the area south of the dog park and wait for backup."

"Copy all, 201, backup is on the way," relayed the dispatcher.

It was dusk now, and the sun had set over the Uncompahgre Plateau to the west, leaving Hannah in that dim window before total darkness enveloped the park. She pulled out her flashlight, stepped into the woods and started searching. Cerise Park had some high-traffic areas near the ball fields, dog park and the river, but the deep middle of the park was still a wild place, which made it ideal for homeless people looking for a quiet place to camp.

Hannah veered off the main walking path and started heading deeper into the untamed portions of the park. The huge pine trees above her filtered out the last light of the day. She came to a small opening in the woods and scanned her flashlight across the grassy patch before moving on. That's when she saw it. A body lay face up at the edge of the clearing. She approached carefully and when she was close, she could see it was a man. Her flashlight illuminated the body and she saw a large pool of blood on the ground, which looked like it had come from a wound on the man's chest. She knelt down and felt his wrist for a pulse; he was dead. She was about to call dispatch when she noticed the man had devil tattoos on his neck and a thin mustache.

She realized he fit the description of one of the guys who had attacked Jake.

32

5

October 2022, Montrose Colorado

Jake walked back up Niagara Street towards the veteran's shelter with his head down. The encounter in the park had left him rattled. He might have had another episode, but he couldn't always remember what was real and what was part of the episode. It all seemed so real. He seemed to recall a dog that was off leash had come at him while he was walking in the woods. The owner of the dog confronted Jake and they got into a fight over something. He didn't remember much after that—it was all kind of fuzzy in his head.

When he approached the parking lot of the veteran's shelter, he saw a police car parked near the entrance. As he walked up to the front door, Officer Hannah Livingston was leaning on the side of the cruiser with her arms crossed, tapping her feet.

"Hey, Hannah, what brings you here?"

"Jake, I need to take you down to the station for questioning," she said, standing up.

"What for?"

"Somebody was killed in the park this afternoon. They wanna question you," she said, clearly uncomfortable.

Jake immediately thought of the encounter with the man and his dog. He couldn't remember how it had ended, but he hoped it wasn't related to whatever this was.

"Do I have a choice?" he asked.

"No, I'm sorry, Jake, I have to take you in. Don't make me arrest you, please."

"OK, fine," he said, walking to Hannah's car as she opened the back door for him.

"Where did you go today?" she asked as she pulled out of the parking lot.

"I went back to Cerise Park," he admitted, looking out the window.

Hannah's eyes widened, and she pulled over to the side of the road, then turned to look at Jake in the back seat. "You mean you just came back from Cerise Park?" she asked incredulously.

"Yeah, that's what I said." Jake was starting to worry. Hannah suddenly seemed different from the woman who'd been so kind and helpful to him.

"What were you doing in the park?" she asked, this time in her cop voice.

"I was looking for something," he said.

"Jake!" she said pointedly, trying to shake him out of his complacency, "There was a murder in the park just about the time you were there. I can't tell you any more, but you're the main suspect. You need to have a solid story when you get to the police station. A detective is going to grill you. Do you understand?" she asked, raising her voice in exasperation.

"Yeah, I understand," he said quietly, then looked out the window, signaling to Hannah that he was done talking about it. She shook her head, turned around and drove him to the station downtown.

"Make sure you ask for a lawyer, OK?" she said, looking at him in her rearview mirror. Jake didn't respond.

When they arrived, a sergeant accompanied Jake to an interview room and gave him a bottle of water. A few minutes later, a tall, thin man with prematurely gray hair, intense eyes and black plastic glasses sat down at the table in front of Jake.

"I'm Detective Davidson. I'd like to ask you a few questions, but I need to inform you that you have a right to have an attorney present if you wish."

Jake thought about what Hannah had said, "Yeah, I'll take a lawyer."

"As you wish," said Davidson, and stepped out of the room.

Thirty minutes later, a tall black woman sat down beside Jake and introduced herself as Angie Johnson, a public defender. She set a brown leather briefcase on the floor next to her before turning to Jake to discuss his situation. She was cordial with the police, but even at thirty, she already had a reputation as a hard-nosed lawyer for her clients. The detectives knew they would not be able to play games with Angie in the room. Jake and Angie talked for about fifteen minutes, then she stepped out and came back in with Detective Davidson.

Detective Davidson took a seat at the small table, set down a file and pulled out a photograph of the victim Hannah had found in the park. "Mr. Hanlon, have you ever seen this man before? His body was found this morning in Cerise Park," Davidson informed Jake. Angie tapped Jake on the arm with one of her long fingers and shook her head, signaling him not to answer. Jake remained silent as Davidson stared at him.

"OK, here's what I know. We have a police report that you were attacked by this man yesterday. He and another man beat you with sticks and you had to go to the emergency room for lacerations to your face and legs, bruised ribs and a mild concussion. In that report, you stated that the man who attacked you had demon tattoos on his neck and a thin mustache." Davidson pulled out a close-up photo of the victim. "I'll ask you again, Mr. Hanlon, have you ever seen this man before?" Angie tapped Jake on the arm again, and he remained silent.

"Where were you today, Mr. Hanlon?" Davidson asked as he returned the picture to the folder. Angie tapped his arm again. "You told Officer Livingston on the way here that you were in Cerise Park today." Davidson looked at Angie to see how she would react. Clearly Jake had not mentioned this to her, and probably thought Hannah would have kept that to herself. Angie looked at Jake with thinly-veiled surprise.

"Did the man have a dog?" Jake asked out of the blue. Davidson looked confused by the question. Angie became furious and quickly interjected, "This interview is over, Detective. I need to confer with my client."

"This is your chance to come clean, Mr. Hanlon. We know you were attacked by the victim and we know you were in the park when he was killed this afternoon. Tell us what happened and the DA will work a deal with you," he said, standing up and staring at Jake. "If you walk out of here now, I can't ensure there'll be another offer."

"My client has nothing to say, Detective," said Angie, and Davidson left the room.

Angie turned to Jake, "What the hell was that? What dog were you talking about? Remember what I said, you don't speak unless I know what you're going to say—no surprises, remember?"

Jake dropped his head into his hands. His heart rate was booming, the tiny room was closing in on him. All he wanted to know was if he had killed the man with the dog. He couldn't remember anything beyond the start of the fight and a red hot rage taking over his entire body. The next thing he remembered, he was walking out of the park.

"Jake," Angie said, touching his shoulder, "Are you alright?" Jake rubbed his temples, not answering. Finally, he raised his head and nodded. Angie stared at him for a long moment, then spoke. "Hey, it's gonna be OK. Let me go talk to Detective Davidson and make sure you're free to leave." She left the room as Jake sat staring in front of him.

In the hallway was a uniformed officer waiting by the door. "Hey, can I speak with you for a minute?" Hannah asked Angie.

"Sure, what's up?"

"Listen, I'm Officer Hannah Livingston. I was the one who responded to the 911 call in the park when Jake was attacked." Hannah paused, looking around and lowering her voice. "I brought Jake his stuff last night at the ER and brought him to the shelter. The nurse told me he'd had some kind of a flashback, where he thought he was back in Iraq. They thought it was probably because of the knock on his head. He told me later that he was a Navy corpsman who worked with Marines in the battle of Fallujah." She looked around again.

"What are you suggesting, Officer Livingston?" Angie asked, crossing her arms.

"I'm just telling you that I think he had a terrible experience in Iraq, and maybe he had some kind of a flashback in the park, ya know? He probably has some unseen injuries. The doctor even noted some previous brain injuries. I just wanted you to be aware, since he probably won't tell you any of that."

"So now you want to help him after you told the detective he was in the park today? He thought he told you that in confidence, as a friend," Angie said, turning to face Hannah directly.

"Listen," Hannah said, raising her voice slightly. "I've screwed up in this department before. It'll never happen again. If a suspect in a murder case shares something with me, I'm bound to inform the chain of command. I can't ignore it. But I dunno... I feel sorry for the guy. I'm a vet myself and I was in Iraq, so I know what a shithole that war was, and he was in the worst of it. I guess I just feel some empathy for the guy, you know? I don't wanna see him get screwed if he's innocent."

Angie looked at Hannah for a long moment, then said, "OK, fair enough, Officer Livingston, I'll take that into consideration."

"Call me Hannah, please," she said, holding out her hand.

Angie shook her hand, then left to find Detective Davidson, returning to the interview room a few minutes later. A technician was just finishing up a DNA swab on Jake's cheek. "You're free to go, Jake," Angie said. "They don't have enough to hold you. They'll be processing DNA found at the crime scene and if nothing matches you, you probably won't hear from them again."

Jake stood up and Angie walked him to the parking lot. "Do you need a ride?" she asked.

"No, I'll just walk, thanks for the help today."

Angie paused. She was about to tread on thin ice, but she was not one to back down when someone needed help. "Listen, Jake, have you ever considered getting counseling? We have some excellent counselors and mental health professionals here in Montrose."

Jake was tempted to get angry or be a smart ass, but he subdued the impulse, "Thanks, Angie, I'll consider it." But he had no intention of considering it. He didn't think there was a person in the world who could erase the memories of what he had seen and done.

6

OCTOBER 2022, MONTROSE COLORADO

Before heading out on her beat, Hannah stopped to see Detective Davidson. He was busy filling out a report on the interview with Jake when she came up to his desk and quietly waited for him to stop typing.

"Do you need me to do anything else, fill out any other reports?" Hannah asked. Davidson stopped typing and looked up at her. "Naw, I've got it from here. What's your feeling about this guy?" He asked, leaning back in his chair. "You spent some time with him in the hospital."

Hannah chose her words carefully. "I don't think he did it, just a gut feeling. He was in the park at the same time, but I just don't see him as a cold-blooded murderer who hunted down this guy and knifed him. He didn't try to hide the fact that he was in the park when I asked him."

"Maybe he trusts you," said Davidson, turning in his chair to face Hannah. "Why don't you check on our Mr. Hanlon once in a while, see if he opens up to you, maybe you'll find out a bit more about him."

Hannah paused. She didn't want to gain Jake's trust just to entrap him. On the other hand, she wanted to keep plugged into this in-

40

vestigation and help Detective Davidson find the murderer. For some reason she didn't fully understand, she wanted to protect Jake too. "OK, I'll do that and let you know if anything comes up."

It was Friday afternoon, and Hannah's shift was over early. The police department had changed her schedule due to a concert in town. After a short drive home, she pulled into her little condo on the west side of Montrose. She lived in a duplex next to an older lady who kept guinea pigs and cats in the same house. Hannah always wondered how anyone could keep those two together. Hannah liked her little place, but wished she could afford a house and a small yard. She had missed her opportunity to buy a house on a police officer's salary. During the pandemic, wealthy buyers from Denver and California moved into little Montrose and snatched up property left and right, jacking up real estate prices. Nonetheless, she liked her homey little condo. She preferred things simple, so the color scheme of her decor was black and white and she kept the place clean and tidy. She also had a two-car garage and a separate place to park her cruiser in front of the garage. She kept an old Toyota Corolla she called The Beater in the garage next to her classic Chevy pickup.

She went inside and immediately thought it would be nice to have a dog greet her, but she didn't think it would be fair to have a dog, given her long working hours and changing schedule. She went into the kitchen, pulled a beer out of the fridge, popped the cap and thought about what she might do tonight. Two weeks ago, she'd met a retired police officer named Susan at San Juan Brews Coffee House, and after a cup of coffee together, Susan intuitively knew that Hannah was dealing with some issues. She'd invited Hannah to a 12-step group meeting that met in Montrose on Friday nights. It was not only for alcohol and drug dependency, but other problems as well. Hannah had attended last week, mostly out of curiosity, and sat through the session without saying anything. She had to admit she'd gotten something out of hearing other people explain their troubles and how they were trying to rebuild their lives.

The meeting had started with a deep dive into one of the 12 steps and then went around the room for anybody who wanted to share. Hannah had a gut feeling she needed to go tonight. They served a little food before the session, which would take care of her dinner, too. She checked her watch—half an hour until the meeting. She slammed a shower, put on civilian clothes, jumped in her pickup truck and headed out.

The meeting was held in a small church that the 12-step organization rented on Friday nights. She walked in and made her way to the dining room, looking around for Susan. She spotted her chatting in the corner with another woman, and when Susan saw Hannah, she excused herself and made a beeline to Hannah. "I'm glad you made it!" said Susan enthusiastically, running her hands through her gray-streaked long blonde hair. She was tall and slim, and Hannah put her at maybe sixty-five.

Hannah looked around the room furtively to see if she recognized anyone. It was hard for her to socialize in the small town, since she knew she might run into someone she had arrested or given a traffic citation to. She relaxed a bit when she didn't recognize anyone.

"Come on, let's grab some food before it's gone." Susan said with a wink. They stood in line, then served themselves helpings of spaghetti, salad and garlic bread, along with a cup of iced tea, and sat down at a table together.

"So, how have you been?" Susan asked as Hannah dug into her spaghetti.

"Pretty busy this week, I've been on the swing shift working till midnight," said Hannah with a mouthful of salad. "Mostly routine, but then there was a murder in Cerise Park."

"Geez!" exclaimed Susan. "Are you investigating it?" she asked.

"No, I just responded to the 911 call and found the victim," said Hannah.

"That must've been gruesome," Susan said, screwing up her face. "I mean, walking onto a murder scene?"

Hannah nodded with a mouthful of salad, "Yeah, stabbed in the chest. Lots of blood," she said nonchalantly.

The two finished their meal and moved into the main room where the moderator presented a lesson on step 3 of the 12-step program—examining past errors. It occurred to Hannah that the lesson was custom made for her. She sat on the edge of her seat realizing she was never going to move forward in her life until she finally dealt with her past. If she left it alone, it would just fester and continue to blow to the surface periodically, like a geyser. After the lesson, the attendees all moved their chairs into a circle and the moderator kicked off the testimony meeting.

"To reiterate," the moderator said in a deep voice, "We're not here to fix each other or comment, we're here to listen and support. Would anyone like to share?" There was silence for about thirty seconds until a man to Hannah's left spoke up. He was large and pink-faced with tattoos on his neck and a half-dozen rings in one ear. "I was addicted to drugs for ten years," he said with confident eyes searching the room. "I lost my wife and my son because of my addiction. But I've been sober now for two years. I've got a job on a ranch, where I work with horses, and I'm so grateful to be here and for the support of this group. I don't normally speak, but you all have inspired me with your stories of courage, so thank you."

Hannah felt her heart begin to beat a little faster. Two more women gave testimonies, then Hannah found herself talking. She hadn't even meant to speak, it just sort of spilled out involuntarily, like a cough she couldn't hold back.

"I served as a military police officer in Iraq in 2008," she began. "I can't explain all the horrors I saw over there, and the way we dealt with it. Most of you probably wouldn't believe it anyway. I provided security for the Green Zone where the Americans worked, trying to keep terrorists and insurgents out of the US base and facilities. There are some incidents that are seared into my heart from that deployment. But I realized after today's lesson that trying to forget them is not working. I have to take some responsibility here, try to find a way to move forward with my life."

She paused and took a big breath as the others waited and watched her sympathetically. "One of the worst things I dealt with had to do with a young girl on a scooter. Our entry points to the base had multiple layers of security so we could stop a vehicle before it approached the final entry gate in case they were carrying explosives and tried to ram the gate. But this girl on a scooter blew past the first vehicle gate where she was supposed to stop for an inspection. Then she gunned her little scooter and aimed right for the final pedestrian gate where I was standing. She couldn't have been more than twelve years old. I can still see her black hair flowing above a red and white dress with pink plastic sandals." She paused again, but then forced herself to continue.

"The week before we'd had a similar incident, where an insurgent on a bicycle bypassed the first gate and tried to make it to the second gate, but he was shot and killed. It turned out he was wearing an explosive vest underneath his jacket."

She was speaking to the people in the room, but her mind was back in Iraq. "So I had that on my mind as the girl on the scooter shot past the first gate and headed towards me. My training and instincts took over and I had to make a split-second decision. I yelled at her, waved my hands, waved my weapon and then shot her four times when she was less than ten yards from the gate."

She stopped and wiped a tear from her eye, "She flew off the back of the scooter and landed face up in a pile of old tires. It turned out she wasn't carrying any explosives. Both of her parents had been mortally injured in a mortar attack by Al Qaeda, and she was trying to get help for them."

Hannah realized she'd been looking down at the floor as she spoke, seeing the images of the young girl laying at her feet, blood spilling from her neck and pooling in the dirt. She looked up and saw the dozen or so men and women crying with her.

She continued. "There's more. Towards the end of my one-year tour, I slept with my best friend Amber's fiancé. Amber had been captured, and I thought she was dead or would never come back, but she was actually rescued. But even if she was dead, I had no excuse for seducing her fiancé, especially while she was in captivity. This weighs on my soul every day. I never thought I was that kind of a woman!" she exclaimed bitterly, screwing up her face in disgust.

"I could blame the war and all the shit I had to deal with, but at the end of the day, I made a terrible decision. My best friend and I had gone through military police training together and we were serving in Iraq at the same time. I broke the most sacred vow of friendship. I would do anything if I could undo that mistake…" Hannah's voice trailed off as she looked up at the faces watching her.

She paused, not sure if she was speaking too long. The bile just kept coming up in waves. "Sometime after that, Amber's fiancé committed suicide. I'd like to think I didn't have anything to do with it," Hannah said, biting her lip and not making eye contact with anyone. "But I can't help feeling that I played a part in that, too. My friend forgave me, and even saved my career when I got into trouble, but we don't speak anymore. I think that's my fault, too. Most of the time I just feel like a shitty human being. I drink more than I should, but it helps me cope," she finished, tears now running down her face.

The people around the circle were wiping their eyes and handing one another tissues. A woman sitting next to Hannah reached over, grabbed her hands and squeezed them. Hannah put her head down and began to sob. She hadn't spoken to anyone about what happened to her in Iraq, and now perfect strangers were hearing for the first time the darkness that she was carrying within her. She looked up and found the entire circle of attendees had moved into a tight circle around her, as if to give her a massive group hug. She wiped her eyes again, quickly gained her composure and stood. The members each gave her a hug before everyone moved to the lobby.

The session ended after Hannah's dark revelations. Susan came up to her before she left and gave her a big hug and whispered into her ear, "I'm so glad you came tonight. Call me if you need anything." She pulled back and slipped a business card into Hannah's hand. Hannah walked out of the church quickly; she didn't want any more hugs. She sat in her truck and stared out the window, feeling completely drained. Slowly, though, ever so slowly, a feeling crept into her heart that this had been good for her, that maybe she had at least taken a small step forward in healing her soul.

7

The interview with Detective Davidson had rattled Jake. He didn't care too much about what happened in his life lately, but he couldn't afford to go to jail, not before he finished what he had to do. It was Saturday morning and he walked down to Main Street to find a barber shop. His baggy jeans, torn flannel shirt, scruffy beard and long hair made him look like a homeless drifter. Unfortunately, most people judged him as unstable, violent, drug-addled or insane. He didn't care what other people thought of him, but he realized their prejudices made him stand out, made him a target. He needed to blend in, not draw attention.

The barber shop was a block off Main, on a side street filled with cars parked by people visiting the local farmer's market. It was an old-fashioned barber shop with two antique barber chairs and a spinning red and white pole out front. The door jingled when Jake stepped inside the small shop and a hulk of a man stood up, set down a newspaper and moved behind the chair closest to the window, pointing to the seat. Jake took off his tattered windbreaker, hung it on the coat rack and sat in the chair. He looked at himself in the mirror—it was time for that guy to go away.

"That's a nasty cut on your head," the barber said in a baritone voice, trying to be friendly. The guy had forearms like ham-hocks and fingers like sausages. Jake reached up involuntarily, touched the cut and felt a flash of anger surge through his mind.

When Jake didn't respond, the barber asked, "What'll it be, buddy?" as he pulled the black cape around Jake's neck, snapping it snug in the back.

"Just a haircut and shave," Jake said, running his hands through his beard for the last time.

"OK, but how do you want your hair?" asked the barber, spinning the padded black leather and chrome chair around and picking up an electric razor with his big paw. It had been so long since Jake cared about his appearance that he was momentarily puzzled.

"I guess whatever looks normal would be good," said Jake. The barber looked confused for a moment, then flicked on his shears and started on Jake's beard. He took off the dense beard with the clippers, dropping big piles of curly black hair on the floor. He then pulled a straight razor from a drawer, sharpened it on a long leather strop, lathered up Jake's face and meticulously scraped the stubble to reveal a smooth, chiseled face. Thirty minutes later the barber was trimming the last of the hair on Jake's neck. He spun the chair around and let Jake look at himself in the mirror.

Jake hardly recognized himself. He used to keep his hair to Marine Corps regulations, even after he was out of the Navy, but he'd let it go years ago. The barber had cut it to collar length, trimmed it off his ears and forehead, making him look much younger than his thirty-nine years. The barber looked equally surprised at the transformation. The scraggly bum who had walked into his shop now looked like a completely different man. He could see Jake's dark brown eyes, which were set above high cheekbones and a Roman nose, and the absence of a beard revealed a strong, chiseled chin. His clean face had a scab on one cheek where the pinecone had landed, and he had a nasty cut on his forehead, but he looked more like a college professor or hedge fund manager than a homeless guy.

"That'll be forty bucks," the big man said as Jake stood. Jake didn't look like he had money and the big guy looked worried, but Jake reached into his pocket, pulled out a roll of cash, peeled off a fifty and handed it to the man. The barber was about to make change and Jake said, "Keep it, thank you."

Four blocks west on Main he found a shop called The Outdoor Store near the City Market grocery store that sold outdoor equipment and clothes. The owner's white lab greeted Jake at the door, sniffing his hand and wagging its big tail. Jake bought a pair of khaki cargo pants, a couple of long-sleeve pullover shirts, a belt, a pair of leather hiking shoes, wool socks, underwear and a canvas oilskin coat with flannel lining. He changed in the dressing room, threw his old clothes in a shopping bag and stepped outside into a crisp fall afternoon. A cool breeze was blowing from the north, but the sun was bright. Jake's makeover was complete. He looked more like a Montrose local who was going hiking in the San Juan mountains than he did his former self.

It was 2 p.m. and Jake felt his stomach rumble. He walked back east on Main Street until he found the Sideline Sports Bar a block south. He pushed open the glass door and was met by a cacophony of loud whistles, shouting and commentary on a half-dozen televisions covering college football games. Football mania was in full swing and the place was packed with fans who were glued to the TV's, shouting and clapping for their teams. Jake found a seat at the end of the bar that didn't have a great view of the TVs, which was fine by him. One of the two bartenders rushed out from the kitchen with two orders of steaming hot wings and set them down in front of a couple to Jake's right. Jake glanced at the bartender and recognized it was Lucia, the former Marine and cook at the veteran's shelter. As soon as she was free, she stopped in front of him to take his order. Her tight jeans and a red and black blouse complemented her raven hair and hour-glass figure.

"What can I getcha?" she asked, clearly not recognizing Jake in his new clothes, haircut and clean-shaven face. Jake smiled, thinking how different he must look to her. "Hey there, Marine," he said, a twinkle in his eye.

She stepped back a second, put her hands on her hips and asked, "Do I know you?"

"Jake from the veteran's shelter," he said. "You made me break-fast yesterday."

"Jake?" she said, squinting her dark eyes and leaning forward. "You look really different."

"I know. I made some changes," he smiled.

"Que Guapo!" she said with obvious admiration. Somehow Jake understood and blushed.

She raised her eyebrows, "Well, you look a whole lot better," she said, pushing hair out of her eyes.

"Why are you working here?" Jake asked. "I thought you were the cook at the shelter…"

"Gotta make ends meet. I cook at the shelter Monday through Friday and bartend here on Saturdays. Rent ain't cheap in this town, lemme tell ya," she smirked. "Now, what can I get ya?"

"Can I get the loaded nachos and a 16-ounce Modelo?"

"Honey, you order like a Mexican," she winked.

"I got a quick question," he said, leaning forward as she was turning to place the order. She turned back with a suspicious look. Jake pulled a tattered map from his pocket and unfolded it on the bar table in front of her. He oriented the map, then put his finger on Cerise Park. "What's on the other side of this road?" he asked, sliding his finger to Chipeta Road, which ran along the western boundary of the park. She looked down and saw that he was pointing to a spot directly across from the west entrance to the park.

"I dunno, some small houses, a trailer park, a few industrial buildings. Why, you looking to rent there or somethin'?"

Jake folded the map up quickly and stuffed it into his pocket. "No, I'm just trying to learn the lay of the land, that's all."

"You don't seem like the average homeless vet we get at the shelter," she said, looking closer at his face.

Jake shrugged, "Whaddaya mean?"

"I dunno, you seem different from the others, that's all," she said.

If only she really knew me, Jake thought. "I don't know what to say to that."

She nodded and headed off to place his order. When she brought him the tall beer, Jake nodded thanks and she moved down the bar to serve a customer who had his finger in the air signaling for another beer.

A different server brought out the nachos and Jake plunged into the stack of cheesy chips, sour cream, salsa and jalapenos.

After he finished his meal, Lucia stopped by and asked if he needed another beer, but Jake said no and asked for the check. He left cash on the bar, including a nice tip for Lucia before he walked out into the waning daylight. The sun was close to setting to the west of town over the Plateau. Jake turned right on Main Street and left on Rio Grande Avenue until he came to the eastern entrance to Cerise Park thirty minutes later. He stepped onto the walking bridge over the river and stopped to look at the swirling rapids below in the moonlight. The turbulent waters looked menacing and reminded him of the view off the back of a Navy ship as the props churned up the water in the middle of the ocean.

He crossed the bridge and started down the walking path that led toward the dog park and the western entrance to the park. After a half mile, he came to the west entrance to the park, checked for cars coming, then jogged across the road. He turned left on the other side of Chipeta then took a right into a small community of battered mobile homes. It was dark now with high clouds covering the stars and moon. Jake estimated the place was home to about ten to fifteen mobile homes. He pulled his hood up over his head and walked quietly down the street, carefully studying each little home.

At the back of the park he came across a faded green and white metal-sided single-wide trailer. Brown leaves from a large sycamore tree that spread its branches above the little home covered the thin patch of grass. An older model Crown Victoria sat in the narrow driveway to the left of the home. Weathered wooden steps led up to a small door. Dim lights were visible through the curtains but Jake saw no movement through the small window in the kitchen that faced the street. He stood under a pine tree in the cul-de-sac and stared at the home, memories tumbling through his brain like pop flares in the desert. Jake felt depressed, angry and sad and he wanted to punch something, release his anger. Finally he turned and headed out of the small trailer park and back onto Chipeta Road. The dark sky above him mirrored his mood as he began the walk back to the veteran's shelter, his mind bouncing between despair, anger and hopelessness.

Jake began to feel a gnawing sense of loneliness and worse, hopelessness. He'd been homeless for too long, and had been out of touch with 'normal' society. The pain boiling in his mind was not something he could tell anyone about, but he thought it would be good to just talk to someone, have a real conversation. He found himself wandering back into the sports bar, hoping Lucia was still there. After all, she'd been a Marine, worked at the shelter, was easy on the eyes and fun to talk to. Most of the college football crowd had left, and the bar was nearly empty except for a couple of hard-core drinkers at the end of the bar and a family eating dinner by the window. Jake spotted Lucia exiting the kitchen and took a seat at the end of the bar. She saw him and came over.

"Back again?" she asked with a smile.

Jake didn't know what to say so he stood there by the bar and just nodded.

"I'm off in an hour, I'll buy you a drink," she stated matter-of-factly. "Hungry?" she added.

Jake shrugged, and she motioned for him to sit. She turned around and pulled another Modelo on tap for him. "Want some more nachos?" she asked, setting the beer in front of him.

"Sure," he said. "That'd be great."

Lucia put in the order, took payment from the family waiting at the register and cleaned up the table by the window. A bell rang and she went to the kitchen window, returning with Jake's loaded nachos.

"Whadya do this afternoon?" she asked, as Jake munched on the cheesy nachos.

"Not much, just walked around to get a lay of the land." It wasn't a lie, just not the whole truth.

Lucia finished up checking out another customer then punched out and grabbed her coat. "You ready?" she asked. Jake threw back the rest of his beer, stood up, put on his coat and followed her out.

She led him across the street and one block west to the Town Hall Tavern, a dive bar for locals. The place was long and narrow with a bar on the left side as you walked in and an open space in the front near the door for karaoke or a single guitar player. The bartender nodded at Lucia. The local bartenders all knew and respected each other.

Lucia led Jake toward the back where it was quieter. Two old locals sat at the other end of the bar watching a game on the TV behind.. The bartender put down a rag and walked over to them. "Hey, Lucia," greeted the young man. He had big rings in his ears and the bolo tie and leather vest he wore made him look a bit like a cowboy.

"Hey, Mike," she said, "Six house tequila shots please."

Mike nodded and headed off to pour the drinks and Jake raised his eyebrows at Lucia questioningly.

"You eat like a Mexican," she said playfully. "Let's see if you can drink like one." Jake wasn't an alcoholic like many homeless veterans, but he did drink once in a while. He knew it wasn't good for him, but with all the trauma he'd experienced, it was the least of his problems.

Mike brought six shots in oversized glasses and a small plate of cut limes. Lucia picked up a glass and nodded for Jake to do the same. "What should we drink to?" she asked.

"The Marine Corps," Jake said, raising his glass to her. She tapped his glass with hers and threw back the clear tequila in one gulp then bit into one of the lime slices. Jake watched her then did the same. It was not great tequila, but at least it didn't taste like gasoline.

"Were you deployed overseas?" Jake asked, as he picked up a lime and bit.

"Yeah, I was in Afghanistan in 2004 - in Kandahar. We were in a beat-up and bombed-out old airport built by the Russians. We lived in GP medium tents and had five gallon buckets for showers. I just remember the mortars landing all the time," she said, staring at her next drink. "I worked in the kitchen making meals for all the snake eaters and support staff on the base. It was pretty rough." She looked up at him. "What about you?"

"Deployed to Iraq a coupla times and once to Afghanistan," he said, not offering more details.

Lucia nodded slowly. "Well, here's to those vacation spots that most Americans never get to experience," she smirked, holding up another shot.

"To great desert vacations," Jake toasted, clinking his glass against hers and throwing back his second shot.

"You ever been married?" she asked, wincing from the tart lime.

Jake shook his head. "Naw, it's not been in the cards for me."

"Why not? Good looking guy like you? You should be beating women off with a stick," she said, snorting a laugh.

Jake looked up at the ceiling for a moment before answering, his head beginning to swirl. "I've just been dealing with some injuries... you know... from the wars."

"Like your balls were blown off or something?" Lucia said, giggling again.

Jake snorted. "No, all that stuff works. It's more in my head," he said, turning to see if she understood. Like most veterans with PTSD or brain injury, Jake didn't like to talk about his issues. If a veteran was missing a leg or an arm, they couldn't avoid talking about it—it was like wearing a giant sign around their neck that said Disabled Veteran. But if they struggle with the unseen demons of war, the invisible wounds of the mind and brain, they tend to keep quiet about it. They know that ignorant people label veterans with mental issues as crazy, nuts or dangerous. Others can't see an actual physical wound and peg them as weak—"Suck it up, man!" is often the recommendation of those who don't understand the hidden wounds of war and have no idea what they're talking about.

Lucia picked up her third shot and glanced at Jake with dark, glossy eyes, indicating with her eyebrows that he should follow suit. Jake reluctantly picked up the last shot. Lucia reached over with her hand and dipped her finger, adorned with a long, red nail, into Jake's tequila, then put it in her mouth and sucked on it.

Oh boy, thought Jake, *I'm not ready for that.* But at the same time, the tequila had demolished his inhibitions. Lucia sipped her last shot as if it was gourmet coffee. Jake threw his to the back of his mouth and went for the lime one more time.

Lucia motioned for Mike, paid the tab, then reached over, took Jake's hand and led him outside. The temperature had dropped and

Lucia's hand felt warm and moist. When they stepped to the sidewalk, Lucia turned to Jake, reached a hand behind his neck and pulled his face down to hers for a long, sensuous kiss. Jake kissed back, but without much passion.

Lucia pulled back and looked up at him, "What's the matter, is it me?"

Jake reached over and brushed her hair back from her eyes, "It's not you, Lucia. I just...I've got some things to work out. I'm not really good to be with right now."

Her dark eyes flared in anger for a moment, then softened. "OK, Jake, I get it," she said, turning and walking away into the blurry night.

Jake stood there under the streetlamp, watching her disappear. "What's wrong with you, man?" he whispered to himself, immediately recalling his visit to the trailer park as the hopelessness and pain boiled up like bile.

Thirty minutes later, Jake stood at the glass door of the shelter and pressed the buzzer for entry. A short, late-night security guard with a goatee and shiny boots opened the door. "You smell like alcohol, buddy," scolded the guard.

"I didn't know that was a crime," said Jake, staring at the guard.

"No intoxication at the shelter—rule number 7," said the guard. "I'm gonna have to report you."

"Do what you need to do, pal," Jake grumbled, pushing past the guard at the entry point and stepping into the hallway that led to his room.

A man sat on a bench in the middle of the hallway, the dim evening light obscured his face. He called out to Jake, "Come over here young man." Jake turned and saw a short, fat guy with a long beard sitting on a bench with his boots barely touching the ground as if he was a kid on a swing.

Jake stopped and stared at him. "Who the hell are you?" Jake asked, still angry from the confrontation with the guard.

"I'm the mayor here," he said, patting the seat next to him as if asking Jake to sit.

Jake remained standing, "Whaddya mean mayor?"

"Well, it's not official, that's just what they call me," the short man stood up and walked to Jake, extending a small hand for a shake. Jake looked at the hand then reached out.

"Don Laverne," the man said.

"Jake Hanlon."

"I heard your argument with the guard. It sounds like you have anger issues."

Jake was about to walk away, but something in the man's voice made him stay. It was the tone, not accusatory, just matter of fact.

"Yeah, probably true. Another of my fine qualities."

"Sit for a spell," the man said, pointing at the bench which looked like it was made for a park. "My knees always hurt so I sit alot."

Jake paused wondering what this guy's game was, then decided to sit.

"I was in the 1st Cav Division early in the Vietnam war in the Ia Drang Valley," the little man said, looking off into the distance. "Toward the end of my deployment a new officer was assigned to our platoon. He ordered us to conduct a mission we all knew was a death trap. He'd only been in the country three weeks. Twenty three of the thirty men in my platoon were killed including the young officer and my best friend."

The man turned to look at Jake who was listening closely, "For years I was incredibly angry. So many of my friends were killed needlessly. If that officer had just listened to us, all those men would be alive." He shook his head and stared at his boots. "I ran through the whole gamut; PTSD, uncontrolled anger, depression, alcoholism." He had Jake's attention, something in his words stirred a memory deep in Jake's mind. "They say time heals all wounds, but it didn't work out for me." The little man paused and looked at Jake.

"Okay, then what worked?"

"Charity." he said, slapping his knee. "I started feeding the poor at a local food bank and somehow my problems began to melt away. I began to look out for others and my life turned around. Maybe it's not the universal solution, but it worked for me."

Jake stood up, exhausted from the day and feeling the weight of pain he carried around each day. The guy clearly meant well, but Jake couldn't handle a lecture right now, "Good to meet you Don," he said, walking down the darkened hallway to his quiet, lonely room.

8

OCTOBER 2022, MONTROSE COLORADO

Hannah's new schedule gave her Sunday off and she figured it would be a good day to visit Jake and see how things were going at the shelter. The idea of reporting her interactions with Jake to Lieutenant Davidson made her stomach turn. It was one of those dilemmas she didn't want to think about right now — help Jake or help her career.

She pulled up to the shelter in her pickup truck and took a big breath before jumping out. *What am I really doing here?* she thought. She didn't have a clear answer, just a gut feeling that she needed to help this veteran for some reason. Plus she had told Davidson that she would look in on him and report anything unusual.

She walked in and almost ran into Jake on his way out. He had his backpack slung on his shoulder and it looked like it was full of his gear. If it wasn't for the backpack, though, she might not have recognized him. His hair was cut neat and trim and his beard was gone, revealing a surprisingly handsome face with deep brown eyes above a strong chin and high cheekbones.

"Jake, is that you?" she asked with surprise.

He stopped outside the door and shrugged.

"What's going on?" she asked, noticing a look of weariness in his eyes.

"They're kicking me out," he said.

"What? Why? What's going on, Jake?"

"They said I came in drunk last night, assaulted the security guard."

Hannah's mouth dropped open. "You assaulted a guard?" she asked incredulously.

"No, I pushed past him when he was giving me the third degree. I barely even touched him. It's fine, Hannah, I don't wanna stay in this place anyway, it's way too uptight for me."

"OK, but why was he hassling you?" she asked, thinking she probably knew the answer.

"The guy said I was intoxicated. You told me there was no alcohol allowed in the place. You didn't say I couldn't even have a drink in town," he said, shaking his head.

She stood there staring at him. The accusation was baseless, but she didn't want to get into an argument with him over the alcohol policy. He'd been asked to leave; it was a done deal. The next thought that came to her made her pulse beat like a small drum, so she suppressed it, for now.

"So what're you gonna do now?" she asked, as they moved into the parking lot.

"I'll just go back to the park," he said, looking down at his feet.

"No, Jake, that's not safe! You know that. You were just attacked there, for one thing. Plus winter is coming. There's gotta be a better option," she said with exasperation.

"Like what?" he said calmly.

Her previous thought came back again like a rock dropped into a pond sending ripples outward. *Damn*, she thought, *in for a penny, in for a pound.* "There's a little one-bedroom studio attached to the condo where I live. It has a separate entrance and everything. A previous owner converted one of the bedrooms into a tiny place to rent out. I've never used it. You can stay there."

"Naw, I couldn't do that," he said unconvincingly.

"No, really, I'm not using it, it's just sitting there vacant," she said, her mind spinning. *What am I doing? I don't really know this guy.*

Jake thought for a moment. "How much would you rent it for?"

Hannah was a little confused. She figured if he'd been homeless, he probably had no money. "You can just stay there for now, I'm not worried about rent."

"I don't need a hand out," he said defiantly.

"Jake, it's not a hand out. I'm not using it, it's empty. Just take it, please. I don't wanna find you in the park again. Besides, it's starting to get cold," she added, putting her hands on her hips, ready for his next excuse. "You can do some painting for me as payment. I haven't done a thing with the place. Really, you'll be doing me a favor." That was a stretch, but she didn't want to think of him camping out in Cerise Park. If he ended up getting a job someday, he could pay her rent.

"I guess if I can pay you in some way, that'll be OK," he said, relenting.

"Great, it's settled then," she agreed, but she was also thinking, *What have I done?*

Jake climbed into her truck and Hannah pulled out of the Veteran's Center parking lot and headed toward her condo. *What am I gonna tell Davidson now?* she thought, *I've got your murder suspect living next door to me?*

"Whadya do yesterday?" she asked, more to make conversation than to interrogate him.

"I got a haircut and a shave, picked up some new clothes, went to Cerise Park then had dinner at a sports bar," he recounted as he stared out the passenger window at the row of brown trees that were losing their leaves.

Hannah hadn't noticed the new clothes; she'd been caught off guard with his haircut and shave, but she glanced down and saw the new boots, pants and jacket he was wearing. Clearly he had some money. And why had he gone back to the park? Davidson was going to have a field day with that information — murder suspect returns to the scene of the crime... to remove evidence?

She didn't comment on the new clothes, being sensitive herself to how people looked at her. With her jet black hair, milky white skin and runner's physique she usually drew the stares of men, and it was not always welcome. She didn't want Jake to feel self-conscious about his looks. She had to admit, though, he'd gone through an amazing transformation, from dirty, scruffy guy living in the park to clean-cut, stylish, handsome man.

She drove down Hillcrest Drive and took a left on Stratford, then a right into the cul-de-sac where she lived. The four units all painted the same off white color faced each other across the cul-de-sac and each had an attached two car garage with extra parking in front of the garage. A few small trees and brown grass made up the common areas between and in front of each unit, creating a sense that they were little individual homes rather than a block of condos.

Hannah pulled into the driveway in front of her unit and looked over at Jake before opening the door. "This is it," she said, nodding at the building in front of her. "I'm in Unit B. Your place is around the back."

Jake nodded slightly but said nothing. Hannah had no idea how long he had been homeless and what it might mean to him to have a place of his own. He scanned the property then looked at Hannah for direction. "Let's go check it out," she said encouragingly, opening the truck door and stepping out into the driveway.

Jake got out of the truck, grabbed his backpack and walked around the front of the vehicle where Hannah stood watching him. She had no intention of bringing him into her side of the condo. Inviting him to stay in the detached studio had been a big enough leap for her. She already shared one wall with the crazy cat and guinea pig lady; what difference would it make to share another wall with Jake?

She led him to the left along a small gravel path that wound around her unit and led to a door on the back of her home. Years ago, whoever had owned the place had gained permission from the HOA to close off a spare bedroom in the back of her unit, add a separate entry door and build in a small kitchenette, bathroom and shower. There was no separate bedroom in the studio, just a full size bed in the left half of the apartment next to a tiny chest of drawers. The kitchen and bath were on the right. The bathroom and shower were the only things enclosed in the room. There was no table, but the kitchenette had a narrow countertop bar and two bar stools, as well as a narrow fridge, a two-burner cooktop, a microwave built into the cabinets and a coffee maker on the linoleum counter. Hannah was able to get a good price on her condo because most buyers wanted a two bedroom unit, not a one bedroom with a separate studio apartment attached out back.

Hannah pushed a four-digit code on the keypad on the door lock and popped open the door. "4902," she said to Jake as she swung the door open. The place smelled a little musty, as she rarely had reason to venture in. Her aunt had visited last year and Hannah had washed the bedding and towels but hadn't re-made the bed, and had left the linens piled on it.

Jake walked in, stopped and scanned the place.

"It's kinda small, but cozy," she said. "It's got everything you need." She moved further inside and started to give Jake the nickel tour. "The linens and towels are clean, I just forgot to make the bed. There's a bathroom and shower back there," she said, pointing to the narrow door in the opposite corner of the room. "And the kitchen is sur-prisingly functional," she said with enthusiasm, realizing that she was repeating the same lines the real estate agent had used when showing her the place two years earlier.

"Lemme look in the kitchen here and see if you have the essentials," she said. "My aunt stayed here a few months ago and I haven't re-stocked the place. Go ahead and make yourself comfortable," she said, seeing that Jake was still standing in the entryway with the backpack slung over his shoulder.

Hannah pulled open the kitchen cabinets one by one, making a note to bring more paper towels, trash bags and coffee filters. She pulled the fridge open and saw that her aunt had left a few bottles of water, a diet RC cola, and a tub of margarine. She inspected the margarine to make sure it wasn't expired. She also found a few cans of soup and stew in the cabinets.

Jake set his backpack on the bed, unzipped it and pulled out a ziploc bag that looked like it held his overnight kit stuff. He went to the bathroom and turned on the water; she assumed he was washing his face.

She moved next to the bed and grabbed the sheets to help him make it when she saw a large knife in a scabbard poking part way out of Jake's bag, like the tongue of a lizard sticking out of its mouth. She recognized the wooden handle and distinctive hilt of a K-Bar. It was the iconic knife used by Marines since World War II. Two thoughts popped into her mind at the same time and fought with each other: the guy in the park had been killed with a knife, and it was also totally natural for a corpsman who worked with Marines to hang on to his K-Bar as the one piece of kit that exemplified service in The Corps. She turned and started when she realized Jake was standing behind her.

9

October 2022, Montrose Colorado

On Monday, Hannah was assigned a day shift. She parked in the back of the new Montrose police station downtown and made her way to the conference room where the sergeant was getting ready to conduct roll call and brief all the officers preparing to start their shifts. Sergeant Jenkins was an old-school cop who had worked tough streets in Los Angeles before joining the Montrose Police force. He told people he liked the small town vibe and the absence of major gangs. Some of the officers called him The Cricket behind his back because of his long skinny legs, high voice and uncanny resemblance to Jiminy Cricket.

At 7:30 a.m. sharp, he kicked off the meeting, "Alright everyone, settle down, listen up." Jenkins paused as the conversations died down. "The road construction is still ongoing off Spring Creek Road. Olivea and Johnson, you two work that and coordinate with the construction crew." Johnson rolled his neck. It was going to be a long day sitting on a construction site, pulling over the occasional knucklehead who tried to speed past the orange cones. Jenkins continued his assignments, "Last night there was a burglary off Marine Drive in the trailer park. Jimenez, go over there, knock on doors, see if anyone saw or heard anything." Jimenez gave a thumbs up from the back row. That was a predominantly Hispanic part of town, and Jimenez spoke Spanish and worked that beat. "We're getting complaints of drivers not yielding at the new traffic circle by the Rec Center. We had a fender bender last night, no injuries. Holcomb, that's in your beat. Spend a little extra time there today. Everyone else, work your beats," Jenkins said, looking around the room for any questions.

"Now, before everyone heads out, Lieutenant Davidson is gonna brief you on the murder we had in Cerise Park last week." Jenkins nodded to the tall lieutenant, who stood up from the first row and addressed the room. "Most of you have already heard that we had a fatal stabbing in Cerise Park around 11 a.m. on Friday. Our victim was a white male, age twenty-eight, named Jimmy Hopkins. Jimmy had an arrest record, including possession and dealing coke in and around Cerise Park. He wasn't a model citizen and some of you may have had interactions with him in the past." Davidson paused, pushed a remote button and Jimmy's face appeared on the screen at the front of the room. "Have any of you seen this man?"

Hannah looked around then spoke, "Sir, Cerise Park has been part of my beat for the last year and I hadn't seen him until I found the body."

Davidson nodded. "Anyone else?"

Officer Johnson spoke up. "LT, I think I pulled him over last year for speeding. As I recall, his tags were expired, too. I'll pull the record on that and send it to you."

"Thank you, Officer Johnson," Davidson said, waiting for any more comments.

When no one else spoke up, Davidson continued, "The coroner reports that our victim was stabbed with a narrow blade like a stiletto, maybe eight inches long. We didn't find the murder weapon in the park, but keep an eye out. The coroner puts the time of death at between 10:30 and 11:30 Friday morning. Forensics has come back, and at this point, we don't have any DNA evidence that points to a suspect."

Davidson scanned the crowd then caught Hannah's eye before continuing. "However, we do have a person of interest in this case. His name is Jake Hanlon. We believe he is a homeless veteran, possibly passing through Montrose. He was attacked in Cerise Park by a man and a juvenile with sticks the day before our victim was killed. It turns out that our stabbing victim was one of Mr. Hanlon's attackers." Davidson paused to let that sink in. An officer whistled softly and the others suddenly were alert, shifting in their chairs.

"We also know Mr. Hanlon was in or near Cerise Park during the time of the stabbing. We have no direct evidence of his involvement in this homicide but he remains a person of interest." He paused for questions, then pushed the remote again, bringing up a picture of Jake on the screen. "This is Jake Hanlon. If you have any interactions with this man, or notice anything suspicious, let me know. Any other questions?" Davidson scanned the room and glanced at Hannah again.

Hannah realized that the picture had been taken when Jake was interrogated by Davidson on Friday afternoon, when he still had a beard and long hair. He was now almost completely unrecognizable from the photo. She suddenly wondered if Jake's transformation had been a coincidence. She was going to mention Jake's new look, but realized it would open up questions about how she'd come across that information and ultimately how she had invited Jake to stay in her studio apartment. She had no desire to bring this up in front of everyone. Davidson was not known for his tact, and she had no idea how he would react. She decided she would tell him in private.

She was on her way out when Davidson called to her, "Got a minute, Officer Livingston?"

"Sure, I was planning to come see you after the roll call," she said a little nervously. "I didn't know you'd be down here briefing us."

"Let's go up to my office," he said, gesturing for her to lead the way. Hannah waited for Davidson to take a seat at his desk before she sat down in the small metal chair in front of it. His desk was clean and neat with only a laptop, a photo of his wife, a pen holder and a pad of paper. He kept all of his ongoing case files on the laptop so there was no mountain of files on his desk. He smelled of Old Spice aftershave. "So," he said, leaning back in his chair, "What's the latest with our suspect?"

Hannah disliked the way he used the word suspect, but she understood Davidson's point—there were definitely a few red flags with Jake. "I went to check on him yesterday and found out he'd been asked to leave the veteran's shelter."

Davidson sat up straight. "What happened?"

Hannah looked down for a moment then spoke. "He came back to the shelter Saturday night after drinking somewhere in town. The night security guard claims Hanlon shoved him. Hanlon said he just brushed the guy's shoulder on the way to his room."

"So it seems we have a violent alcoholic," Davidson said, rubbing his hands together.

"Sir, I wouldn't jump to that conclusion from this one incident," Hannah said, hoping she wasn't going to piss off the lieutenant.

"What would you call it then, Officer Livingston?" Davidson said, squinting his eyes at her.

"Well, I feel partially responsible," she said. "When I dropped him off, I told him there were no drugs or alcohol allowed in the shelter. I didn't know he wasn't allowed to have a few beers in town and come back in."

"Do you know for a fact that he just had a few beers?" Davidson asked, twirling a pen in his hand.

Hannah thought for a moment, "No sir, I don't."

Davidson nodded, "Almost all of the homeless I've encountered have a drug or alcohol problem, or both. Do you think it's safe for us to assume that Mr. Hanlon has this problem, too?" Davidson asked, as if lecturing a new cop.

Hannah knew it would be pointless to offer up her gut feeling about Jake now or remind Davidson of the fact that many police officers also had alcohol problems. "I suppose that's a fair assumption, sir."

"And what about shoving a security guard. Is that a type of violence?" he asked with the tone of a sixth-grade teacher. Hannah didn't want to argue the point about whether it was a shove or rubbing shoulders with the guard, so she remained silent.

Davidson nodded like he had won a point, "And where do you think our suspect is now? Did he tell you where he was headed?"

"He said he was going to go back to Cerise Park," Hannah replied, working up the nerve to tell him the rest of the story. "I didn't think that was safe for him after he was attacked, so I invited him to stay in a detached studio apartment on the back of my condo." She stopped momentarily. "Just until he can get himself sorted out," she added quickly.

Davidson scratched the gray stubble on his chin. He looked like he was about to rip into her. "Well," he said calmly, with no small amount of sarcasm, "I guess you'll be able to keep a better eye on our murder suspect now." Hannah nodded in acknowledgement but did not respond.

"Is there anything else you can share about Mr. Hanlon at this point?" Davidson asked, rocking back in his chair.

"He has a knife," Hannah said reluctantly, waiting for Davidson's reaction.

"What? You've seen the knife?" he almost yelled, leaning forward on the desk and getting closer to Hannah.

"Yes, I saw part of a knife sticking out of his backpack. It's a K-Bar, standard issue Marine Corps knife."

"I'm familiar with a K-Bar," Davidson said, looking a little disappointed.

"It's quite a bit bigger than the stiletto you mentioned, but I thought you'd want to know," Hannah said, trying to make up for the fact that she hadn't brought it up at the briefing. "He got a haircut and a shave too; he looks different from the photo you put up."

"That would have been a good thing to bring up at roll call," Davidson growled.

"I wanted to let you know first," she said, "See what you wanted to do with the information." It wasn't a lie. "I can get a picture of him now," she offered.

Davidson looked appeased, "Yeah, let's do that, Officer Livingston. See if you can get a good headshot and bring it to me."

"Will do, sir," Hannah said, wondering how she was going to take Jake's picture without alerting him.

"Anything else then?" he asked.

"No sir," she said, standing up to leave. Davidson nodded and Hannah walked out, feeling like she'd just left the principal's office.

Davidson picked up the phone after Hannah walked out. "I've got an assignment for you," he said to the person on the other end. "Come see me this morning."

———◇———

Hannah's shift was mostly uneventful. She pulled over a couple of speeders and a guy from Arizona with both turn signals broken. She broke up a fight at a gas station and took a report of a stolen motorcycle. At the end of her shift she responded to an accident on Townsend where two high school kids ran a red light at the entrance to the school parking lot and got T-boned by a pickup truck. Fortunately, no one was injured because the truck driver had slammed on his brakes at the last moment, slowing his momentum considerably. Hannah directed traffic in the middle of the road while two other officers took statements from the drivers and onlookers and a tow truck worked on removing the two damaged vehicles.

The sun was setting earlier every day and she arrived home as the late afternoon light cast long shadows across her yard. She took a shower and put on jeans and a sweatshirt. She decided to go check on Jake; maybe she could figure out a way to get his picture for Davidson.

As she walked around back to the studio, she saw two empty paint cans in the grass next to the house. She knocked on the door and Jake opened it holding a paintbrush in one hand.

He stepped back and let her in. "Wow, you work fast," she complimented, scanning the apartment, which was completely repainted in a light coat of gray. She was a little ticked that Jake hadn't asked her about the color, but she had to admit it was a nice neutral that looked really good.

"I've got a little trim to finish up," Jake said, returning to the corner near the bed and getting down on his knees. He dipped his brush into a half full can of paint on a flat piece of cardboard and proceeded to run the small brush slowly over the remaining white baseboard trim. Hannah stood there for a minute admiring his work, then had an idea.

She pulled out her phone and said, "I wanna take some pictures of this and send it to my aunt. She'll be happy to see I've got a new color for the next time she comes for a visit." She took a few pictures of the walls, then waited for Jake to finish his trim and stand up. When he did, she shot a photo of the wall behind him and just caught Jake at the edge of the picture looking back at her. She took a couple more shots of other areas just to make sure he didn't suspect anything.

"Well, whaddo you think?" he asked, looking around the room.

"I think it's fantastic! What do I owe you for the paint and brushes?"

"Nothing. I don't like handouts, this is just a down payment for letting me stay here. What else can I do to help?" he asked.

Hannah blushed slightly as this good-looking man, flecks of paint in his dark hair, tight, paint-spattered T-shirt, jeans and bare feet stood there staring at her.

"I wanted to get rid of this old carpet," she said quickly, pointing to the weathered carpet underneath the bed, "Put down some linoleum, make it easier to clean and maintain."

"I can do that," Jake said. "Just lemme know what kind you want."

"You did so well picking out the paint, I trust you to pick out a good color for the floor," Hannah said, knowing she was terrible at picking out and matching colors, part of the reason her color scheme in her condo was black and white. "I'll leave you the keys to my old truck. You can use it to pick up materials when I'm at work. And I insist on paying for the flooring. You can give me free labor, but I'm gonna pay for the flooring."

Jake shrugged as if to say, "Suit yourself."

"I was going to order a pizza. Why don't you join me? I can bring it over in about 45 minutes."

Jake hesitated, then said, "Sure."

A driver in a small pickup dropped off the pizza and Hannah brought it and a couple of cold Cokes to the studio. The door was open, so she walked in and was hit by the pungent smell of new paint.

"Jake?"

"I'll be out in a second!" he called out from the bathroom. After a couple of minutes, he came out of the bathroom wearing the same jeans, but now he had on a clean T-shirt and boots.

"It kind of stinks like curing paint in here," Hannah said.

"Yeah, I've been smelling it all day, so I'm used to it."

Hannah suggested they eat outside, behind the apartment. She was not going to invite him into her condo. "I'll be right back," she said, setting the pizza box on the counter. "I've got a couple of folding chairs we can use."

She returned from her garage and popped open the two chairs as Jake brought the pizza and Cokes out from the studio kitchen. The sun had just set and there was an orange glow to the west directly in front of them on the horizon. It was a crisp fall evening and Hannah was glad she had on her sweatshirt, but Jake looked comfortable in his short-sleeved T-shirt. They sat side by side with their backs to the studio wall, watching the last dance of red light up the sky as they ate.

Hannah was curious about Jake. She knew so little about him other than that they had both experienced the Iraq war. She knew people thought she was pushy, so she tried to be tactful. "You don't seem like most homeless people I've met," she said suddenly.

Jake finished chewing. "What are most homeless people like?" he asked, throwing the ball back in her court.

"Well, they seem to have mental health issues and substance abuse problems," she said, immediately remembering the incident at the hospital where the nurses had told her he'd had some sort of flashback.

"What makes you think I'm any different?" he asked.

She hadn't expected him to throw himself under the bus like that. "I dunno, you just seem more put together, like you have your problems under control."

Jake took a sip of Coke before responding, "I'm trying to work some things out in my life right now. To be honest, I do have some big problems, but I'm finally at the point where I think I can make a dent in them, finally address them," he said, looking over at her with eyes that pleaded for understanding.

That was a much more honest answer than Hannah had expected, probably more honest than anything she would have told someone she'd just met. She still struggled with her experiences in Iraq, so she could only imagine what Jake was going through after his tour in Iraq and then somehow becoming homeless.

"How long have you been homeless?"

"It's been about two years now," he said, taking a bite out of a slice of pizza and wiping the corner of his mouth with the back of his hand.

"Are those problems you mentioned related to your deployment, to the Battle of Fallujah?" she asked, turning to face him. "I only ask because, to be honest, I'm still wrestling with my experiences in Baghdad as an MP." She didn't think she'd get Jake to open up unless she was honest with him and shared some of her own issues. She told him about shooting the girl on the scooter in the Green Zone. "I keep thinking I wiped out an entire generation. The girl's parents were killed in a mortar attack and then I killed their only child," she said quietly, as darkness settled over them.

Jake was silent for a long moment. Then he said quietly, "I got my best friend blown up, and couldn't save him as he bled out."

Hannah was silent; she wanted to give him space to continue if he needed to.

"That's one of the things that I'm trying to work out. One of the reasons I've become an 'urban camper'," he joked, turning to her with a smirk.

"Urban camper; I like that," smiled Hannah. "It sounds more PC than homeless," I'm gonna use that with my colleagues from now on. They'll get a kick out of it." She didn't ask anything more about Iraq, as he seemed unwilling to talk more about it at the moment.

A brief silence fell between them before Hannah said, "Hey, I just wanted to let you know that if you want to talk more, I'm always available."

He looked at her in the waxing moonlight and Hannah thought she saw tears in his eyes. "Thanks," was all he said, though he sounded a little choked up.

"Ya know, I just started going to this 12-step program, and it's been good for me. If you're interested, I can take you sometime."

"I don't think that's my cuppa tea," he said, "But thanks for the offer."

She nodded, and after a minute tried to shift the conversation. "Where did you grow up?"

"San Marcos, a town north of San Diego," he said tersely.

"Is your family still there?"

Even in the twilight, Hannah could see the darkness come across his face and his jaw tighten. "I don't talk about my family."

"Oh, I'm sorry," Hannah said quickly, feeling caught off-guard.

"It's OK. I really appreciate the pizza," he said, standing up and signifying that the Q&A session was over.

"No problem, I appreciate the paint job. It looks great!" As she walked back to her condo, she realized two things simultaneously: Jake had a lot of secrets, and she was beginning to feel something for him beyond simple veteran to veteran kindness.

10

APRIL 2004, IRAQ

A week after Martinez, Davis and Tony Luongo were blown up by the IED, Jake was moved from the medical triage tent back to work with his squad. Staff Sergeant Crawford had been called to a quick meeting with his platoon commander and been given a new assignment. The squad was ordered to position themselves down an alley and provide a quick reaction force, or QRF, to their sister squad that would be assaulting a building being used by the insurgents to fire rocket-propelled grenades on the Marines flooding into Fallujah. With Crawford's squad of thirteen Marines now down to ten, the platoon commander had assigned Crawford the QRF duty thinking it would be easier than being the assault force.

At 0700, a line of Humvees rolled down a main north-south road that the Marines had named Highway 1. They passed a mosque on the left and an empty dirt soccer field on the right before halting at the intersection of Highway 1 and a narrow side street they had designated 24-A. Their target building lay two blocks down road 24-A at the end of the dead end street.

The assault force squad, led by a tall, gangly Marine from Louisiana named Anton Ledoux, were in the first three Humvees. Ledoux,

80

known as The Ragin Cajun by his squad mates, was famous for his fiddle playing when the platoon was in the barracks. Marines would circle around him at night and Ledoux would regale them with foot-stompin' Cajun tunes.

Ledoux's Marines dismounted from their vehicles and lined up along the building to their right, taking aim at all the structures around them where gunfire might erupt. Ledoux was preparing to lead his men around the corner, where they would be exposed to fire from the insurgents in their target building down the road.

He gave the order on his radio and the squad marched forward around the corner with every other Marine splitting off, running and taking up positions on opposite sides of the narrow street as they moved toward the target building. It was eerily quiet for the first twenty yards and then all hell broke loose.

An RPG whooshed out the top window of the target building in front of them like a dragon spitting fire and smashed into the wall on the left side of the alley, spraying two Marines with razor-sharp shrapnel and fragments. One of the injured Marines fell immediately to the dusty road while the other one limped forward to help his injured comrade.

As soon as the RPG landed, Crawford ordered one of his QRF Humvees to round the corner and fire their mounted heavy weapon into the window on the target building to suppress the RPG-firing insurgent. The big 50-caliber machine gun spewed lead into the window with a deafening sound, like a hundred ten-pound hammers hitting an anvil. Spent shells flew out of the ejection chamber, bounced off the top of the Humvee and clinked to the ground in a pile of hot brass.

Shards of brick and wood splattered around the window from where the RPG had come as the heavy machine gun tore up the wall and window. Moments later, insurgents fired another RPG from a lower window at Ledoux's Marines on the other side of the street. This time the round smashed into the road near Ledoux's second line of men, exploded and sent shrapnel spewing into the men. Two more went down. The assault on the target was now stalled as Ledoux regrouped and put his remaining Marines to work dragging their wounded buddies into cover.

Ledoux jumped on his radio. "Bulldog 1, this is Gator 1, I need QRF here now! We have four wounded and we need to suppress the RPG's in the objective."

Crawford answered back as several of his Marines stood around listening to the dire situation on their radios. When a Marine is in trouble, they can count on other Marines to march through hell to rescue them. "Roger all, Gator 1, we're comin' in hot behind you."

Crawford was in the midst of giving his men orders when Jake ran up to him, his face ablaze with determination. "I'll take out the RPG's!" he yelled at Crawford and then ran around the corner and sprinted up the street as AK-47 fire erupted from another blown-out window on the target building, slapping the ground with bullets all around him as he zig-zagged up the middle of the street.

Crawford had no time to stop Jake, he had to organize the QRF. He gave them a quick plan and led the way around the corner and into the line of fire to help the pinned-down Marines. Within two steps of rounding the corner, a sniper's bullet rang out and caught Crawford in the forehead, killing him instantly. The remaining eight Marines in Crawford's squad, seeing that their leader was dead, continued on with the plan. Four instantly hit the ground around the corner and fired continuously into the openings in the target building ahead of them while the other four sprinted for the cover of an abandoned vehicle twenty-five yards away.

Meanwhile, Jake ran the last thirty yards to the ground floor door of the target building. He stood against the base of the structure to catch his breath, switched the safety off of his M4 rifle, pushed open the door and charged in.

The space was dimly lit and littered with empty boxes of ammunition, but against the far wall he spotted movement. Within seconds, a young girl in a black abaya revealing only her dark eyes stepped out from the stairwell, holding an AK-47 in front of her, but not aiming it at Jake. Jake kept his rifle pointed at her. "Put it down!" he yelled, gesturing with his left hand for her to set the gun down. To his horror she slowly raised the AK-47 to her shoulder as if she had never shot it before and was trying to figure out how it worked. Jake had time to yell at her twice, "NO, PUT IT DOWN!" But she perched it on her shoulder and took aim at him. Jake realized in an instant that he would rather take that bullet than kill her, but he had to protect his Marines, he couldn't let another Marine die on his watch, he had a mission. He pulled the trigger, squeezing off a two-round burst and the girl was thrown back against the wall, crumpling into a black ball.

At that moment, something flipped in Jake's brain, and from that point on, he would have only periodic and fleeting memories of what happened next. He ran to the corner near the girl, looked down at the dark red pool near her bare feet, let out a blood-curdling yell and charged up the stairs toward the second floor.

Before he could reach the second floor, a man appeared at the top of the stairs, saw Jake charging up and lowered his AK-47, but before the man could aim down the stairs, Jake let go a volley of three rounds. The insurgent pulled the trigger as Jake's bullets ripped through his chest and the rounds from the AK-47 ricocheted off the ceiling above Jake's head.

Jake took the last few steps two at a time before stepping over the dead fighter in front of the door to the second floor. He heard shouting from inside the room, as if whoever was in there was trying to find out if their fellow fighter was still alive. Jake didn't wait for an invitation. He pulled a grenade off his chest, reached for the doorknob, opened the door, pulled the pin and tossed the grenade into the back of the room.

The Marines from Jake's squad who were leap-frogging down the alley heard the explosion and saw smoke and debris blown out the lower window. It could only mean one thing—a grenade from inside the building had exploded. The Marines continued covering each other's movements with fire as they ran toward the target building.

Jake counted to three after the grenade exploded, then burst into the room. The air was thick with smoke and dust. He looked down the barrel of his weapon, but could barely see his own rifle sights because of the debris floating in the air. He felt for the wall to his right and slowly moved along it until he came to the first corner. He took a ninety-degree turn to the left and again moved along the wall, his senses acutely attuned to any sounds or movement ahead of him. He came to the far wall where the insurgents had been firing out the window. His grenade toss had reached this far and he expected to find one or more dead or injured fighters there. Sure enough, as he approached the window, which was at about waist level, he saw one man lying in a pool of blood. The grenade had ripped open his back, spraying the man with steel fragments, an RPG launcher lay at his side. The air in the room was starting to clear as the debris settled and Jake saw something moving in the far corner. He stepped carefully toward the movement until he came to another horror scene. In the corner, a woman was lying on her side with blood streaming from her ears from the overpressure of the grenade. A piece of wood about the size of a pencil was stuck in her left eye. She looked at Jake with her right eye, then lifted the black cloth of her abaya to reveal a baby lying on its back underneath the cloth.

The woman gestured with her hands in a lifting motion towards Jake. He realized she was pleading with him to pick up the baby. She wasn't asking help for herself, she wanted him to save her baby. Jake looked down at the infant and saw that it was very young, maybe three months old or less. The baby was wiggling its arms and legs and looked uninjured. Jake began unconsciously reaching for the baby when something stopped him—it felt like a black hand on his heart. He pulled his hands back, believing in his gut that this baby wasn't being used as a booby trap, but he couldn't take the chance. He had to clear one more floor of this building and protect his Marines.

He stepped over the baby, shook his head at the mother and walked back to the stairs. He checked his magazine, changed it for a full one off his chest pouch and peered around the corner to the last set of stairs. Putting his weapon to his shoulder, he crept up the twenty or so steps to the top floor. The door to the room was open and Jake peeked inside, leading with the barrel of his gun. At that same moment, a man on his right who was hiding behind the door grabbed Jake's rifle barrel. Jake wouldn't let go and the two men fell to the floor wrestling with the gun. The insurgent was a big man, had a huge head like a five-gallon bucket, with a long black beard and hands like ribeye steaks. He and Jake rolled on the floor and the big Arab ended up on top. He wrenched Jake's weapon away but was unable to turn it and fire because Jake was too close to him. The man sat astride Jake and pressed the gun sideways into Jake's neck, trying to use the handguard to choke him. The man was strong and had the benefit of gravity and leverage as he pressed the rifle into Jake's throat. Jake's arms couldn't hold back the weapon anymore. He knew he had one move left, it was now or never, do or die. He released his right hand on the gun and the man shoved it harder into Jake's windpipe.

Jake would be done in ten seconds, but with his free hand he reached for the K-Bar knife on his hip near the floor, unsnapped the safety catch, grabbed the knife by the handle, raised his arm just as he was about to pass out and slammed the blade into the side of the man's head with all his strength. The insurgent let go of the weapon, reached up to feel the knife sticking out of his temple and toppled over to his right.

Jake scooted out from under the man: he was already dead. He retrieved his knife, picked up his M4 rifle and rubbed his throat. His windpipe was nearly caved in, but at least he could breathe. He scanned the rest of the room, saw it was empty and slowly made his way downstairs. When he got near the second floor, he heard noises. He was about to toss in another grenade when he recognized the voices as men from his squad. He stepped into the room and saw them all huddled in the corner near the woman and her baby. One of the Marines reached down to pick up the baby and Jake yelled, "NO!!"

but nothing came out except a squeak. A bomb detonated, blowing everyone across the room. Jake was tossed out the door, tripped and rolled down the stairs.

11

October 2022, Montrose Colorado

An early season storm brought moisture down from the north, pelting the Western Slope of Colorado and the surrounding lowlands in sheets of rain and sleet, while the numerous peaks surrounding Montrose valley above 9,000 feet were left covered in snow after the clouds cleared the next day. The weather in Colorado could be unpredictable, but there were plenty of sunny days to make up for the few days of stormy weather.

Hannah was assigned another day shift on Tuesday during the worst of the storm. Rain or early snow usually brought more car accidents and this Tuesday was no exception. Hannah flicked the lights on in her cruiser as the tow truck in front of her tried to pull a car out of the irrigation ditch. The driver, an elderly man, had been on his way to the grocery store when he was caught in a mini-deluge, lost sight of the road and slid off to the right into the ditch. He was terribly upset, so Hannah had calmed him down, called his wife to come get him and waited for the tow truck to haul away the car. They were on a narrow two lane farm road that was now blocked by the tow truck, leaving single lane traffic only. She stood outside in her yellow raincoat directing cars with a lighted wand as rain poured off the brim of her cap. When the tow truck finally pulled away, she climbed back in her car and was about to head home for the day when a call came in reporting an accident off Chipeta Road, less than a mile from her position.

Hannah threw on her siren and boxed around the row of farms to her left, turned on Spring Creek Road then made a left on Chipeta. The rain was still pummeling the road and cars had their headlights on for safety. Heading south on Chipeta, she came to the scene of the wreck. A driver who had seen the accident was standing in the rain outside her car when Hannah pulled up. Hannah jumped out of her cruiser, realizing she was the first officer on scene. The rain was now blowing in her face, but she could see a car flipped over on its hood, upside down about ten yards off the side of the road and at the bottom of a small embankment.

She threw on her coat and ran toward the car. The woman who had seen the accident was waving her hands so Hannah stopped to find out what she could.

"I saw it all!!" the woman shrieked, pointing near the upturned vehicle.

"What happened?" Hannah asked hurriedly.

The woman appeared to be in her late fifties and was wearing black and gold gym clothes. Her blonde hair was sopping wet and she was beside herself. "It was going too fast, it flipped!" she exclaimed, then wiped rain and tears from her eyes.

Hannah didn't wait for the rest of the story. She ran to the side of the road and climbed down the slick, muddy embankment. She could tell the car was some kind of sporty Japanese model with fancy rims and tires. She knelt down to peer through the shattered upside down passenger window so she could see the driver. Shards of broken glass in the mud and grass cut into her knees. The driver was still upside down with his seatbelt in place. The first thing that caught Hannah's eye was the empty vodka bottle laying on the inside hood of the car, now below the man's head.

"Son of a bitch," she whispered as she shouted to the man. "Hey, are you alright?"

The man turned his head to Hannah, his glassy eyes trying to focus on her and said, "Huh?" His long hair hung upside down, and he didn't seem all that aware of what had happened. Hannah wanted to reach in there and punch him in the face, but she got the better of her instincts. She needed to check the rest of the vehicle for survivors. "Is there anyone else in the car?" she yelled at the man. This time his face twisted into a tight ball of grief as he tried to speak, but no words came out.

Hannah grabbed her flashlight and scanned the back seat. The rain was still coming down in buckets, obscuring her vision. She stood up and moved to the other side of the upturned car and panned her flashlight across the muddy ground in front of her, and that's when she saw a flash of pink.

A young girl, maybe ten years old, had been flung from the vehicle as it flipped over and was now pinned underneath the top of the car. She was on her back and her long dark hair covered her face. The car was resting on her stomach and her lower body was trapped underneath.

Hannah shined the flashlight in her face and brushed away the girl's hair. Her eyes were closed but Hannah saw the slightest rise and fall in the girl's chest as she tried to breathe. Protocol was to let the EMT's extract a person in order to minimize additional injuries, but Hannah saw blood spilling from the girl's mouth, a sign of internal injuries. She couldn't just wait and watch her die. She heard sirens in the distance, but this was life or death. She dropped to her knees and began digging under the vehicle so she could maybe pull the girl out. The ground was soaked and the clay-like mud clung to her hands as she pulled gobs of it from under the vehicle. She stopped and repositioned herself with her butt on the ground and her feet against the car for better leverage. She grabbed the girl's arms and pulled as hard as she could. The girl's arms stretched, but she remained stuck. Hannah felt like she was pulling the girl's arms out of their sockets. She scooted closer so she could reach under her arms and then she pulled for all she was worth, yelling at the top of her lungs as the frustration and adrenaline hit her.

She felt the girl move slightly so she repositioned herself to get a better grip and pulled again, this time using her legs more. Again, the girl moved a few inches but was stuck in the suction of the mud. Hannah reached down, grabbed the girl's pants at the waist and let out a thundering roar as she pulled with everything she had. This time the girl's body slid all the way out and Hannah fell onto her back in the mud with the rain lashing her face. She looked up from the ground and saw Officer Jorge Jimenez staring down at her. Jimenez worked the beat just north of her area and rushed to the scene when he heard the call go out. Within a few minutes, two EMT's kneeled next to the girl as Jimenez grabbed Hannah from behind and lifted her off the ground.

"Hey, are you OK?" Jimenez asked, as he wiped away some of the mud from her face.

"Yeah, I'm fine," she gasped, trying to regain her breath and looking down as the EMT's started CPR on the girl. "There's a drunk in the driver's seat," she said, nodding her head towards the car.

"Alright, I'll take care of him, are you sure you're OK?" Jimenez asked, looking warily at her. Hannah didn't realize it but she was completely covered in mud and blood and looked like a monster from a horror movie.

"Yeah, just go get the guy," she said and Jimenez gave her one more look and ran around to the other side of the car.

She moved to where the EMT's were working on the girl. She didn't want to bother them, but she could see the frustration in their faces as they tried to revive her. Hannah bent over to look at the girl's face and suddenly felt light-headed. Instantly, her mind took her back to Iraq, back to another dead girl laying in the dirt, another one she had failed to save.

She stood up and turned away, her breath coming in short gasps. She felt herself sweating as her heart raced in the cold wind. She tried to step up the embankment to her patrol car to get a drink of water, but the incline was greasy with slick mud and she fell to her knees. She stayed there in the mud on her knees and put her head in her hands.

Suddenly a voice above her was shouting through the cold, slashing rain and she looked up to see Sergeant Jenkins, The Cricket, standing at the top of the embankment. "Hang on," he yelled in his high voice, immediately sizing up the situation. Jenkins rushed to the back of his patrol SUV, pulled out a length of rope and tossed one end down. Hannah stood, grabbed the rope with her slick hands and Jenkins pulled as she trudged up the steep ditch through the slick mud.

"Damn, Livingston, you look like hell!" Jenkins exclaimed, coiling the rope as wind and rain lashed them. "I'm sending you home, I'll get your report tomorrow. We'll take it from here." Another Montrose police car was parked along the road and a Montrose County Sheriff was pulling up as well.

"Are you hurt?" Jenkins asked.

"No," she replied, wiping her hands on the front of her pants.

"Here," Jenkins said, tossing a wool blanket to her from the back of his car.

"Can I stay and see if the girl survives?" asked Hannah.

"No," replied Jenkins firmly. "You're shivering and covered in mud and blood. Go home, take a hot shower, get a good night's rest and come see me tomorrow." He turned and started barking orders to the officers on scene.

Hannah took one more look back at the EMTs who were still on the ground working frantically on the girl—it was not a good sign. She climbed into her patrol car with the blanket wrapped around her shoulders, put her hands on the wheel and began to sob, for the little girl crushed under the car, for the anguished girl on the scooter she'd shot in Iraq, but maybe most of all for the innocent girl she used to be who had died along with these other little girls.

She sat there for about fifteen minutes to pull herself together and then drove home in a stupor. To say it had been a bad day would be the understatement of the year. It was times like this that she wished she had someone at home waiting for her, but it seemed that was not to be.

She pulled into the driveway, took off her boots outside her door, and trudged inside, making a beeline for the freezer where she kept a bottle of tequila. She had been so good, resisting the temptation to open it for weeks, but tonight was different. She sat down on the blanket, uncorked the bottle and poured herself a tall shot of anejo. That's when there was a knock at the door.

Who the hell is that? she thought irritably, standing up and walking to the entryway in her wet socks. She opened the door and found Jake looking back at her in her muddy uniform, but he said nothing.

"I brought you something," he said with a sly smile. "Something to thank you for helping me out."

Hannah looked down and saw that he was holding a leash. A motley tan and white dog with a single floppy ear was sitting quietly behind him. Her jaw dropped at the sight of the little guy, and at Jake's impetuous act, but also at the almost desperate need she felt to let the dog curl up on the couch with her.

"This group, Underdog Rescue, had a tent set up in front of City Market with a bunch of rescue dogs, so I walked over and had a look. They rescue abandoned dogs from the reservations in Utah, clean them up, give them their shots and pair them with good homes. I figured you could use a friend," Jake said, looking down at the dog who was wagging his tail.

Hannah was speechless, but she squatted down to greet the dog and he walked up to her tentatively and licked her hand. Despite all the logic in her head that told her to tell Jake to take it back, she instantly fell for the little guy. She reached down to pat his head and he put his ears back and looked up at her with big golden eyes.

"What do I say, Jake? I don't even have any dog food and I can't leave him alone all day while I work," she said, backtracking on her own thoughts.

"I know," he nodded, lifting a small bag in his other hand. "I got him some food and treats and I can watch him while you're at work." That last statement stuck with her and kept her awake that night, with its implication that Jake intended to be around tomorrow, next week, next month and who knows how long. She had thought of him as a transitory, interesting person, a fellow Iraq veteran she could help for her own penance, a wounded soul on his way to whatever destiny had in store for him. She hadn't considered the fact that he might become a fixture in her life.

"Well, I—" she stammered, "I mean, he's here, so I guess we should get him settled," she grinned, moving back from the door and letting them both enter.

"What's his name?" she asked, as the dog, still on the leash, began to sniff around and explore Hannah's living room.

"They called him Armando, but you can name him anything you want. They said he's only 10-12 months old so he'll probably respond to whatever name you give him." Jake set down the bag of dog food and held the leash as the dog explored the room.

"Armando's fine, I guess," she shrugged, looking down at him as he wagged his tail. He was about thirty-five pounds, she guessed, and had a black spot over one eye, making him look like a sweet little bandit.

"What happened to you?" Jake asked finally.

Where do I start? thought Hannah. She took a seat at the table and sighed heavily, and Jake sat across from her, still holding Armando's leash. "I was first on scene of a car wreck where a young girl was tossed from the vehicle and pinned underneath. I pulled her out from under the car, but I'm not sure she made it. The EMTs were working on her when my sergeant sent me home."

Jake nodded as Armando sniffed Hannah's feet.

"I need to take a shower," she said, changing the subject.

"I think Armando would appreciate that," Jake teased, breaking the tension with a smile. "I'll see you tomorrow then," he said, standing up.

"No, stay and have dinner with me," Hannah blurted out. "It's been a helluva day." Her next thought was, *I've just invited a stranger to stay in my house while I take a shower.* But something in her mind clicked and said, *It's OK. Trust.*

Jake sat back down slowly and scratched Armando's ears. "What do you want for dinner, maybe I can get it started while you're in the shower," he suggested.

"It's top-notch fine dining," she said with a smirk. "Grab any two Lean Cuisine meals from the freezer and microwave them. There's lettuce in the fridge for a salad, too."

Jake stared at the opened bottle of tequila on the table then looked at Hannah and asked, "Whaddaya wanna drink?"

Hannah looked at the tequila bottle, suddenly realizing that she didn't need it, that she'd grabbed it as a lifeline, maybe a lifeline that connected to nothing.

"I'll have water," she said. "There's bottles in the fridge."

Jake let the leash go slack and Armando nuzzled up against Hannah's knees, sniffed her hands and wagged his fluffy tail.

"I think he likes your mud smell," Jake joked.

Hannah laughed, bent down and gave Armando a kiss on the head, scratched his ears, then stood up and went to the shower. In the bedroom, she undressed to her underwear, threw her muddy uniform into the laundry hamper, and stared down at her duty belt holding her service pistol. She picked up the belt and carried it into the bathroom with her, setting it on the counter. The weapon had become such an integral part of her life that she took it everywhere.

When she returned to her bedroom after her shower, she saw that Armando had nudged open the door and was lying on the floor beside her bed with his nose between his paws staring at her. She beamed at the thought that her new furry friend would be waiting for her every day when she got home. "Hey, buddy, I'll have to get you a dog bed," she said, petting his back. She put on sweats, let her wet hair hang down her back and led Armando back into the kitchen.

Jake had heated the two meals and placed them on plates he found in the cupboard. He'd also made two salads and set up the meal on her small dining table.

She took a seat with her back to the wall and Armando crawled under the table and lay down at her feet.

"I think he's taken to you already," Jake said, sitting across from her. "There's Swedish Meatballs and Shrimp Linguine, take whichever one you want," he said, pointing to the two plates on the table.

"Shrimp sounds good to me," she said.

"I was hoping you'd take that," Jake said with a grin. "I love Swedish Meatballs. Do you remember those meatballs they used to serve at the DFAC in Iraq? It was like they were made of rice or something."

"Yeah, I remember," Hannah said. "They were so dry they sucked the moisture out of your mouth."

"Yep, they sure did. You could use them to soak up spills, like cat litter."

Hannah laughed. "OK, they weren't that bad."

They finished their meal and Hannah sat back in her chair and looked at Jake, saying out loud what had been bothering her all night, "I really hope that girl made it. Normally you're supposed to let the EMTs extract victims. But blood was coming out of her mouth, and I thought she might die from internal bleeding." She shook her head and looked down at Armando.

"You did the right thing," Jake said emphatically. "I was a corpsman, I would've done the same. You assess the situation and make the best call. Internal bleeding is life-threatening. Believe me, you did the right thing, Hannah."

Hannah wanted to believe that, but she was also afraid she might have hurt the girl by yanking her out of the sucking mud under the car. She'd seen too many dead and dying people in Iraq and the thought of being involved in another child's death was unthinkable to her. "I just can't be responsible for another kid dying," she said aloud, remembering that she didn't like to show vulnerability, and wondering why the hell she'd just said that.

A dark cloud seemed to cross Jake's face just then and he reached down to pet Armando, seemingly more for his own comfort than for the dog's.

"What is it, Jake?" Hannah asked, sensing his mood shift. She moved over to the couch and motioned for him to join her.

"It's nothing," he shook his head, standing up and taking a seat at the opposite end of the couch, but Hannah knew it was something. Her contact with death this afternoon made her impolite, less willing to put up with the phony veneer of life.

"Bullshit," she said. "What is it?"

Jake rubbed his face with his hands then spoke with a distant voice, "I shot a girl in Iraq, too," he said quietly, then took a deep breath before continuing. "I entered a building and this young girl wearing a black abaya held a gun in front of her like a broomstick. I told her to drop it, but she raised it to her shoulder and aimed at me." He looked down. "I finally double-tapped her and moved on. I had to protect my squad from some RPG-slinging insurgents. They'd already injured four Marines with rockets."

Hannah could picture the scene exactly as he described it. So many of the battle scars of Iraq were deeply etched in her mind, like a map carved into stone. She sensed Jake was still torn about his decision to shoot, just like she was. Killing a child might be self-defense legally speaking, but that didn't make it feel any better. The guilt and shame stay with you forever. She didn't ask any more questions, but reached her hand over and placed it on his arm. Jake looked up from Armando, who was lying at the foot of the couch, and into Hannah's eyes. She held his gaze for a moment, then pulled her hand back.

What am I doing? she thought. Armando stood up and moved toward the door.

"I'll take him out," Jake said, grabbing the leash and walking out into the moonlight with Armando at his side.

12

October 2022, Montrose Colorado
(The next morning)

Jake opened the driver's side door of Hannah's pickup and gazed down at Armando, "Jump in, pal, I'm not lifting you." Armando looked up at Jake then figured it out quickly and leapt straight on to the vinyl bench seat in the old Chevy 1500 short bed. Having lived as a wild dog by himself on a reservation for months, Armando was keen to go wherever it was warm and dry. When Jake slid into the driver's seat, Armando scooted to the passenger side and looked over at Jake as if to say, "Where are we going?"

Jake pulled on the lap belt and drove out of Hannah's complex, heading west toward Murdoch's farm and ranch store. It was the ideal place for outdoor life in Montrose, as they stocked everything a rancher or outdoorsman would need plus tools and guns. Jake parked, snapped the leash on Armando and walked him into the store. Now that it was fall, they were selling warm clothes, jackets and gloves. The place smelled like pumpkin spice candles. Jake read the aisle signs and made his way to the back of the store where they kept the guns.

He stood at the glass counter staring at the large collection of pistols. "Anything I can help you with?" asked a large man behind the counter, his stomach poking through his Murdoch's store vest. He wore a cowboy hat and a gold earring.

Jake looked down at the array of pistols again, then asked, "Do you have a Ruger SP101?"

"Sure," the man said, pointing to a different counter. "All the revolvers are over here." Semi-automatic pistols had largely replaced revolvers in law enforcement, military and civilian use, but many people loved the simplicity and reliability of a revolver.

The man pulled a set of keys from his belt, opened the glass case from behind, set a small rubber mat on the counter, pulled out the short gleaming revolver and placed it on the mat like he was presenting a fine piece of jewelry.

Jake picked up the gun, expertly flipped open the 5-shot cylinder, ensured it was empty, closed the cylinder, looked down the sights once then said, "I'll take it."

A little surprised at the quick sale, the salesman nodded, picked up the gun and locked the gun case. "I'll need to see your ID. We have to run a background check, and it might take half an hour depending on how backed up the FBI site is."

Jake showed no emotion, but inside his heartbeat sped up. *I wonder if this background check will look at my VA mental health records?* He'd been on the periphery of the federal government long enough to know that many branches were like little fiefdoms and didn't share all their information with each other for various reasons. He was counting on bureaucratic inefficiency. He handed the man his ID and looked down at Armando, who was sniffing the floor. "I'll take my dog out for a walk and be back in a bit."

"First I need you to fill out this online form," the man said, turning a laptop computer around and putting it in front of Jake on the counter.

Jake stared at the questions, his heart still banging. He had the thought to turn and head out the door right now, but he needed to do this. He started typing. Most of the information was run-of-the-mill personal data for the FBI to run a check—name, DOB, place of birth, citizenship, etc. He came to the block where he had to enter his place of residence and he put in Hannah's address. It then asked if he had ever been arrested or charged with a felony, and he typed in "No." The salesman walked over to serve another customer dressed in hunting garb as Jake entered the rest of his information. The last few questions were about domestic abuse—Jake froze. His hands shook as he filled out the domestic abuse section. His mind spun, he began to sweat and thought he was going to have another episode. "Get it together, man! You've got to do this," he whispered to himself.

He wiped his brow and glanced over to see that the salesman was showing a bolt action rifle to a customer wearing camo hunting gear. Jake powered through the questions, answering "No" to several domestic abuse questions. *If only*, he thought, glancing at his answers one more time before digitally signing the document.

"You done?" the salesman asked, leaving the hunter to fondle the long gun for a moment.

"Yes," Jake replied, turning the laptop around for the man to see.

"OK, everything looks good," the man said, reviewing the answers. "Give it about half an hour to process for approval."

Jake nodded, and led Armando down the aisle and out the door. The sun was bright, but a cold wind cut through him. He zipped up his jacket, looked south and saw that the San Juan Mountains had a splash of white on their peaks. The rain in Montrose overnight had resulted in more snow in the high country.

Armando sniffed at the bags of animal feed in the parking lot and Jake led him to a large patch of grass he found near some apartments behind Murdoch's. He wanted to let Armando run around off leash, but he wasn't sure the little guy wouldn't run away. His head was still spinning after answering those questions. He hadn't anticipated questions on domestic abuse. Jake looked around, and when he saw he was alone, he pulled his jacket up to cover his mouth and screamed into it, as if expelling a band of demons from his gut. It was either that, he knew from experience, or the pain and trauma would build up and blow to the surface at the wrong time. Armando looked back at Jake with fear and surged ahead on the leash, as if trying to put distance between himself and this man who had roared like a bear.

"It's OK, come 'ere, boy," Jake said, regaining his composure and kneeling down, trying to comfort Armando. The dog moved tentatively toward Jake and licked the back of his hand. Jake scratched his ears then stood up and they started back to Murdoch's.

The man at the gun counter had the pistol in a small black plastic case when Jake returned. "Everything went through," he said with a nod, picking up the gun case. "I have to walk it to the checkout register for you."

"I need a box of shells for that, too." The man pointed to the shelf where they kept the .38 and .357 rounds. Jake chose the more powerful box of .357 bullets.

Jake finally relaxed a bit as he and Armando followed the salesman to the front of the store. He paid cash and they returned to the truck.

They both sat in the front seat for a few minutes as Jake looked out the window, lost in his thoughts and memories. He popped the pistol under the seat, started up the truck and drove off.

He stopped at the east parking lot of Cerise Park under a large oak tree, let Armando out and walked over the river bridge into the park. He followed the cement footpath heading north for a few hundred yards, then turned off the path into the tangled woods. Eventually he came to the site where yellow police tape tied to trees formed a small perimeter. He stood at the edge of the site and stared into the small space, trying to remember any details. He looked hard at the area and walked around the perimeter, Armando at his side staring up at black birds squawking in the trees. Jake studied the site inside the tape from several angles. Finally, he walked the perimeter one more time, peering down at the ground. All he saw were the footprints of a dog or coyote that had approached the site and left the same way. *I don't remember this*, he thought. He was afraid he had been here, had done something terrible, but he had no recollection of the place. He knew he'd had an altercation in the park, he remembered bits and pieces of it, but he couldn't remember where, or when or with whom. He sat down on a stump and put his head in his hands. His mind felt like pieces of a jigsaw puzzle scattered on a table, memories that sometimes clicked together to tell a story but other times reflected a shattered life. He rested there for several minutes until Armando nudged him with his wet nose. Jake stood up and knew now, more than ever, that he needed to finish what he came to Montrose to do.

He walked Armando back to the path and followed it to the north-west side of the park, where it opened up to another parking lot. He saw a man walking off to his left near the ball fields. He thought he recognized him as a shopper with a blue ball cap and Carhart jacket that he'd passed in an aisle at Murdoch's, but he couldn't be sure.

He led Armando to the sidewalk exiting the park until the two stood at the intersection of Chipeta Road. He looked both ways and crossed the street, walked Armando south along the road until he came to the trailer park again and took a right turn. He knew where he was going this time and walked quickly down the road until he reached the end of the cul-de-sac.

He slowed his pace and stooped down to pet Armando, plucking a few goat head stickers from his fur that the little guy had picked up in the park. While he was attending to the dog, Jake studied the shabby green and white mobile home at the end of the road. The rusted Crown Vic was missing from the small driveway to the left of the trailer. The place looked empty. Jake scanned around to see if any of the neighbors were outside, but he saw no one. He took a chance, walked quickly to the mailbox in front of the trailer, opened it, reached in and pulled out a piece of junk mail, and stuffed it into his pocket.

He quickly walked Armando out of the trailer park, his heart racing and his head spinning. When he got back to Chipeta Road, he reached into his pocket and pulled out the piece of junk mail. Stamped on a small sticker on the flyer for new windows was the name and address of the owner of the trailer. Jake read the name and his jaw hardened—now he knew for certain.

He looked at his watch; it was 3:30 p.m. "Let's go, boy," he said, giving the leash a tug. Armando stood up from the ground where he'd been lying as he waited for Jake. They walked back through the park together, not stopping until they reached the parking lot where Hannah's truck sat. On the way, they passed the dog park, where they found one of those water fountains that fills a little bowl near the ground so dogs can drink. It was a cool day, but they had walked a mile or two, so Jake pushed the stainless steel button, water filled the little bowl and Armando drank heartily, pausing to look up at Jake as if to say, *I've never seen one of these.*

On the way back to Hannah's, the junk mail in Jake's pocket felt like it was radioactive. The implications of what it meant settled in his mind like a tick burrowing under his skin. He knew with certainty what was coming, but he couldn't deal with it right now—he needed a diversion, something to get him through the night, something to ward off the nightmares he knew he'd have tonight. He pulled into a liquor store off Main Street and bought a bottle of cheap tequila with a red skull imprinted on it. "Perfect logo," Jake said to himself.

The woman behind the counter had blue hair that had once been blonde and was wearing a Broncos T-shirt. "Beautiful day, huh? I wish I was outside or somethin'." She was obviously bored and wanted to talk. Jake just nodded. "Will that be it then?" she asked, seeing she wasn't going to get conversation out of him.

"Yes, thanks," he said, paying for the bottle and leaving. He drove back to the condo, parked in guest parking and walked Armando around to the studio. He didn't have an outside chair so he sat on the ground leaning against the house. He left the leash on Armando, but let him wander a bit in the unfenced back area, figuring the leash would slow him down if he decided to do a runner. Armando sniffed around the back yard and explored the smells of the plants and animals, constantly looking back at Jake for reassurance.

Jake uncorked the death's head tequila and drew back two long gulps right out of the bottle. It went down smoother than he expected for a cheap brand. Hannah was coming home soon and he didn't want to make a scene, but he had his own problems to deal with. Armando finished exploring and lay down next to Jake in the brown grass, both of them watching the orange glow to the west. Jake reached down to pet him and took another swig off the bottle with his other hand—that's when Hannah rounded the corner.

"That ground is damp," she said, bending down and calling Armando. The dog stayed sitting beside Jake, as if unsure who his master was. Jake reached over and nudged Armando to stand up and greet Hannah. She gave him a pet and scratched his ears. Hannah saw the bottle of tequila next to Jake and a frown crossed her face. *Last time I checked, she had a bottle of tequila on her coffee table*, Jake thought.

"I'm gonna grab some chairs," she said, standing up. "Come on, boy," she called in a sing-song voice, patting her thigh. Armando looked at Jake again for confirmation and Jake said, "Go on, boy." She soon returned with the two folding chairs they'd used when they had the pizza. Jake helped her unfold them. She set them against the wall and they both sat down facing the dying light of the day.

"How was your day?" he asked.

"Pretty boring, really," she replied. "We had classroom training in the morning and I just gave out a few traffic tickets in the afternoon."

"What was the training about?" Jake asked.

"The first part was just a refresher about use of force—you know, when to shoot, when to tase, when to fight, stuff like that." Jake nodded. "The second part was interesting. It was a brief by a DEA agent explaining that they believe a sophisticated drug gang was moving into the west of Colorado after gaining a foothold in the Denver metro area. I was pretty shocked. I mean who would think we'd be dealing with those kinds of hard core criminals here. I didn't think little Montrose was fertile ground for big time drug dealers."

Jake nodded in silence. In his wanderings, he'd seen people go crazy for fentanyl and other opiate type drugs. All you had to do was give vulnerable people a try of the stuff and you could create customers for life. He didn't know how much time Hannah had spent in big cities, but he'd seen the devastation firsthand. He could see how any up-and-coming town would be an attractive market for drug dealers; they were just getting in on the ground floor.

"You must've had a hard day," Hannah said. She made it sound like a question and turned to look at Jake, nodding at the bottle of tequila on the ground under his legs.

Jake suddenly had an intense feeling that he wanted to tell her everything, describe what he'd done today and why, tell her about his past, let her know all the demons he was fighting... but he couldn't. He had a feeling that just telling someone like her, someone else who had experienced loss and trauma in war, would be good for him. But he couldn't do it, couldn't bring himself to open those dungeon doors. Plus he had plans. Anything he told her would probably ruin his plans and maybe hers too. He opted for half-truths.

"I went to Murdoch's today, had a look around at their dog stuff and tools. It's a pretty cool store."

Hannah nodded, "That's all you did, window shopping?"

Jake couldn't tell if she was being subtly critical at his lack of accomplishments today or just curious. He needed to tell her more. He picked up the tequila, took another drag on the bottle and offered it to her. She shook her head.

Again he felt the urge to confide in her, explain all that had happened to him, but his brain shut down his mouth. He did share a few things, though. "I walked over to a trailer park on the other side of Chipeta," he said, omitting his stop at the site of the murder.

"Why go there?" Hannah asked, her brows furrowed in confusion.

"Remember I told you I got my best friend blown up?" he said, looking off into the dusk.

"Of course," she said, sitting up a little straighter.

"It's a bit of a story," he said, his tone warning her.

"I've got plenty of time."

"Well, the gist of it is that we were assaulting the second story of a building in Fallujah and we knew the enemy was gonna fight. As we lined up for the assault, Tony stepped in front of me and took my spot in the line-up. That was my position in the stack, you see, where I always was. Tony said we couldn't afford to have the corpsman injured, like he somehow knew something was going to happen. I should've resisted, but I let him do it." Jake paused and shook his head.

"We cleared the room, but there was a baby crying in the back of the room. Our point man Davis picked up the baby and that set off an IED. Davis was killed instantly, Martinez bled out in a matter of seconds. Tony was third in line and took a piece of shrapnel in his gut. It should've been me. I was blown backwards, but just shaken up."

He sighed deeply. Hannah sat forward in her chair, listening intently. "I dug into Tony, but I couldn't stop the bleeding. There was a gusher somewhere hidden that I couldn't find. I fished around in his stomach for as long as I could, but couldn't stop the bleeding. Tony knew it was the end. He got pale and lost the strength to resist. He put his hand on me and told me to please tell his mother that he loves her." Tears fell from Jake's eyes as he continued, "He died in front of me, and it should've been me. He was my best friend and the greatest guy you could ever meet." Wiping his eyes with the back of his hand, he reached down to pet Armando, who had now moved between the two chairs, but Jake didn't realize Hannah was petting him, too. He accidentally put his hand on top of hers and quickly pulled it back, "I'm sorry, I didn't mean anything," he said.

Hannah lifted her hand off Armando and placed it on Jake's arm. "I'm glad you told me this, Jake. I'm so very sorry. That fucking war did nothing but chew up everyone who was there. It's like it took on a life of its own, like it became a monster." Jake wanted to pull his arm back from her touch for several reasons, some of which Hannah wouldn't understand, but then she slid her hand on top of his hand and squeezed his fingers. "I'm here for you, just remember that," she said softly, looking him in the eye.

"You asked me where else I went today, that's why I told you this story," said Jake, turning to her and slowly pulling his hand back. "I was never able to tell Tony's mother what happened, how he died, that I was there, that he loved her." He stood up and walked around in a small circle, shaking his head. "I just didn't have the guts to meet her, to tell her the details of what happened, tell her how I should have been the one killed, how he took my place." He stood there with his back to Hannah, looking up into the stars that were beginning to show their light against the darkening sky. "This is one of the things that's haunted me." He paused for a long moment, but Hannah waited. Then he continued, "It's one of the reasons I became homeless... not the whole reason, but one of the reasons. I'm trying to set things right."

He turned around to face Hannah. "I found out she lives here in Montrose. I've been walking to her home and checking it out, but I haven't been able to muster the courage to knock on her door."

Once she'd left Jake and returned home, Hannah sat on her couch with Armando at her side. She'd fed him and now he was laying on his back with his paws in the air, letting Hannah scratch his tummy.

Everything Jake had told her this evening was rolling through her head in waves of emotion. She wished she had someone to talk to about him; her feelings were complicated. She had probably burned the bridge with Amber, her former best friend. The only other person she could think of was Susan, the retired police officer who'd invited her to the 12-step meeting. She decided to call her.

"Hey, Hannah! How ya doin'?" Susan cheerfully answered the phone.

"I hope I'm not calling too late?" Hannah asked.

"No, not at all, honey, what's goin' on with you?"

"I was wondering if we could meet for a quick drink tonight." Hannah bit her lip, worried it was too spur of the moment for Susan.

"Of course, where do you wanna meet?" Susan said.

"How about The Horsefly in twenty minutes?"

"Works for me, I'll see you there."

Hannah gave Armando a bone, locked up and drove to the brewpub. The Horsefly Brewing Company was a Montrose landmark with a popular following. They had excellent craft beers, a good menu for pub food and great service.

She found a small booth by the window and scanned the room while she waited for Susan. The place was about half full with a few old timers at the bar and some families and couples eating at tables. A waitress appeared to take her order, her long, shiny dark hair falling over her shoulders. Hannah thought she was probably Filipino.

"What can I get you?" she asked.

"I'm waiting for a friend, but I'll have two iced teas with chips and salsa."

The girl nodded and scurried off. Susan had told Hannah at their first meeting that she was a recovering alcoholic, which was why she attended the 12-step program, so Hannah wasn't going to drink in her presence.

Suddenly, an older man with a huge beard who'd been sitting at the end of the bar stood up, pointed at the bartender and started yelling, "Who are you to tell me I've had enough?!" He was slurring his words and Hannah instantly sized up the situation. She was off duty and didn't want to get involved, but she couldn't allow the guy to start a fight or hurt someone. She waited to see what the staff would do.

A manager at the other end of the bar left her customers and approached the man from behind the bar. "Sir, I'm going to have to ask you to leave. You've had enough to drink and you're yelling at my staff."

"No one can tell me I've had enough! I've got rights, too. I wananother beer."

"Sir, that's not going to happen. We would be negligent to serve you any more alcohol," the manager said calmly, leaning forward to emphasize her point. The drunk reached across and pushed the manager, and she fell back but the bartender caught her.

"This is bullshit," he slurred, swiping his arm across the bar, sending bottles flying and glass shattering onto the floor. Suddenly, he felt a chokehold around his neck and dropped to the floor, reaching for the arm around his neck.

"I'm an off-duty Montrose police officer," Hannah said to the man and the crowd of gawkers. She loosened her hold, but held the grip around his neck in case he tried anything. In less than a minute, sirens sounded and an officer from the Montrose PD entered. He saw Hannah on top of the guy and walked up to her.

"Whadda we got, Hannah?" Officer Jackson asked.

"This guy is drunk and they wouldn't serve him anymore so he pushed the manager and broke a bunch of bottles."

Jackson nodded, "OK, thanks, I've got 'im now," he said, snapping a set of handcuffs on the man. He lifted him to his feet and marched him out the door. "Let's go, buddy, you're goin' for a ride."

Hannah stood up and everyone in the bar broke out in applause. Surprised and embarrassed, she smiled and raised her hand to dismiss their cheers before heading back to the table, where Susan was now sitting.

"That was impressive," Susan nodded with a smile. "Nice take-down."

Hannah was still full of adrenaline, her heart racing. "Yeah, it's hard to be invisible in this small town," she smirked. In reality, she loved the occasional opportunity to use her jiu jitsu moves. She'd practiced a little jiu jitsu in the Army and found it pretty helpful as an MP. Countless criminals found themselves on the ground after an altercation with Hannah, wondering what the heck had just happened.

"So, what've you been up to... I mean besides practicing WWF moves?" Susan teased.

"Well, I've been helping this homeless guy, a veteran, and I wanted to get your take."

"OK, sure, tell me about it."

Hannah told her everything, from Jake's attack all the way to her conversation with him earlier that evening, including how she was beginning to have feelings for him.

Susan listened without interrupting. Hannah was finishing the story when she added, "He actually got a dog for me, Susan! I've always wanted a dog, but I never had the time. It's like he sensed I needed it." She paused, knowing she was about to tell Susan what was really on her mind. "It's like the police officer in me is saying I should keep him at a distance, be wary. But the woman in me sees a kindred spirit, an Iraq war veteran damaged by war, but who's not giving up, and is still moving forward, trying to make a new life. He's considerate, good looking, kind in his own way, and generous. He's also a bit of an introvert and he's definitely keeping some secrets. After what happened with my best friend's fiance, I thought I didn't deserve to be with another man, that I was totally unworthy... but with Jake, I dunno, I feel something. I thought it was the connection of two vets, but now I think it's deeper. I actually care about the guy. Is that crazy? Am I falling in love with a homeless man? Am I crazy?" Hannah asked. She shook her head as if mystified by her own decisions.

Susan smiled. "You're not crazy, honey. Affection, love, compassion, whatever you call it, goes where it goes, right? It's a feeling, not a thought. It flows like a river and you can't stop feelings any more than you can stop the flow of a river. But that's not the same as making a conscious choice to have a relationship with a guy."

Hannah nodded, listening intently to her friend who had a lot more experience than she had.

"The key is trust. You may have feelings for a guy, but do you trust him? Are you ready to be vulnerable and open up to him? Lemme tell you a story." Susan took a sip of her tea and continued. "My first husband was a cop, too. I knew it was probably a big mistake," she smirked. "Everything was great for the first two years, until one day I found out he was heavy into online porn. I had no idea. I confronted him, he got angry and denied everything. At that point, I lost trust in him. We split a little while after that." She sat back in her seat and sighed. "All I'm saying is that a relationship must come with feelings and trust. You have to have them both, you see what I mean? You could have feelings for someone, deep feelings, but not trust them completely either."

Hannah nodded. "Yeah, that makes sense. I didn't think of it in those terms."

"I'm not telling you what to do about Jake," Susan clarified, raising a finger for emphasis, "I'm just telling you that from my experience, feelings are not enough to sustain a relationship."

Hannah took a sip of her tea and looked across the table at her new friend. She was puzzled over the idea of what trust really is, how you know you have it before it's too late, how you measure it. She figured it all came down to a gut feeling. She had trust in her fellow police officers because they had a common bond and she knew them, and it was the same with the soldiers she'd served with. She thought of Jake in the same way and just trusted him implicitly. It was the bond of brothers, the sacred oath to look out for each other. But Jake was no longer a soldier and clearly he'd had some trauma after the war, hit rock bottom and become homeless along the way. But Hannah was a lot less judgmental about homeless people than her fellow cops. "But for the grace of God," she always reminded herself. The crap she'd experienced could have easily overwhelmed her, and in some ways it still did, but it hadn't resulted in the loss of her job and homelessness. And she knew that her brushes with death and darkness made her more sympathetic to people who'd taken a serious beating in life.

"Thanks so much, Susan, you've given me a lot to think about. I really appreciate being able to talk to you about all this."

Susan reached across the table and touched Hannah's hand, "Honey, I hope you know you can reach out to me for anything, OK? I'm glad we're friends."

Hannah felt her own trust in Susan's friendship was growing. "So am I. Thanks, Susan. And thanks for coming tonight on such short notice."

"No problem. Hey, we're having a meeting again this Friday if you wanna come?"

Hannah bit her lip. She didn't want to let Susan down, but that last meeting took a lot out of her, even though it was a net positive. She knew she needed to dig up some more weeds in her mental garden, but the prospect of that left her feeling bloody and dark. *Can I ever move forward without dealing with the past?* she thought, though she already knew the answer. "I'll let you know. Thanks for the invite," she smiled.

13

OCTOBER 2022, MONTROSE COLORADO

Detective Joe Davidson was not a man to let things lie. Tall and thin with a slash of gray at his temples, he looked patrician, like he belonged to the staff of an ivy-league school. His school master looks belied an indomitable determination to solve cases. He'd cut his teeth in Oceanside, California, in the narcotics unit, and had an enviable rate of arrests. He'd been there when fentanyl started to show up in the back alleys of North County, San Diego, and he'd seen it grow into a destructive epidemic that was ravaging California cities. How he'd ended up in small-town Montrose, Colorado was a point of gossip among his colleagues in Montrose. Some said he'd gotten in trouble with the police chief in Oceanside, others said his wife had had a nervous breakdown. What very few knew was that his teenage son had died when he was given fentanyl at a high school party in Oceanside.

The other reason for Davidson's move to Colorado was his gambling problem. He played the ponies at Del Mar and Santa Anita so frequently that his Chief caught wind of his debts. It was a vulnerability he couldn't risk in a detective, it made him too susceptible to bribes. The Oceanside Police Chief politely suggested a change of location for Joe, but it wasn't really a suggestion: it was move on or be fired. The chief was worried that his son's loss to an OD and his gambling problem would damage Davidson's impartiality when dealing with drug dealers in Southern California. He didn't need Davidson going into revenge mode.

Davidson sat in a booth at Denny's off south Townsend Avenue. The tall booth seats gave him a measure of privacy that he couldn't find easily in other coffee shops. Arturo Gonzalez walked in, spied Davidson in the back corner, and came over. Davidson had used Arturo as a confidential source in Oceanside and when he took the job in Montrose, he cajoled Arturo to come out and work with him again.

Gonzalez had been recruited into the Logan Heights gang in San Diego as a kid and grown up in the drug trade. Joe had picked him up on a drug bust near Carlsbad, California and decided to turn the kid into a snitch rather than put him in jail. In fact, Arturo had been looking for a way out of the drug and gang business. He'd married a pretty girl from El Salvador and wanted to start a new life and a family. He was smart enough to figure that his odds of making it to thirty were not good on his current track. He also had the advantage of being able to blend in anywhere like a chameleon. He was of average height and weight with no real distinguishing marks, except maybe his dark mustache. As a drug runner, Arturo had displayed a knack for disguises and deception, making him a natural for Davidson's purposes. Davidson had helped him relocate to Montrose and put him to work figuring out how the drug trade worked on the western slope of Colorado. Even though the little western slope towns of Colorado paled in comparison to 3.5 million people in San Diego County, there was a quiet, but expanding drug business growing here.

Davidson nodded as Arturo took a seat in the red vinyl booth across from him. "What's up, Artie?"

"Same old, same old," said Artie in a slight Hispanic accent. His brown Carhart coat, jeans and John Deere ball cap made him look like he worked on one of the many local ranches or farms in the Montrose valley.

"You want coffee or somethin'?" Davidson asked.

"How about a full breakfast?" Artie asked, flashing his trademark smile. "I got news for you, boss!"

Just then a tired-looking waitress with a pen in her hair stopped at their table, "What'll it be, guys?" she asked, pulling the pen out and snatching a notebook from her pocket.

Davidson, who was sipping on his bottomless cup of coffee, had already eaten at home but he nodded at Arturo to order.

"Chorizo con huevos por favor con tortillas de maíz."

"Why did you order in Spanish? She didn't understand the shit you were sayin'," Joe asked gruffly after the waitress walked away.

"Boss, she understood completely. Plus, it's my job to sprinkle Spanish culture everywhere I go," he grinned.

"Are you sprinkling it or tinkling it?" Joe asked, poking fun at Arturo's cultural pride.

"Ha Ha, boss. When I'm done, this whole town will speak Spanish."

"I think it's already on the way, Artie," Davidson said, sipping his coffee. "So, what did you find out?" he asked, looking at his watch. Arturo liked small talk but Joe needed to get back to the station for another meeting.

"Well, the big news is that your man bought a gun at Murdoch's."

"What?" Davidson said with quiet shock, leaning forward in the booth.

"Yeah, he walked straight back to the gun section, bought a pistol and one box of ammunition."

"Geez," Davidson breathed, leaning back and scratching his chin. "So he passed the FBI background check?"

"I guess he had to, boss. I watched him fill out the application on a computer."

Davidson shook his head in disbelief. "I knew this guy was up to something. I can't believe he passed the screening."

The waitress appeared with a hot Mexican breakfast for Arturo and Davidson waited until she left before speaking again. "Did you see what kinda pistol he bought?"

Artie nodded as he chewed on a corn tortilla. He swallowed and said, "It was a revolver of some kind, but I couldn't see the make and model. I was in the next aisle over. It had a short barrel, stainless coating, black grip."

Joe nodded, guessing either a Smith and Wesson or Ruger. "Short barrel like five inches?"

"No boss, more like two to three."

Joe nodded again. The only reason for a barrel that short was because it could be easily concealed. A barrel that short wouldn't be very accurate beyond fifteen feet, but it could be easily hidden on someone's body.

Artie took another bite of spicy eggs and spoke as he chewed, "He went to Cerise Park again."

"Don't tell me he visited the crime scene?" Davidson was dumbfounded.

Artie nodded as he took another bite of eggs and salsa.

"You gotta be shitting me!" Davidson exclaimed, more to himself than to Artie. "What did he do there?"

Artie took a sip of coffee then spoke, "He kinda just looked around."

"Like he was looking for evidence he left behind?" asked Davidson, a hint of excitement in his voice.

"I was off in the treeline using my binos so I didn't have a perfect view." Artie looked at Davidson, trying to prepare him for his observation. "He looked kind of confused to me, boss."

"Whadya mean confused?" Davidson asked irritably, sitting back and sensing Artie was not fully committed to Davidson's theory about Jake.

"Well, it wasn't like he was looking for one thing, like a lost knife or something. He circled the whole site and even went down a path once looking at the ground, like he was studying it, trying to figure out what happened."

"Artie, that sounds like a guy looking for lost evidence. Maybe he dropped something on the trail and was trying to find it."

"I don't know, boss, I think he was just studying the place. That's my hunch, anyway."

Davidson was getting frustrated. "I don't need your feelings, Artie, I just need to know the facts about what you saw. Leave the theories and suppositions to me."

Artie shrugged. He'd learned it didn't pay to cross Davidson. "Whatever you say, boss."

"Did he come home after the park?" Davidson asked, his tone softening.

"Naw, he walked out the west end of the park with his dog."

"Wait a minute," Davidson said. "Where'd the dog come from?"

"Oh, I forgot to tell you, he had a mutt the whole time. Some brown and white spotted thing." Davidson stared at him. He was going to rip into Artie for leaving out the detail, but decided to let it go.

"Anyways, he walked outta the park, went south on Chipeta and walked into that trailer park off the west side of the road."

Davidson frowned and narrowed his eyes at the mention of the trailer park. *What the heck was Hanlon doing there?* he wondered.

"I couldn't follow him closely, boss — he woulda made me. It was a narrow dead-end road. The guy walked down the lane, spent about fifteen minutes doing something and then walked back out."

"You couldn't see where he went, what he did?" asked Davidson with urgency.

"Naw, like I said, he woulda spotted me instantly."

Davidson sat back and thought about this new information as Arturo finished his breakfast. Several things Artie had observed bothered him, because they didn't square with his plan for Jake. He could certainly dismiss Artie's "gut feeling" that Jake wasn't looking for evidence he'd left at the site; that was total conjecture. But why did Jake buy the gun legally at Murdoch's? By doing that and completing the FBI background check, he was forever tying himself to that weapon. Any illegal use of the gun would be connected directly back to him. That didn't follow the normal pattern of criminals. Most crooks look for a gun on the black market, steal one somewhere, or try to buy one for cash from a private gun owner. This guy was an enigma. And then there was the visit to the trailer park. What the heck was Jake up to there? Davidson's experience told him that wasn't a random stroll —

there was a reason Hanlon visited that trailer park, and he intended to find out what it was.

Arturo wiped his plate clean with his last piece of tortilla and sat back with a satisfied smile on his face. "So, whaddo you want me to do now, boss?" Davidson drained his coffee and laid out his next instructions for Artie.

Artie headed out and Davidson was about to leave when his phone rang. He looked down at the number. *Shit!* He hesitated, then picked up.

"Hello."

"You missed a payment," said a voice with a Slavic accent.

"I know, I'm working things out. I've got a plan."

"Not good enough detective. How is your wife doing?"

"You leave my wife out of this."

"Pay your debts," the man said and hung up.

Davidson slammed his phone down on the table, then picked it up. He placed a sports bet on an app then stepped outside to his car.

On the drive back to the office, Davidson mulled over his options after what Artie told him. He had to tell Hannah that Jake had bought a gun — there was no way around it. She had to know that for her own safety. But at the same time, he was afraid that if she kicked him to the curb for buying the gun, he would do a runner and they would lose him. She couldn't confront him about the gun because he would know he was being followed. She'd have to concoct some other excuse to boot him out. Davidson couldn't control how Hannah would take the news, and one thing he hated was not being in control.

Back in his office, he called the shift supervisor, "Jenkins, it's Davidson."

"Hey, Detective, what can I do for you?"

"Is Livingston on duty?"

"Yeah, she's on patrol right now."

"Can you have her come see me?"

"Sure, her shift's almost over. I'll bring 'er in early."

"Thanks, Jenkins, I appreciate it."

"Anything I need to know about?" Jenkins asked. "She in trouble or somethin'?"

"No, no, nothing like that. She's just helping me on that murder case in a small way." Davidson wanted to keep the fact that he was using Hannah to spy on Hanlon a secret for now.

"Got it. I'll send her your way."

"Great, thanks, Jenkins."

Thirty minutes later, Hannah was walking upstairs to Detective Davidson's office. She'd received the radio summons from Jenkins while writing a ticket for a snowbird from North Dakota who had no license plate on his trailer. She ran through possible reasons Davidson wanted to see her and none of them seemed good. It was definitely about Jake and probably some kind of bad news. Her black duty boots made a clomping sound as she stepped from the stairs onto the upper floor where the detectives and administrative staff had offices. Hannah was taken aback when Davidson smiled at her as she entered.

"How was your day, Hannah?" he asked, sitting back in his chair with a pencil in his hand. Now she was getting more concerned. Davidson wasn't the type for first names and small talk.

"Typical day in Montrose, sir, nothing out of the ordinary," she said, sitting down and waiting for him to get to the point.

Davidson leaned forward. "I need to inform you that Hanlon bought a gun."

Hannah was momentarily stunned. This was not the news she was expecting. *What the hell was going on?*

Seeing the shocked look on Hannah's face, Davidson filled in the blanks, "He bought a short barrel stainless revolver yesterday at Murdoch's." He let that sink in before continuing. "The fact that he bought it outright, with a background check, tells me he probably doesn't intend to use it for a crime. Obviously, we could tie it to him instantly through ballistics."

"I guess that makes sense," she nodded, her mind spinning as she wondered why Jake would have bought a gun. *Unless, of course, he doesn't care if he's tied to the gun, or plans to kill himself.*

"As you know, a short barrel revolver like that is often used for self-defense," Davidson said.

That's true, Hannah thought, but knew it would also be perfect for killing up close.

"I had to let you know, for your own safety," Davidson continued. "I wouldn't blame you if you kicked him out," he said, though it was obvious that his concern was manufactured. Hannah knew now where he was going with this conversation.

"But if he's put back on the street, Hannah, there's a good chance he'll disappear. Right now, he's our prime suspect in that murder. You know that." He stopped talking and let Hannah consider his words.

Hannah was used to living around guns, lots of guns, and didn't have an innate fear of them. They were just tools to her, to be used at the right time and place to solve a problem. Her real concern was Jake—why did he buy the gun? Did he have a plan to use it, or was it just self-defense? He had been brutally attacked in the park and ended up in the hospital. That would be more than enough for many people to want a gun. The thing that bothered her the most was that Jake had lied to her by omission by not mentioning it when he talked about going to Murdoch's. She knew the guy had secrets, but this was a big one.

She recalled what Susan had said last night about trust. She felt Jake had broken it in some way. On the other hand, who was she to throw stones? She'd slept with her best friend's fiance! And her ex-boyfriend had been a crooked Grand Junction cop implicated in a murder plot! Those personal failures and betrayals haunted her as much as the face of the young Iraqi girl she'd shot. The one positive thing that came out of her mistakes was a willingness to overlook or forgive the failings of others. She understood, viscerally, what it meant to screw up big time, become an outcast and lose the important people in your life.

"OK, Detective, I'll let him stay in the apartment."

"Are you sure?"

She wasn't sure, but it was the best decision she could make at that moment, given everything she knew. "Yeah, I'm sure. I'll be alright." She was going to ask how Davidson knew that Jake had bought a gun, but she already knew the answer. He was having Jake followed.

"He also visited that trailer park off Chipeta. Any idea why he would go there?" Davidson asked, closely watching Hannah's expression.

"It's his Marine buddy's mother," she explained. "His buddy died in his arms in Iraq and he was supposed to tell the guy's mother about it, but he got cold feet. He felt bad and came to set things right."

Davidson nodded. "What was the Marine's name?"

"Longo, Lungo, something like that. Tony was his first name," she replied, remembering the conversation with Jake.

Davidson jotted down a few notes then looked at Hannah. "This is good information you're collecting, keep it up, Officer Livingston. There might even be a promotion at the end of this thing."

Hannah nodded, but felt like a scumbag inside for spying on Jake.

14

October 2022, Montrose Colorado

Hannah had the day off and decided to go for a dirt bike ride. When she was seven, her dad had bought her a mini-bike and then as she got older he continued to buy her larger bikes. She was an only child and in the back of her mind she'd always felt like her father wished she was a boy. She did her best to win his respect and love—she'd learned to hunt, shoot, fish and wrestle, along with riding dirt bikes. When she was fifteen, though, her parents were killed in a car crash, and Hannah went to live with her mother's sister, Becky. She was completely devastated by the loss and often felt like she would drown in her grief. But Aunt Becky, who hadn't been able to have children, showered her with love and attention, and became the perfect surrogate mother. Hannah felt like Becky loved her for who she was, not for what she could do.

Against the odds, Hannah flourished under her aunt's love and care. She gave up extreme sports, with the exception of dirt biking. Her aunt was not wealthy, but she helped Hannah pick up a used dirt bike and drove her to places to ride near their home in southern Utah. Dirt biking was the best connection Hannah had with her father—they had loved riding together. It was also the one activity that helped her clear her mind of all the crap in her life. When she was riding, she couldn't think of anything else but being in the moment—all the past and future problems melted away and she became one with the bike and the trail. Between her aunt's love and the zen-like feel she got from dirt biking, Hannah moved past the tragic loss of her parents. Then, after high school, Hannah joined the Army as an MP out of respect for her father, because he'd been an MP in the Army in Vietnam.

After her stint in the Army, she moved to Montrose because her best friend, Amber, a fellow MP, was from the area and moved back here after her tour and captivity in Iraq. Hannah followed her friend to the western slope of Colorado and became a Montrose police officer. Her betrayal of Amber in Iraq had eventually come to light and the friendship had fallen apart. At the Montrose police disciplinary hearing where Hannah almost lost her job because she had been led astray by her shit-bag ex-boyfriend, Amber had testified on Hannah's behalf. Even though Hannah had betrayed her, Amber unexpectedly spoke highly of her at the hearing, saying that she trusted Hannah with her life and asking the panel to take into account the heroism Hannah had displayed in Iraq. The senior police officers were swayed and voted to retain Hannah. But Amber and Hannah had since drifted apart, the wounds seemingly too deep.

She parked at the Peach Valley trailhead and let Armando run around and sniff while she unloaded her bike. It was a cool fall morning, so Armando could nap in the truck while she took a ride. Peach Valley was her favorite local riding place because of the diversity of the terrain. The lower part of the riding area was a series of adobe foothills that offered generally fast and flowy trails. Above this line of foothills, the topography changed to pinyon pines, junipers, sage and steep rocky trails. At the eastern edge of the riding area, the terrain dropped off almost vertically into the Black Canyon of the Gunnison National Park.

After she put on her helmet and gear, Hannah loaded Armando back into the truck and started her bike, letting it warm up for a while. Finally, she strapped on her goggles and headed toward her favorite trail, Eagle Valley. She rode an older KTM 250 2-stroke that fit her well, being both light and powerful. She kept telling herself that someday she would buy a new bike, but her little orange mustang had never let her down.

The trail was like a secret path used by train robbers back in the day. The narrow opening, a vertical fissure in the rocks, wound through a tight, rocky canyon. The trail was epic. It had just enough technical features to challenge a good rider. Hannah cleared a long slab of stone then came to a rock ledge with a 15-foot drop to the left that she had to ride around. The ledge was only a few feet wide but had a steep run up, so she had to hit it with momentum. She stopped at the bottom to scout the best line, then hit the throttle and bounced over the ledge. Scraping her handguards on the rock wall, she cleared the obstacle with a sense of exhilaration. There were two more tricky rock step-ups, but Hannah cleaned them all.

At the top of the trail, she took a sip of water from her pack before starting up Spikes Trail, named for a local renowned rider. Spikes had a few technical step-ups at the bottom, but then opened into a faster flowing trail. At the end of Spikes, she parked her bike, took off her helmet and walked ten feet to the edge of the Black Canyon National Park. The chasm below her seemed like it came out of nowhere and belonged to another planet. Sheer black and brown rock walls plunged a thousand feet below. At the bottom of the canyon, she could see the deep blue strip of the Gunnison River raging down the canyon through a series of white, foamy rapids.

She sat on a rock overlook staring down at the majesty of the canyon. It always amazed her that this incredible geologic feature was right in her back yard. The beauty of the canyon was truly awesome, and gave her a sense of the wonders of this world. She munched on a power bar and reveled in the view.

Her focus on riding the dirt bike had blotted out all other thoughts, but now in this serene place, she thought about Jake and what Davidson had told her yesterday. When her busy mind was finally silent, she realized that she wasn't afraid of Jake now that he had a gun—he could have just as easily killed her with the K-bar knife. No, she was afraid of what Jake had in mind for the gun, what it meant for him and for her. What demons did he carry or what fears did he have that would be solved by using that gun?

The only explanation that made sense to her was suicide—it was common for a combat veteran from Iraq to take their own life after a long bout with depression and hopelessness. Jake had obviously had his share of problems that resulted in homelessness. And yet, he was quite different from other homeless vets she had encountered. He also seemed like he was doing better recently, not worse, like he was making traction toward progress in his life. She tried to recall what he had said to her the other night. "I have some problems, but I think I'm finally making a dent in them," or something like that? The bottom line was that the gun didn't make her worry about her own safety, but it did cast a shadow on Jake's future. Buying it seemed like it was a regression for him, a step toward more problems, not away from them. From

Hannah's perspective, it seemed like it might lead to confrontation, darkness, incarceration and no real future for Jake.

That she had concern for him, maybe more than concern, was another source of pain. *Why am I always attracted to lost causes? Why can't I meet a nice accountant with a BMW and a condo in Telluride?* She knew the answer instantly—those people bored her. After her deployment to Iraq, she had no time for fake people living fake, shiny lives. She wanted real relationships with real people—people who laughed and cried, who were dealing with mental and physical pain, who valiantly fought a good fight every day against the absurdity of this life, who knew loss and triumph but kept moving forward. Jake was one of those souls, as was she. A veteran of the terrible Iraq war.

She strapped her helmet on and rode back down the same trails to the trailhead. Daylight savings was in effect now and the sun was already creeping towards the horizon. Back at her truck, she opened the door and let Armando out. He bounded from the truck, wagging his tail and running in circles, clearly excited to see her as she loaded her bike back into the bed of the truck. The last few days he had really bonded with Hannah. "OK, buddy, come 'ere and gimme a kiss," she said in the playful tone she reserved for Armando, squatting down and letting him lick her face.

The sun was still warm, beating down on the white adobe clay and reflecting back to Hannah. She reached into the dented Coleman cooler in her truck bed, pulled out a bottle of Gatorade and sat on the tailgate staring off toward the impending sunset in the west. After doing his business nearby, Armando jumped effortlessly into the truck bed and lay down next to her on the tailgate. "I'm getting used to this dog thing," she said aloud, reaching over and rubbing Armando's nose. Armando, still panting from burning energy around the parking lot, looked happy to rest for a bit next to his master.

"Well, what should I do, boy?" Hannah turned to Armando. "You spend more time with him than I do. Should I trust him?" Armando's golden gray eyes reminded Hannah of speckled marbles her aunt had kept in a box in the closet. Armando looked up at Hannah with those glassy eyes but gave no obvious sign of his opinion of Jake. "You're not a lotta help here, buddy." She felt good, physically and mentally, after the dirt bike ride. It was as if some black carbon had been blown out of her system. She finished her drink as the wind blew gently through her messy hair and began to cool her off.

"We better roll, hombre," she said to Armando, jumping down from the truck bed. She drove home as Armando stuck his head out the window, smelling the farm animals, fresh cut hay and corn harvesting they passed along the way.

She pulled into her driveway, unloaded the dirt bike, put it in the garage and went inside to take a hot shower. She threw on sweats and tossed a Lean Cuisine into the microwave. After wolfing down the overly salty meal, she made a cup of tea and walked around the back to check on Jake, Armando trotting at her side.

Jake was sitting in a folding chair, leaning against the house and watching the sunset with a beer in hand. "Hey, Hannah," he said, looking up at her as she rounded the corner. Armando ran to Jake and squealed as Jake grinned and scratched his ears enthusiastically.

"I think he likes you more than me," Hannah said, standing in front of them.

"Naw, it's just his way of saying hi," Jake reassured her. "Lemme show you something," he said, standing and walking to his apartment door. He pushed it open and motioned for Hannah to step inside.

Hannah walked in and saw the new flooring. It was a brown and gray wood pattern that perfectly matched the paint. "Wow!" she exclaimed, turning to him. "It looks amazing. When did you do it?"

"I put it in yesterday when you were at work. It's vinyl. The pieces click together, so it's pretty easy to install and waterproof too."

"It really looks great, Jake," she said, nodding. "Thank you so much!" she said, turning to him. "How much was it?"

"It was about a hundred bucks—got it on sale at Home Depot."

"Well, I can't thank you enough," she said, looking into his eyes.

"Like I said, it's the least I can do to pay you back for your kindness."

Hannah was taken aback. She'd been described as many things, but kind wasn't usually one of them. Jake definitely saw her in a different light than most people. Something lit up within her at the idea that she could be a kind person. In her mind, she was tough, generous, honest, hardworking, but not really kind. She was glowing with the new view of herself as maybe having some nugget of kindness in her.

"Hey, ya know, I was thinking," Jake began slowly, pulling her out of her thoughts. "Maybe I could use some of that 12-step meeting stuff you mentioned after all."

A deep warmth seeped into Hannah's heart.

15

OCTOBER 2022, MONTROSE COLORADO

Hannah returned to work the next morning. Jake sat out back sipping black coffee and watching the leaves blow gently around the back yard — *maybe a storm was coming*, he thought. Armando sniffed around the wet, decaying leaves, chasing off a black bird that landed in the small patch of grass that made up the back yard. Jake's plans had led him to this moment, but he needed to steel himself for the finale. Even though he realized long ago that he had to do this, the thought of it made his heart race. *It's all come down to today*, he thought. *All those years and today I'll finally make things right.*

He drained the dregs of his coffee, went inside and whistled for Armando. "We're taking a road trip, boy, saddle up," he said, putting the coffee cup on the counter and grabbing a small bag under the sink. He looked at the note he had left on the counter and read it one more time. They walked around the front to Hannah's side of the townhouse and jumped in her old pickup truck.

Jake drove up Main Street, took a left on Chipeta and parked at the north side of Cerise Park near the dog park. A gray Toyota Tacoma with tinted windows pulled in behind him and parked at the other end of the parking lot.

Knowing he would be leaving Armando in the truck, Jake let the dog play in the dog park for half an hour. Armando was wary of other dogs, but he found a white doodle-something that was playful and the two of them chased, jumped and barked at each other. Finally, when they both lay down in the shade of a large pine tree, their tongues wagging, Jake called Armando and snapped on his leash. He led him to the dog watering station and made sure Armando drank his fill. He put Armando in the cab of the truck, rolled the windows down halfway, grabbed a small backpack and started walking out the west end of the park. He took a left on Chipeta, walked a few hundred yards along the side of the road, then turned into the road leading to the trailer park. He walked past a few parked cars and trucks and made his way to the battered green and white mobile home at the back. The Crown Vic was parked next to the trailer. As he walked closer, memories spilled into his head and he knew he was about to have an episode — he needed to get this done.

He walked to the side of the trailer, passing a yard gnome and a small painted turtle, up the cracked wooden steps, past a faded plastic owl and knocked on the door. To his left, a cracked window was slightly open and he could see three leprechaun figurines on the window sill. After a few moments, he heard shuffling inside. The door opened slowly and a woman with shoulder-length gray hair, jet black eyes and a deeply lined face stood in front of him. She was wearing a knitted shawl and a heavy wool skirt. At the sight of Jake, her eyes flared like streaking comets.

"Hello, Mother," he said calmly.

"Aren't you gonna invite me in?" he asked, deadpan.

She said nothing, and stepped back from the doorway. Jake walked in and looked around. The room smelled like cigarette smoke and Dinty Moore beef stew. A little wooden shelf in the corner held a collection of glass frogs with their legs hanging over the edge, each one playing a different musical instrument. There were no family photos anywhere in the room. To the left of the door was a tattered brown couch facing an old Zenith TV. Across from the couch and next to the frog shelf was a single tattered recliner with a knitted blanket on the headrest. The kitchen was to the far right near the front of the single-wide, and the bedroom and bath were in the back of the trailer. In front of the couch was a small scratched and dented wooden coffee table, the kind you saw at the Salvation Army store for ten bucks.

Jake took a seat in the recliner, as his mother remained standing by the door with a dumbfounded look on her face. "Sit down, Mother, we've got some things to talk about." Jake pointed to the couch and emphasized the word mother as if it was the most important part of the sentence.

Maybel Hanlon scrunched up her face as if she was going to laugh or cry, then cautiously sat down on the couch. She held her hands together in her lap, trying to suppress their shaking.

"How long has it been?" Jake asked. She said nothing. "It's been twenty years, nearly a quarter of a century. That's kind of a long time for me not to get a Christmas card, don't you think?"

Maybel shifted in her seat uncomfortably, "I... I didn't want you to think about me, I felt it was best for you after everything that happened," she croaked in a husky chain-smoker's voice.

"Wow, Mother, your concern for my well-being is heartwarming. Maybe we can take a little walk down memory lane together, recall some good ole times." The woman sat stone-faced, except for a twitch in her left eye. "Do you remember when I was six and Frank broke my arm?"

"He was your father, you should call him that, at least. Have some respect," Maybel said.

"Don't make me laugh, Maybel," Jake said. "Father is not what I would use to describe him. Son of a bitch, maybe, but not dear old Dad. Anyway, do you remember that incident when I was six?" he asked again, raising his voice a little. She looked down at her skirt and picked at a loose thread.

"Frank was in one of his moods and he broke my arm because I spilled my milk. What I remember most about that incident is when the school nurse asked you what happened and you told her I fell down the stairs." He paused and glared at her. "I was six years old and you were the only one who could have protected me from that monster, but all you did was cover up for him. Do you know what it's like for a six-year-old to come home, afraid every day, wondering what his father would do to him and knowing that he can't even trust his own mother to look out for him?" Jake sat forward, unable to hide the pain in his voice. Maybel wouldn't look at him.

"How about the time he knocked three of my teeth out in sixth grade and gave me a concussion? That time the CPS lady came to our home after one of my teachers filed a complaint. You said I crashed my bike into a telephone pole. I remember that you were very convincing, showing her the pole and even the scratches on my bike."

"Your father was a complicated man. Vietnam changed him," she explained, but sounding more like she was pleading with him.

"No, he wasn't complicated, Mother, he was pure evil! But you... you pretended to be my mother when it suited you, but at every opportunity, you aided and abetted that piece of shit!" Jake was yelling now. These were words he had needed to speak for too long, and now they were coming out like a volcano. Maybel shrank back into the couch as if she'd been punched in the gut.

Jake paused and took a breath to calm his tone. "You destroyed my childhood. Everything bad that's happened to me is rooted in your betrayal of the most sacred duty of a parent, to protect their child," he growled, his voice cracking. "I would've been better off being raised by wolves or living on the street. You and that animal nearly destroyed me. I've had hard times in the Navy, but none of it compares to the shit you two inflicted on me," he said, shaking his head.

"I would ask you how you feel about that, but I already know the answer. You'll give some bullshit excuse about how you were a victim, too. That you didn't have a choice. Well, Mother, I'm here to give you some choices," Jake said, lowering his voice.

He reached into the small backpack at his feet and pulled out a stainless steel revolver, making sure Maybel saw it. He flicked open the cylinder, turned it so she could see that it contained five bullets, then snapped it shut. Her whole body began to tremble as if she had just been plunged into ice water.

"Here are your choices, Maybel," Jake said calmly, standing up and placing the revolver on the table in front of his mother. He sat back down, making sure she realized that she could reach the gun before he could ever get to it.

"Choice number one," he said, leaning back in the recliner. "You take that gun, stick it to the side of your head and blow those rotten brains all over this shitty trailer. This is where you take responsibility for enabling the horrific, constant abuse of your only child, where you finally acknowledge what a piece of shit human being you have been, and send yourself to hell as a small penance for failing at the most basic duties of a human being." He waited to see how she would respond, but she was frozen, so he went on.

"Option two is that you pick up that gun, aim it at me right now in this chair and pull the trigger. Put me out of my fucking misery, Mother. Finish what you started so many years ago when you decided to destroy your son's future. You'd be doing me a favor. My life came off the rails because of your abuse and neglect. I've just been waiting for you to finish the job my whole life." He stared at her and had expected to see evil, but all he saw was a worthless woman shaking like a leaf, tears welling up in her eyes.

"Option three is the one where you don't take any action, the one that I figure is most likely because it's what you've done your whole life. If you will not take responsibility for your failure as a parent, and you won't finish off what you started and put me out of my misery, you will force me to kill you, to put a bullet in the head of my mother, to send you to the lonely grave that you deserve." Maybel began to sob.

"Please, Jake," she wailed, wiping her face with the back of her hands.

"So what's it gonna be, Mother?" Jake ignored her pleas and suddenly felt an episode coming on, and knew he had no time left. He couldn't let it happen here, in front of her. No, he could never let her see that. His head was in a vice, his breathing fast and shallow, lights danced across his eyes. He stood up, nearly fell over and walked to the door, wobbly as a drunk. He pushed open the door, almost fell down the steps and stumbled down her driveway to the cul-de-sac. He walked as fast as he could out of the trailer park, across Chipeta and back into the park. He thought he could make it to the truck if he ran, so he started sprinting, his heart pumping, the poison in his head becoming diluted with his rapid heart rate. Finally, he reached the truck and tore open the driver's door, gasping for breath. Startled, Armando stared at him and whimpered. Jake put on his lap belt and lay down on the bench seat in the truck. Armando moved over to give him room, then rested his head on Jake's shoulder as Jake passed out.

16

MAY 2004, IRAQ

The battle for Fallujah was largely over, but the Marines and Army were tasked with mopping up pockets of resistance. The insurgents who had not been killed or captured during the main battle had either fled to another Sunni stronghold to the west, or gone underground in Fallujah. It was this later group that was causing big problems. The ISIS and Al Qaeda fighters had now switched from direct combat with the Marines to subversive attacks, the most horrific of which was the use of EFP IEDs. Ironically, explosively formed projectiles were developed by oil companies in the United States in the 1930's, and now they were being used to devastating effect as land mines and personnel mines against Americans.

The vulnerable point for the insurgents was that they had to place their homemade EFPs in the ground or in locations near where American or Allied vehicles traveled. This is where the US military sought to interdict the process. Through drones in the sky, observers, informers or spies, they tried to identify the location of the mines before they could be employed, or best of all, catch the insurgents in the act of emplacing the mines.

When Sergeant Crawford was killed by the sniper and three other members of the squad were killed by the booby trap IED in the building, Jake had once again been reassigned to another squad in the platoon. His new squad leader was Sergeant Anderson. Everyone called him 'The Beast' because he spent every free minute pumping iron in the makeshift gym the Marines had built at their forward operating base just outside the perimeter of Fallujah. Coffee cans filled with cement and rebar served as impromptu weight-lifting equipment for the small contingent of hard core weight-lifters at the FOB. It was undoubtedly a stress reliever for the combat weary Marines. Anderson, known as the mayor of the gym, spent so much time there, even the men in his squad began to worry about whether he would be able to plan their next missions.

The squad received their orders the next night. Careful intelligence work had determined a location where the ISIS fighters would likely be placing buried EFPs. The Marines had let some of their local sources think they would be using a new road for logistics that headed west through the middle of Fallujah. In reality, they planned to use a different road on the outskirts of town to resupply troops. The ruse was a trap to catch some of the insurgents in the act of placing IEDs.

Anderson gathered his squad together, gave them the plan and supervised the loadout of two armored Humvees. Their mission was to drive down a narrow road, walk the last part on foot, where they suspected insurgents would be emplacing mines, and call in an artillery strike on the fighters as they were digging and working. The Company Commander of the Marines had been clear that they needed to minimize civilian casualties, and one way to do that was to have Marines who were close to the location call in the specific coordinates of the insurgents laying the mines.

The two Humvees rolled out of the makeshift operating base at 2300 hours on a moonless night in the Iraqi desert. They kept their lights off and drove with night vision goggles, trying to be as quiet as possible. At 2335, they pulled over at a pre-designated spot and hid the vehicles inside an abandoned garage. The seven Marines stepped out into the cool night. There were rolling blackouts in Fallujah after the fighting and it was eerily dark as the men spread out and patrolled up the street under a canopy of stars. The buildings around them were badly damaged from the fighting, with blown out windows and shattered bricks causing it to look like an earthquake had hit. The streets were littered with trash, old tires, and damaged cars along the road, making it difficult to navigate.

Anderson led the squad up three more blocks, and then they took a right on a road they called Main Street. It was a prominent thoroughfare where merchants had set up their small shops up and down the road before the heavy fighting. Now it was abandoned. Anderson signaled to his men and the squad split up, with three of them quietly taking up firing positions on the north side of the road amidst the empty carts and shops, and Anderson and the three remaining men finding concealment on the south side of the road behind a jumble of merchant tents and tables.

"Beast 2, this is Beast 1, over," Anderson said over the radio to his other fire team across the street.

"Beast 1, we're in place," replied Corporal Roberts from the other fire team.

"Roger," answered Anderson. "Beast 2, have your men scan to the west of our position, we'll watch to the east. Lemme know if you see anything."

"Roger, Beast 1, Beast 2 out."

Anderson then set about placing his three men in the best positions to see what was happening down the road to the east of their location. Roberts did the same, ensuring they had a good view to the west but were well concealed. Jake was now in Robert's fire team and took up a position underneath an upturned wooden cart. The other Marine in their fire team, Private Kooken, had found a good spot peering out from underneath a merchant's canopy. The two fire teams were not directly across from each other. During planning, Jake had come up with the idea to offset the two fire teams by about 25-30 yards, giving each unit a better view down their respective parts of the road, without unduly separating the two teams.

Sometime after 0400, Jake thought he saw figures in the road fifty yards ahead of his position. "Hand me those binos," Jake whispered to Kooken. The two had been trading off the binoculars every half hour. Jake crawled over, and met Kooken half way.

"You see somethin'?" Kooken asked. This was Kooken's first mission in Iraq and he was as jumpy as a cat. He had just finished infantry training at Camp Pendleton and been sent to Iraq as a replacement for men injured or killed in his platoon.

"Not sure," Jake said quietly, taking the binoculars and peering down the dark road. Sure enough, he could clearly see two dark figures with shovels working along the side of the road.

Jake motioned for Roberts to crawl up to his position and the fire team leader crept under the cart next to Jake. "Whadya got?" he asked.

Jake handed Roberts the glasses. "I see two guys down the road with shovels, digging on the side of the road."

Roberts took the binos and stared into the lenses for nearly a minute. "Yeah, I see 'em too," he whispered to Jake. He handed the binoculars back to Jake and pulled out his squad radio.

"Beast 1, this is Beast 2, over."

"Go ahead, Beast 2," replied Anderson.

"Beast 1, we've got two guys digging along the road about forty meters west of our OP." The road to the west had a slight bend in it, so Anderson couldn't see the two men digging from his position.

"Copy all, Beast 2, I'm coming over to have a look, out."

"What the hell is he coming over here for?" Roberts whispered to himself within earshot of Jake. "Doesn't he trust me to call it in?"

"He's a new squad leader," Jake explained. "He's just trying to get it right."

"Well, it's bullshit," whispered Roberts. "He's exposing our position so he can confirm what I've already told him."

A moment later, Anderson crept out from his hide site, looked up and down the street for any sign of movement, and started walking slowly to Robert's site. Suddenly an RPG came whooshing out the top window of a building above where the insurgents were placing the IED's. The terrorists used a spotter above them to provide overwatch when they were laying an IED. The spotter had seen Anderson step out of the shadows and walk down the street. The RPG round skipped twice then exploded into an abandoned cafe next to Anderson's Marines.

Anderson ran back to his men, making sure they were all OK. Another RPG rocket flew out of the same window and landed closer to Anderson's fire team, throwing rocks and debris all over them. The men from Robert's fire team were shooting up at the window, trying to suppress the fire. Anderson quickly called back to the forward operating base for fire support. He'd already written down his own position and he quickly calculated the ten-digit grid coordinate for the building where the RPG's were coming from. Suddenly, machine gun fire erupted in front of his site—someone had crept up on their position and opened fire. Anderson and his team returned fire and killed the machine gun operator. Anderson picked up the radio handset again and read off the ten-digit grid coordinates to the artillery crew before returning fire again at another insurgent sneaking up on their location.

In less than a minute, the Marine artillery crew on the outskirts of Fallujah fired a single 155mm artillery round. Following a large thumping sound, the round squealed through the air, then landed directly on top of Anderson and his three Marines, killing them all instantly.

As an investigation would later reveal, in the heat of the melee, Anderson had given the artillery crew the coordinates of his own location instead of the coordinates for the building from where the RPGs were being fired.

Roberts, Jake and Kooken looked back from firing at the building to see the result of the artillery round. "Shit!" yelled Roberts, "We're hitting our own guys! Jake, you and Kooken get over there and see if any of them are still alive. I'm gonna contact the arty team." Jake and Kooken nodded, slid out from their concealed positions and ran back up the road to what remained of the other fire team.

Roberts yelled into his radio handset, "CEASE FIRE, CEASE FIRE."

"Roger, Beast, we copy, cease fire," replied the radioman from the artillery squad.

"You hit Beast 1's position!" Roberts yelled into the mic. "We need an emergency extract, only three friendlies remain. We're taking fire from both ends of the road!"

"Copy all, Beast 2, QRF is on the way as well as Cobra." The Marines used the AH-1 Super Cobra attack helicopter as heavy fire support for ground troops. The narrow helo could be loaded with a wide variety of armament to include rockets, but it was most known for its 20mm gatling gun, which could hold up to 750 rounds of ammunition, including rounds that detonated on impact. Roberts passed on the coordinates of their position as well as the two locations they were taking fire from. In less than a minute, he heard the distinctive whine of the Cobra's engines as the bird made its way up the deserted streets of Fallujah to their position. When the helo was within sight, Roberts threw out an infrared chemlight to better identify his position for the helo pilot. The chemlight would be invisible to insurgents but show up like a bright light with night vision goggles.

In the meantime, Jake and Kooken were sorting through what was left of Anderson and his three Marines. The shell had been deadly accurate, landing perfectly on top of their location. Whatever wasn't destroyed by the explosive blast was shredded by the shards of metal and shrapnel that spun like flying saw blades from the explosion. Jake knew as soon as he approached that there would be no survivors.

"Kooken, wait here and keep an eye out." He ordered the young private to lay down and keep watch down the street toward the enemy.

He didn't want the kid to have to see what remained of the Marines inside the carnage of the blast area. Jake cautiously approached the small crater that was still smoking. It was dark and he tripped over something. He looked down and saw a leg inside a boot laying at his feet, completely severed from the rest of the body. "Oh my God!" he whispered, searching the rest of the blast site. Eventually, he found a torso missing the head, another leg and boot, an arm with the hand attached and something that might have been a head. The rest was gone, either vaporized or blown somewhere else. He piled the body parts all together so they could be collected and identified later, then he threw up so violently that he was sure the inside of his stomach would come out his mouth. He was about to call Roberts on the radio when he heard the Cobra flying down the street.

The Cobra pilot saw the IR chemlight from Roberts and turned his machine on a dime to fire at the building where the RPG's had come from. The 20mm high-explosive shells literally tore the building apart, destroying anything inside. Next, the pilot moved up the street where fighters had been firing on Anderson's position and took aim down the alley. Two distinct muzzle flashes were seen by the pilot as insurgents attempted to fire on the helo. The Cobra turned in their direction and unleashed a wall of lead, obliterating everything in the street and turning the area into rubble.

At the same time, a quick reaction force of eight Marines in two armored Humvees tore down the street toward the stranded team. They saw the remains of the smoke grenade and pulled up to Robert's position, each Humvee taking up a firing position down opposite ends of the road.

"Jake, whadya have over there? The QRF is here," said Roberts over the radio.

"We're on our way back," answered Jake. He didn't want to tell Roberts over the radio about the carnage he'd seen; he needed to tell him in person. He grabbed Kooken from his hide site and they ran back to Roberts.

"Where are the rest of our guys?" Roberts asked, as Jake and Kooken returned.

Jake looked at the rookie Marine and said, "Go look under the cart and see if you can find the binos, I think I left them there." The wild-eyed young private hustled off to look.

"They're all dead," Jake said softly to Roberts after Kooken left. Roberts was stunned. He had served with this squad for over a year now. These were his brothers.

"I'm gonna go have a look," Roberts said. Jake tackled him and held him to the ground as Roberts began to struggle.

"Don't go over there, Roberts. There's nothing for you there. I'll take care of it," Jake said, letting Roberts get back on his feet. Jake grabbed a couple of body bags out of the Humvee and slowly returned to the blast site.

17

OCTOBER 2022, MONTROSE COLORADO

Armando was licking the sweat off Jake's cheek. For the past hour, he had been passed out in the truck in a kind of catatonic state. Armando had squeezed into the corner to avoid Jake's unconscious movements, but now Jake was finally asleep. Armando needed to go outside, so he pawed at Jake's ear.

Jake awoke from the episode as he always did, like a drowning man being pulled from the bottom of a lake. He gasped for air as if his lungs were on fire and sat up in the cab of the truck. It took him a few minutes to figure out where and even who he was. He ran his hands through his hair and looked at his watch. It was 4:15 p.m. and the sun was low on the horizon.

"Buddy, I'm so sorry!" Jake said to Armando, realizing how long the little guy had been sitting inside with him. He snapped on the leash and walked Armando to the dog park. Inside the gate, Jake unleashed him and let him run around and do his business. There were still a few dogs milling about, with owners who'd presumably just gotten off work. Jake was groggy, but he watched Armando play with a Golden Retriever and a German Shepherd. Armando was faster than the other dogs and had more agility, but eventually the German

Shepherd caught up to him and Armando lay down and began panting in submission.

Jake was about to call Armando and leave when he noticed two men in deep discussion at the far end of the park. The shorter man, who was smoking, wore a black leather jacket, and a pitbull lay at his feet. The taller man had his back to Jake, but he turned slightly and Jake caught a glimpse of his profile—it was that detective from the Montrose Police. *What was his name again?* Jake racked his memory. *Davidson, that's it.* Suddenly Armando appeared at his side, panting, and Jake felt it was a good time to leave so he gave him water and loaded him back into the truck, then stood and stared off to the west.

An overwhelming weariness settled on his mind and body. The episodes always left him with a feeling that life was short, that he might never wake up from the coma-like state, that all his flailing to find happiness, or at least peace, was just a useless joke. He thought of his mother. She had never laid a hand on him, but she had allowed his father to beat him mercilessly, even watching sometimes silently. Did his father terrorize her too? He hadn't seen that, but it was a possibility he couldn't dismiss, a possibility that she was a victim too in some ways. She had looked so frail and frightened when he saw her; a far cry from his memories of the ice-mother who showed no emotion when he was being abused. Did she deserve to die for the abuse of her child and for being a terrible mother? Up until now, Jake thought the answer was yes. His father was dead, and she was the last link in that chain of terror that he was determined to break free of. But now, in hindsight, Jake realized that he didn't want to be a part of any more death and suffering. At his core, he realized that just confronting her at last was the real win. The act of finally telling her what she had done to him and how it had ruined his life was enough. The look on her face had been what he needed to see. He realized he could walk away now. He had done his duty, forcing her to acknowledge her role in his abuse. Her death would not grieve him, but he didn't want to be the instigator.

A new feeling flowed into his mind like fog rolling into a bay—he wanted Hannah to be proud of him. He wanted a relationship with her, whatever that meant. She had been generous and kind when no one else had given a shit about him for so long. Even more than he wanted to see his mother pay for her cruelty, he wanted to have Hannah in his life. It suddenly became clear that the two desires could never co-exist. He could inflict revenge on his mother or he could continue to see Hannah, but not both.

He jumped in the truck and sped back to the trailer park. He passed an older Toyota Tacoma parked in front of another trailer, then pulled up in front of his mother's home, opened the driver's side door and sprinted around to the front door of the trailer. He banged on the door but heard nothing. Her car was in the driveway, so she had to be home. He banged again and yelled, "Mother, open up!" but got no response. He tried the door, but it was locked. He peered through the cracked window next to the door with the white lacy curtains and saw his mother standing in the living room facing the window. "Mother, open up!!" he yelled. "It's OK, everything is OK, I forgive you, just open up!" Maybel stood there stone-faced holding the pistol. "Mother, NO!!" he yelled and smashed his hand against the window, cracking another pane.

Maybel slowly raised the pistol and put it to the side of her head. "Mother STOP!!" he yelled, banging both hands on the windows. His mother said very clearly, "I love you, Jake," then pulled the trigger.

Hannah pulled into her driveway after a long day at work. She had responded to a disturbance at the City Market parking lot. A young man, clearly on drugs of some kind, was yelling obscenities and threatening customers outside the store. Hannah had called for backup, but couldn't wait, as the man grabbed an empty shopping cart and was ramming people with it.

"Put it down!!" Hannah had yelled as she bolted out of her patrol car. He ignored her and ran off with the cart, aiming it at an elderly couple exiting the store. He bashed the cart into the man and knocked him to the ground along with all their groceries. The woman began screaming.

Hannah pulled out her taser and shot the deranged man in the chest from fifteen feet away. He slammed to the ground and went into convulsions, as 1200 volts rippled through his body. She waited until he lay there quietly then turned him onto his stomach so she could cuff him, and that's when she noticed him foaming at the mouth. She figured he must be on some opioid trip, so she pulled out a bottle of Narcan nasal spray from a pouch in her duty belt and gave him two sprays before he started vomiting.

Her backup, Officer Canberra, arrived and she told him to call the EMTs. She turned the man to his side so he wouldn't be face down in his own vomit. The ambulance arrived within five minutes. The same two EMTs who had attended to Jake in the park jumped out of the ambulance, acknowledged Hannah, triaged the guy and loaded him into the back. After a moment, they sped off.

On her way home that afternoon, Hannah received a call from another officer that the man had died of an overdose of fentanyl. At first she was relieved that he hadn't died due to the taser shock, but then she felt a surge of sadness. She was a combat veteran and had seen death up close many times, but something about this man's death hit her hard. He looked like he was around thirty. He had his whole life in front of him and now it was lost, spilled out of him in a parking lot because of a poison that destroyed his life.

The waste of the guy's life, the pain that his family and friends would feel, the loss of his potential all crept into her head like a scorpion quietly scuttling into the corner of a room. Police officers were not supposed to get emotionally attached to the people or situations they encountered; this was preached at the police academy and reinforced at police stations everywhere, but it was like asking them not to be human. Hannah was usually able to remain detached, but once in a while an incident or a victim slipped through her armor. She kept seeing the frightened look on the man's face as he spewed out the poison from his system. When she had him on the ground, she'd seen his eyes roll back and in her gut she felt he wasn't going to make it.

She took a quick shower, changed into jeans and a sweatshirt and stared at a bottle of tequila on the shelf in her kitchen. The desire to pound a few glasses as an antidote to her dark feelings was almost overwhelming. "Screw that," she said aloud and walked around the back to retrieve Armando and check on Jake. It wasn't quite dark yet but it was unseasonably warm. The door to Jake's studio was ajar so she gently pushed it open.

Jake was curled up on the bed and Armando was laying next to him with his paws on Jake's leg. Hannah stared at the two for a moment before speaking. "Is this what they call male bonding?" Armando's tail began to wag, but Jake remained quiet and motionless.

"Jake, are you OK?" she asked slowly, beginning to feel alarmed. *Was he on drugs? Was her decision to let him live in her studio finally coming back to bite her?* She walked over to the bed and quietly sat down beside him. "Hey, Jake... are you alright?"

Jake opened his eyes and Hannah was taken aback. They were red, bloodshot and filled with more pain and anguish than she'd ever seen. Suddenly, she remembered being at the bedside of Amber's fiance in Iraq when Amber had been captured. Chris was completely devastated at the news that Amber had been taken by an Al Qaeda terrorist. He was a wreck and in the throes of deep, visceral pain. That's when she'd made one of the biggest mistakes of her life and slept with him... she told herself it was to comfort him. It not only destroyed her relationship with Amber, but it shattered her own self-image.

Looking at Jake now, she felt torn. There was no way she was going to sleep with him, but he was suffering deeply and needed comfort. She was normally not a very affectionate woman, partly due to her time in Iraq and being a police officer and partly due to her nature. She knew she had many good qualities, but she was not affectionate. It was a trait she admired in others, but couldn't find in herself, at least not yet.

She put a hand on Jake's shoulder and let it rest there. He looked straight into her eyes and the depth of anguish she saw was so great that she had to look away. He was lying on his side facing her when suddenly Armando stepped over Jake's back between Hannah and Jake, as if he wanted to be in the center of whatever was going on. He lay down with his back to Jake and looked at Hannah as if to plead, "Sorry, I can't come with you, I'm needed here right now."

Hannah reached over Armando and grasped Jake's wrist, gently pulling his arm over Armando's back so he could snuggle the little guy. She stood up to leave when Jake reached his hand across Armando's back and held it open to her. She looked at his face again and saw the eyes filled with pain and let her hand slip into his. She felt calluses and the strength in his large hand. She sat down on the bed and just held his hand. It could have been twenty minutes or an hour, but eventually Jake fell asleep holding her hand. His breathing deepened and slowed. Hannah looked at her watch and felt her stomach grumble; it was 7:45 p.m. She was about to gently pull her hand away and go make dinner when Jake suddenly yelled something indistinguishable, startling her. His hand squeezed Hannah's harder, causing her to wince, but then it relaxed. She sat there on the edge of the bed for another thirty minutes, then softly withdrew her hand and stood up in the darkness. Armando opened his eyes and looked at her but remained curled under Jake's arm. She quietly stepped out of the studio and closed the door.

18

OCTOBER 2022, MONTROSE COLORADO

"Artie, meet me at Denny's at 8," ordered Davidson into his cell phone as he stood outside the Montrose Police station smoking a cigarette. For his own reasons, Davidson never brought Artie into the station. He didn't want any of the other officers to know who his CI was and didn't want Artie captured on a security camera.

"OK, Jefe, see you there."

Thirty minutes later, Artie walked into Denny's shaking snow off his Carhart jacket. An early fall storm had dumped three inches in Montrose, covering the city in a blanket of white. Artie saw Davidson in his usual spot and headed over to the quiet corner booth.

"I already ordered that greasy breakfast for you," Davidson said as Artie slid into the seat across from him. Two cups of coffee were sitting on the glossy wooden table, steam rising into the air.

"It's not called a greasy breakfast, boss, it's Chorizo and eggs, a Hispanic delicacy."

"Well, that shit would turn my stomach inside out. What's the latest with our man?" Davidson asked, trying to get information out of Artie before breakfast arrived.

Artie poured cream into his coffee, stirred it then looked at Davidson, "Kinda strange day for the guy."

"How so?"

"Well, I followed him to the dog park at Cerise." Artie looked at his boss then continued. "He lets that dog out into the dog park for a while, puts it back in the truck and sets off on foot out the west entrance. I had a feeling he was heading to that trailer park off Chipeta again so I got ahead of him this time and parked in a place where he wouldn't notice me." Just then the waitress set down Artie's breakfast with a side of tortillas.

Davidson looked impatient as Artie started to make a burrito out of the eggs and chorizo. He took a bite and continued. "So he goes into the trailer at 10:40. There's a car next to the trailer, so I figure someone's home. He kinda stumbles out about 11:00 then heads back the way he came. I'm hidin' in the truck as he passes, but I get a look at the guy and he looks sick."

"Whaddya mean sick?" Davidson asks.

"I dunno, he was pale and practically runnin' like he's gonna pass out or throw up or somethin," Artie explains after stuffing another tortilla in his mouth. "He walks back to Cerise Park, climbs in the cab where he'd left the dog and stays in there until after 4. I can't see him in the cab so maybe he's taking a long nap, or sleeping off a bender or somethin. So I sit there in my truck for like five hours and he finally comes out and takes the dog back to the park."

Suddenly Davidson realized that he'd been in the park about the same time that Hanlon had entered the second time. He never saw the guy, but then again it was dusk. He wondered if Hanlon had seen him or the man he was talking to—that would not be good.

"So then what does he do?" Davidson asked as Artie swept the remains of his chorizo and eggs into a tortilla.

"This is where it gets weird," Artie says, sitting back. "The guy is standing by his truck just staring off into the distance for like fifteen minutes, then he practically runs to the cab, jumps in and hauls ass back to that trailer. I follow him and park where I can get a look at what's goin' on."

"So what time was this?" Davidson asks, jotting into a small notebook he'd pulled from his coat pocket.

"About 4:45," Artie said. "So the guy parks, jumps out of the truck like it's on fire and runs to the door of the trailer. He bangs on the door but no one opens it, then he bangs on the window. I'm maybe a hundred yards away, so I can't hear anything. He stands there looking in the window and banging on it, then he drops his head, walks slowly back to his truck and drives back to where he's living."

"How long would you say he was at the door?" Davidson asked, sipping his coffee.

"I dunno, maybe five minutes tops, boss."

"I need you to be more precise with time, Artie. That's what I'm paying you for," Davidson said in a voice that left no room for argument.

"OK, boss, sure thing," Artie nodded.

"So what's your take on what he did today?" Davidson asked. He had his own theory, but wanted to see what Artie would come up with.

"Someone was there in the trailer both times," Artie said, looking up and thinking. "He came flyin' back for some reason, I mean the guy was haulin' ass like he was being chased."

Davidson nodded. "OK, got anything else on Hanlon for me?"

"Nope, that's it, boss."

"Fair enough," said Davidson, looking at his watch. "Now, what about that little guy?"

Artie shifted in his seat like he was uncomfortable. "I been busy trackin' Hanlon, boss, but I did get some info on the guy."

"Go ahead," Davidson said impatiently. He was not one to accept excuses.

"I followed him once and your hunch was right, he's dealing to people in the park. One of my sources said he's not sellin' retail, he's a wholesaler to other small-time dealers."

"Is it fentanyl?" Davidson asked, a little more grit in his voice.

"Yeah, boss, that's what my sources say."

Davidson sat back and sipped his coffee. His suspicions had been confirmed. *Not only that, the guy had been stupid enough to lie to me*, thought Davidson.

"So what's my priority, boss? Who do you want me to follow?"

"Focus on the dealer. I wanna know more about his transactions, what his patterns are, what days and times he visits the park. I wanna know when he farts and what he eats for lunch, you got it?" Anger had infused itself into his voice.

"Don't worry, boss, I'm on it."

On the way back to the station, Davidson mulled over everything Artie had told him about Jake. He couldn't stop wondering why Hanlon had raced back to the trailer like a madman. That didn't add up.

At his desk, Davidson went back through his notes from when Hannah had told him why Jake had visited the trailer park. He found it: Hanlon was visiting the mother of a Marine friend killed in Iraq, a guy named Tony Lungo or Longo.

On a hunch, Davidson found the address of the trailer and punched it into the city database. It came back with an owner named Maybel Hanlon. Davidson stared at the name for a few moments, then whistled to himself, "Well, Mr. Hanlon, seems like you've been lying."

He began to dig into all the online police and FBI resources he could access on Maybel Hanlon and a grim picture emerged. The San Diego Sheriff's Department and the Oceanside Police Department had visited the home of Maybel and Gerald Hanlon seven times between 1986 and 2001, all based on complaints from teachers, neighbors and school counselors about child abuse. None of the complaints ever resulted in any criminal charges or attempts to remove the child, Jake Hanlon, from the family. Davidson dug deeper and found that Maybel had worked for the North County child protective services for twenty-two years before she was fired in 2000. "Geez," he said aloud. "No wonder. The cat was in the hen house."

Maybel moved from Oceanside to Montrose in August 2002, after her husband Gerald was killed by a hit-and-run driver in March of that year. The police were not able to close the case on the hit-and-run, so it was still an unsolved homicide.

Davidson read every complaint against the parents he could access in the databases. Not all were accessible but the three he did have access to made the hair stand up on his neck. "How in the hell did they let those people keep custody of that boy?" he asked himself, leaning back in his chair and trying to figure out what all this meant. If Hanlon had visited his mother in the trailer park, why did he make up the story about his Marine buddy? What was he doing visiting his mother, anyway, if the complaints were true? He picked up his phone and called The Cricket.

"Jenkins," said the high-pitched voice of Sergeant Jenkins.

"It's Davidson. Is Livingston on duty?" he asked without preamble.

"Yep, you need to see her again?"

"Yeah, somethin's come up. Can you send her to my office?"

"You got it, Detective."

Twenty minutes later Hannah parked her unit and entered the station. She had just finished working a wreck near Main Street where some clown slammed on his brakes on the icy road and skidded into a Montrose County snow plow truck. The first snow always brought out the worst drivers. The driver had stated that the accident shouldn't have happened because he had four-wheel drive. Hannah tried to explain to the driver that four-wheel drive meant nothing once your vehicle lost traction and started skidding across an icy road. The guy looked astounded, thinking some widget on his car had failed rather than acknowledging that he had entered the intersection too fast.

She stomped the snow off her boots and headed upstairs to Davidson's office. He stopped typing on his laptop and leaned back in his chair when he saw her. "Take a seat, Officer Livingston," he said, gesturing to the chair in front of his desk.

He cocked his head and paused a moment before speaking. "I've got some new information on Hanlon." He let that sit for a moment. Hannah didn't react, but her heart jumped a beat. *What else has he dug up?* She was more and more confident that Jake was not the killer of the guy in the park.

"You know how you told me he's been visiting his Marine buddy's mother in the trailer park off Chipeta?"

"Yes," Hannah nodded, not sure where Davidson was going.

"Well, it turns out that was bullshit," Davidson said with a smug smile. "The trailer belongs to Hanlon's mother, Maybel Hanlon. His father was killed in a hit-and-run in SoCal in 2002 and his mother moved out here a little while after that."

Hannah was momentarily shocked. Having lost her parents at an early age, she was always moved by the thought of someone getting a chance to visit their mother or father after a prolonged separation. *But why had Jake lied to her?*

"I did some digging and it turns out that Hanlon's parents were both grade-A creeps. I found a half dozen complaints against them for abuse of Hanlon. There were allegations the father beat him and even worse shit than that." Davidson let that sink in.

Hannah's head began to spin. The one crime she couldn't abide, the one that she hated to come across in her police work, was the abuse of a child. The near-helpless kids were always so damaged by the people they trusted most, and the awful parents deserved to be taken out back and beaten with a bat, as far as she was concerned.

"So did CPS or law enforcement take him away? Did they ever charge the parents?" she asked, sitting up attentively.

"Naw, that's another pisser. Get this, the mother worked at CPS, so she probably knew how to get these things quashed," he said with a sneer.

Hannah shook her head in disgust, realizing now that Jake may have become homeless from a combination of his awful upbringing and his combat experiences in Iraq. But he'd still lied to her. She knew he probably had his reasons, but it was a breach of trust that she couldn't ignore.

"I think we should interview the mother," Davidson said. "It may be a dead-end but she might have information on Hanlon that ties him to the murder in the park."

Hannah noted that he'd said, *'We should interview the mother.'*

"Well, I still have a couple hours left on my shift and that's my beat, so why don't we go together?" she suggested, almost involuntarily.

Davidson winced as if he'd bitten down on a small rock in his soup. Hannah was sure he would say no, but then he nodded and stood up. "Yep, let's go."

They walked downstairs together and jumped in Hannah's cruiser. The sun was out and the snow was starting to melt, leaving a dirty slush on the roads. She drove up Main, took a left on Chipeta and a right into the trailer park, parking in front of the green and white mobile home at the end of the cul-de-sac. A Crown Vic was in the driveway.

They both got out and Hannah tapped her pistol handle out of reflex. She'd been to enough domestic calls to know that things could go pear-shaped real fast.

Davidson walked up the narrow driveway with Hannah right behind him. At the top of the stairs to the trailer there was a small landing with barely room for both of them. Davidson looked at Hannah then knocked on the door. Hannah stood behind him to his left, her hand touching her holster. There was no answer. Davidson knocked again, this time with force. "Mrs. Hanlon, this is Detective Davidson with the Montrose Police Department, please open up."

As Davidson waited for a response, Hannah moved her head to the left and peered through the cracked and broken window next to the door. Beyond the thin white lace curtains she could see the lower half of a body lying on the floor. "I've got a female on the floor!" she reported.

Davidson leaned over, looked through the window, nodded and then rammed the flimsy trailer door with his shoulder. The lock broke immediately and they rushed into the small room. The scene in front of them told a story they had both seen many times. The woman lay face up on the floor with a large pool of blood encircling her head and upper torso. In her right hand lay a stainless steel five-shot revolver with a three-inch barrel. Her index finger was still sticking through the trigger housing of the gun.

"Check for a pulse," Davidson ordered. "She looks long dead, but let's be sure. I'm gonna call forensics, an ambulance and the coroner," he said, returning to the front porch to get away from the stench.

Hannah pulled a set of rubber gloves from a pouch on her belt and snapped them on. She stepped gingerly around the body until she stood at the head of the woman she assumed was Jake's mother. The woman had been beautiful in her time, Hannah noted, with sharp facial features, long black hair that was now streaked with gray and delicate features and hands. Hannah bent down and felt for a pulse—nothing. She put her fingers on the woman's cheek and it felt cold; she was dead. She was about to stand up when she noticed the corner of a small photograph under the couch near the woman's left hand. She guessed the woman had been holding the photo when she killed herself, assuming it was a suicide, then dropped the photograph as she fell, causing it to slide under the couch.

Hannah reached under the couch and grabbed the picture. It was a 5 x 7 photo of a woman holding the hand of a little boy. Even though it was an older picture, Hannah could tell it was the woman lying dead on the floor. She had the same beautiful face, petite build and high forehead. The boy looked to be somewhere between eight and ten years old. He was holding the woman's hand and looking at the camera without a smile. In fact, neither of them were smiling. The photo reminded Hannah of one of those pictures from the late 1800's, where people would stare into the camera lens without showing any emotion, as if happiness was some kind of sin. Hannah stared at the boy and thought she recognized Jake's large eyes and strong chin, but she couldn't be sure.

She turned the photo over and saw handwriting on the back in blurry blue ink that read, "I ran over the son of a bitch to free both of us. I love you." Hannah read it again. Maybel must have been talking about Jake's father. Davidson had mentioned that the father, Gerald, had been killed in an unsolved hit-and-run back in San Diego County. It looked like Maybel's last act was to admit to killing her husband. But who was she confessing to on the back of the photo? Then she realized it was meant for Jake, a final act to show him that she was not all bad.

For reasons she didn't fully understand, Hannah put the photograph in her pocket.

Davidson stuck his head back through the doorway. "She dead?"

"Yeah, stone cold," replied Hannah.

"We need to go pick up Hanlon. I'm sure that pistol is the one he bought at Murdoch's," Davidson said. "I can hold him for a couple of days while forensics goes through the crime scene evidence. He probably staged this to look like a suicide. I'll have an officer go pick him up and bring him in," he said, stepping back into the room and putting on the rubber gloves that Hannah handed him.

"Why don't I bring him in?" Hannah suggested. "He's at my home and he knows me and trusts me. There won't be any confrontation. I can't promise that if a stranger shows up to arrest him."

Davidson scratched his chin and looked at her as he considered the request. "OK, but call me once he's in a cell."

"Will do," Hannah nodded. "You need anything else from me here?"

"Naw, I gotta go over this site, go ahead and grab Hanlon."

19

OCTOBER 2022, MONTROSE COLORADO

When she pulled into her driveway, Hannah went straight from her car to Jake's studio and knocked on the door. Armando barked in warning and after a moment, Jake opened the door warily. Hannah pushed the door in angrily and stepped inside. "You lied to me," she said without preamble, hands on her hips and an edge in her voice.

Jake stepped back and sat down on the edge of the bed with a heavy sigh, trying to pull himself together. He was still recovering from the episode and from watching his mother kill herself. He looked like a beaten man.

Hannah took a deep breath and got control of her temper before continuing. "You told me you were visiting your Marine buddy's mother in that trailer park, Jake. But Detective Davidson found out the truth." She left out the part about his mother being dead. She wanted to see what Jake's responses would be to her questions.

"I did lie to you," he admitted, once he'd gotten his bearings and realized what was happening. He reached down to stroke Armando, who was by his side.

"But why?" Hannah asked, almost pleadingly.

"I was embarrassed," he said quietly, looking at the floor.

Hannah understood why he might have felt embarrassed, but it didn't square with her way of looking at things. She had lost her best friend's trust and vowed to never lie to a friend again. But of course, she hadn't been in Jake's shoes. She knew the answer, but wanted to hear it from Jake. "Why were you embarrassed?"

Jake ran his hand through his dark hair, then looked up at her and sighed again, leaving his hand on Armando's back. "My parents abused me. After all these years, I'm still embarrassed about it. It makes me sick. I've never told anyone about it."

"What kind of abuse?" Hannah regretted asking the question as soon it came out of her mouth, but she was still angry he'd lied to her, so she overstepped. "Sorry, you don't have to answer that." But Jake looked at her with a pain she'd never seen before.

"You want me to spell it out?" he asked, his voice rising and beginning to crack. "You want all the gory details? You wanna hear how they locked me in the basement, did terrible things to me?"

"No, no! I don't want to hear that. I'm sorry, Jake, I didn't mean... it was just the cop in me."

Jake put his head in his hands and squeezed his temples as if he was trying to press the images out of his head.

Hannah sat down on the bed next to him. She reached over and put her hand on his shoulder. "Jake, look at me." He turned his head slowly and stared at her with bleary eyes. "I just came from your mother's house. Davidson is still there. What happened there, Jake?"

"Is this the cop asking or Hannah?" Jake asked, wiping his eyes with the back of his hand.

"It's me, Hannah," she said softly, wishing now that she had changed out of her police uniform. "Davidson has it out for you for some reason. He knows about the gun you bought and he's gonna pin this on you and probably tie it to the murder in the park, too. I don't know him that well, but he has the reputation of a pitbull." She paused to see his reaction as Armando licked the back of her right hand.

Jake ran his hands across his face as if to wipe the strain away. "I left home at seventeen and joined the Navy. I never confronted my parents about what they did. My father was killed in a hit-and-run and my mother moved out here. For years, I've dreamed of confronting her. It became almost an obsession," he said, shaking his head. "It's one of the reasons I became homeless." He stopped and looked at her. Hannah watched him and listened without interrupting.

"Anyway, when I found out she lived out here, I knew I had to see her once and for all. I couldn't get on with my life until I saw her. I was so angry, Hannah. I wanted revenge for what they did to me. So yeah, I bought the gun, scouted out her house and went in to talk to her."

"How did that go?" Hannah asked, again chastising herself. *Just shut the hell up, Hannah.*

"She didn't take any responsibility. She tried to say she was a victim too, but I knew better. I wanted to kill her on the spot, but instead I left the pistol on the table in front of her and told her to either shoot herself or shoot me, or else I'd come back the next day and finish it one way or another."

Hannah tried not to show the shock she felt at hearing him say that he wanted to kill his own mother.

"I left her trailer and went back to Cerise Park where I'd left Armando in the truck, and I had an episode that knocked me out for hours. When I woke up in the cab of the truck, I knew I didn't want to be responsible for another death. Ya know what I mean? After Iraq and all that slaughter, I just couldn't be part of any more death." He looked at her as if pleading for understanding.

Hannah may have been hard as nails — at least that's how many would describe her — but she knew what he was feeling. There comes a point in a good person's life when too much violence just spills over the edge, as if we humans are only meant to take so much of it, and too much of it is poisonous to a good soul. She suddenly realized why he might be having these episodes.

"I do know what you mean, Jake," she said, rubbing his shoulder and thinking of the little Iraqi girl who tried to charge the gate on her scooter.

"After I left her, I realized in my heart that just confronting her was all I needed. I didn't want her to die because of me. I ran back to the trailer and banged on the door to take back the gun, but she didn't answer." He paused, the tears rolling down his face. "I looked through the window and saw her with the gun to her head. She looked at me and pulled the trigger," he said, sounding shocked, then dropped his head and covered his eyes with the palms of his hands. Silence descended for a moment, until he added, "I just left after that and came back here."

The story rang true and aligned with what she'd seen in the trailer. She didn't know why, but she believed him completely. She leaned over and wiped the tears from his face with her fingers. He looked up at her with bloodshot eyes and then hung his head. Hannah gently lifted his chin and gave him a kiss on the cheek. His skin was warm and salty.

"It's going to be alright, Jake," she reassured him, pulling back before she got in over her head. "But Davidson ordered me to bring you in."

At that moment, Hannah made a fateful decision. "I'm going to my place to shower and change. I have a friend from Texas who has a hunting cabin near the Black Canyon National Park." She pulled out a pad and pen from her pouch. "Here's the address," she said, jotting it down on the pad. "Take my truck and go there."

"I can't do that, Hannah, I'll be putting your career in jeopardy," Jake said, standing.

"Listen, we don't have a lot of time. Just do this until I can figure things out," she implored, urgently pressing the paper into his palm.

Jake looked away for a moment, then turned back to her and nodded. "OK, but just for a couple of days. Then I'll turn myself in."

"OK, good, start packing, I'll be right back," she said, heading out the door.

It was completely dark outside when she returned less than fifteen minutes later. She pushed the door open. Jake had packed his scant belongings into his duffel bag. "Take this," she said, holding out a flip phone.

"What's that for?" he asked.

"It's a burner phone I found. I keep it for emergencies. Call me if you need anything and I'll keep you updated," she said, handing him the phone and charger.

Jake reached out and warily took the phone, sliding it into his bag.

"There's one more thing," Hannah said, reaching into her pocket for the photo she'd taken from his mother's trailer. "I found this under the couch near your mother. I think it fell out of her hand when she hit the floor."

She held the photo out, but Jake just stood there, as if he was afraid of what it might show. Finally, he reached across slowly, took it and stared at his mother holding his hand when he was a child. He began to tear up again, but Hannah spoke. "Look at the back," she said quietly.

Jake turned it over and read, "I ran over the son of a bitch to free both of us. I love you."

He stared at the words for over a minute, then let his arm fall to his side, the photo gripped between his fingers. "What've I done?" he said aloud, but to himself, not Hannah.

Hannah didn't know what she could say to help and realized it was now or never to get him out of the house. "Take Armando with you. I don't wanna leave him alone all day. You can be company for each other." Armando stood up and wagged his tail as he looked back and forth at the two humans, seemingly agreeing that this was the best solution.

20

Hannah dreaded the call, but dialed Davidson's cell. "Have you got 'im?" Davidson asked, getting straight to the point.

"No, he took off." Hannah hated lying to Davidson, but she was in too deep now. "He must've known someone would discover the body and bailed."

"Damnit!" yelled Davidson. "Is he on foot?"

"No, he took my truck," Hannah said.

"Shit," he breathed. "We'll talk about it tomorrow, I've gotta get a BOLO out on him right away and get a judge to issue an arrest warrant."

"Are you still at the crime scene?" she asked.

"Yeah, forensics is here and the coroner just left."

"Anything else jump out at you?" she asked, hoping for any tidbit that might exonerate Jake.

"No..." he paused like he didn't want to say more, but then added. "I pulled the serial number off the pistol. I'll check with Murdoch's tomorrow to confirm it was the one Hanlon purchased, but I'm sure of it. I gotta go." He hung up abruptly without another word.

Hannah lay in her bed that night staring up at the ceiling. *What have I done?* kept rolling through her head. *Did I just let one rash decision ruin my life?* She'd been in this mental space before and hated the feeling that she'd just set things in motion that she couldn't control and that might come back to bite her. But equally compelling was the feeling that Jake was about to get railroaded. He'd made some bad decisions, but they were understandable, and she felt in her gut that he wasn't a murderer. It was a terrible moral dilemma. She knew Jake's combat experience in Iraq was the tipping point for her—she just couldn't see a fellow Iraq veteran handed one more shit sandwich. She finally drifted off to sleep in the wee hours of the morning, with the image of Jake holding his mother's hand in that photograph.

Davidson stood up and walked to the podium. The Cricket had just handed him the remote. "Detective Davidson has a few words for you before you head out today," Jenkins said, taking a seat in the front row.

"Some of you may have heard that we discovered a body yesterday in a trailer park off Chipeta Road. The deceased has been identified as Maybel Hanlon. Her son, Jake Hanlon, is our lead suspect for the stabbing in Cerise Park."

Davidson paused for effect as the officers in the audience nodded and whispered to one another. "Hanlon is at large. We've issued a BOLO for him and we have a warrant out for his arrest." Davidson scanned the room. Hannah sat stone-faced toward the back of the room, gripping the armrest on her chair. Davidson's gaze fell on her and she refused to look away, even though her heart was racing and she could feel sweat beading on her neck.

"All shifts need to be on the lookout for this fugitive. He may be driving an older brown Chevy 1500 short bed, license plate RGH35J." Hannah's heart almost jumped in her chest. He hadn't identified her as the owner of the truck, but one or two of the officers who knew her well would put two and two together. "He's considered armed and dangerous. Do not attempt an arrest on your own. If you identify him, call it in, follow him and wait for back-up." Davidson looked around. "Any questions?" No one raised a hand.

"OK, officers, let's get after it and be safe," said The Cricket, taking Davidson's place at the podium.

"Hannah, can I see you for a minute," Davidson asked, approaching her as everyone filed out of the briefing room.

"Sure," she said calmly, but her mind was racing. She expected a royal ass-chewing from him, if not a full interrogation. They walked in silence to his desk upstairs and sat down. Hannah leaned forward and tried to look at the pictures on Davidson's desk rather than his face as she waited for him to speak.

"How the fuck did Hanlon get your truck?" he asked, pressing his elbows on his desk and pushing his upper body forward in an aggressive pose.

"I let him use it when I was at work," she said matter of factly. In fact, Davidson already knew that, since Artie had followed Jake in the truck several times.

"How did he know to run before you got home?" There it was, the silent accusation.

"Like I said," she continued, "He must've known we would come looking for him, since he'd been at the scene."

"He wasn't just at the scene, he killed her, Livingston," Davidson spat out. "Ballistics confirmed the pistol found at the scene was the one he purchased from Murdoch's."

"But why would a guy purchase a gun legally and complete a background check just to use it to kill his mother two days later?" Hannah asked. She had to figure out if Davidson knew something he wasn't telling her. "He could have killed her with a kitchen knife. Why go to all the trouble of buying a gun?"

Davidson sat back and chewed on the inside of his lip, clearly not pleased with Hannah throwing shade on his case. After a few tense moments he spoke. "The guy was homeless, so clearly his elevator didn't go to the top floor. He killed the guy in the park, so killing a second time, this time a crime of passion, was no big deal."

Hannah wanted to point out that there was no evidence linking him to the Cerise Park stabbing other than his proximity in the park, but she didn't want to aggravate the lieutenant and seem sympathetic to Jake. She kept her mouth shut.

"Hanlon killed them both," he said, making clear that the topic was no longer open for discussion.

"If he has any contact with you, I need to know about it asap, understood?"

"Of course, sir," she nodded.

"OK," he said in a softer voice, leaning back into his chair. "I need you to take another look at the crime scene in Cerise Park, you were the first one on the scene and discovered the victim. Go out there and search the area again where you discovered the body. I have a feeling he ditched the murder weapon near the scene even though our officers never found it." As a small town police force, Montrose PD didn't have a dedicated crime scene investigation team, but relied on regular officers who were cross-trained in CSI as a collateral duty. Hannah was one of those.

"Why would the killer leave the weapon there?" Hannah asked.

"I think Hanlon killed the guy and stashed the knife somewhere nearby for the same reason he left the pistol at the trailer park. Either the guy is stupid, has a death wish or he's got mental or substance abuse issues that keep him from thinking straight. Killers are not usually rational like you and me, Hannah."

Like you and me, Hannah thought to herself, *as if we're always the rational ones.*

"Do me a favor. Go back to Cerise Park where you found the victim. I know our officers have already searched the area, but I really think that the knife's still there somewhere. See what you can find, yeah?"

"I'll do my best, but what makes you think I can do better than the others?"

"Let's just see what happens, OK, Livingston?" said Davidson dismissively.

Twenty minutes later, Hannah parked her police SUV at the west entrance to Cerise Park and walked south down the path toward the crime scene. The sun had melted the snow except for a few dirty white patches in the shade underneath tall pines. At the site, the yellow crime scene tape was still in place, wrapped around three trees that formed a triangular perimeter around where the body had lain. Hannah ducked under the tape and walked to where she'd found the body. An outline of white paint in the dirt represented the position of the victim. Surrounding the outline was a flat area of about ten square feet covered in pine needles. Beyond the pine needles were shrubs, small rocks and undulating terrain that led to a fifteen foot deep ravine to the south. She stepped back outside the crime scene tape and started at the edge of the pine needles and walked slow concentric circles around the scene, pulling back bushes and tree branches to get a good look underneath them.

The sun shone beams through the trees, taking the edge off the chilly morning. A squirrel high up on a branch chirped away as Hannah circled his territory. As her search circle expanded, she came to the edge of a dense thicket filled with thorny plants that were nearly impossible to walk through. She scoured the edge of the brambles and suddenly she saw something shiny and black. She bent over to have a closer look and saw a long stiletto-looking knife laying at the base of one of the thorny plants. She gasped, amazed at the idea that this could be the murder weapon and had been missed by the other officers but found by her.

She pulled out a set of rubber gloves from a pouch on her belt, snapped them on and reached down to pick up the knife, and that's when she noticed the tracks in the muddy ground near the knife. There were one or two small human footprints alongside several large pawprints. She studied the pawprints and had to do a double-take. It was clear that the animal had two hind paws but only one front paw. She pulled out her cell phone and took pictures of the footprints and dog tracks.

She gently grasped the knife from the handle and held it up in front of her face to study it. The blade was about eight inches long, black and sharp. The handle was made of some kind of plastic or epoxy with small ribs in it. The dark blade made it hard to see for sure, but she spotted what looked like blood stains on the tip. She pulled a small evidence bag from her pocket and slid the knife into it with the blade upwards. She pulled her gloves off and walked back to her cruiser. The possible ramifications of what she'd found rolled through her head like giant waves crashing against a flimsy dock.

What if this has Jake's DNA or fingerprints on it? she thought. "Well then, that settles that," she said aloud. "I'm not protecting a murderer."

But what about the footprints and pawprints? Suddenly her memory clicked—the guy who had witnessed Jake being beaten up and called the police had a three-legged dog! He was also a small man, maybe five-foot-four, if she recalled correctly.

What was he doing near the site and the knife? she wondered. The guy obviously walked his dog regularly in Cerise Park, but this was a pretty big coincidence.

Davidson was on his computer when his cell phone rang. He looked at the number and picked it up.

"She found it," said Artie the snitch, barely above a whisper.

"When?" asked Davidson.

"Ten minutes ago. She bagged it and now she's walking back to her car."

"Are you sure it was the knife she found?"

"Yeah, I'm set up in a perfect spot in the trees and I've got binos on 'er. It was definitely the knife. Want me to follow her?"

"No, she might make you. If she doesn't bring me the knife or if she tries to clean it, I'll know she's helping Hanlon. If she brings it to me straight away, I know I can trust her."

"OK, boss, is there anything else for me to do?"

"Yeah, get back on the little man's tail."

Fifteen minutes later, Hannah stood in front of Davidson's desk with the evidence bag in her hand. He was on the phone but said, "I'll call you back," when he saw Hannah with the bag.

"You found it?" he said, like a kid who'd just come across buried treasure.

"Yeah, it was about fifteen yards from the site underneath some thick brush," she said, opening the bag so he could see the knife inside. "I guess the others missed it." She set the bag on his desk.

Davidson cleared his throat. "Yeah, they're stretched pretty thin these days and I think they've been a bit careless. That looks like it," he proclaimed. "I'll have the lab check for DNA and fingerprints."

"There was one other thing," she said.

Davidson looked surprised. "Yeah, what's that?" he asked warily.

"I saw fresh tracks in the mud near where I found the knife," she said. "Like a small man's boot and some pawprints from a dog. The strange thing is, the dog only has three legs."

Davidson twisted in his seat. "What are you, an expert tracker?" he asked sarcastically.

"I hunt elk," she replied. "I'm decent at reading tracks."

"Oh," he nodded. "Well, it was probably some guy walking his dog and got interested in the crime scene tape," he suggested.

"Well, here's the thing," Hannah said carefully. "The guy who called 911 after Hanlon was attacked in the park was a small guy with a three-legged dog. That's a big coincidence, don't you think, Detective? I mean how many three-legged dogs can there be in Montrose, and at that spot in that park, of all places?"

Davidson put on a fake smile. "How could you tell it was a three-legged dog?"

"It was pretty obvious. The two hind paw prints were clearly visible, but there was only one forepaw. I followed the dog's tracks around—it was clearly missing a front leg."

"I'll look into it, thanks for your attention to detail, Livingston," Davidson said, standing up and indicating that the meeting was over.

As Hannah walked back downstairs she had the distinct impression that Davidson was not happy to hear about the tracks she'd found.

After she left, Davidson picked up his phone and dialed.

"Yeah, what's up," a voice answered.

"Meet me in the parking lot of the dog park in fifteen minutes," Davidson said.

"I'm doin' some business right now," said the voice on the other end.

"It's not a request," Davidson growled, ending the call and heading out of his office. Fifteen minutes later, he sat in the driver's seat of his unmarked vehicle in the nearly empty parking lot on the west side of Cerise Park. He looked at his watch and cursed. Ten minutes later a black Chevy Tahoe pulled up alongside his car.

"Why do drug dealers and pimps always drive black SUV's?" Davidson asked after rolling down his window.

"Because we fucking like them," Ardon Donnelly said above his half-lowered and darkened driver side window.

"Are you sitting on a phone book in there?" Davidson mocked.

"OK, asshole, did you bring me here just to bust my bawls?" Donnelly said in his thick Boston accent.

"We got a problem," Davidson said, resting his arm on his window sill. "The officer I sent out to the crime scene spotted footprints near the knife... your footprints."

"That's bullshit, what is she, Daniel Boone or somethin'?"

"It was your three-legged mongrel, dumbass. She saw his prints next to yours and remembered you as the guy who called in the beating on Hanlon."

"She said my name?"

"She didn't remember your name, but she sure remembered you and your pit. And your name'll be in her report of the attack."

Donnelly glared at Davidson and shook his head. "You wah supposed to have pinned the stabbing on that homeless guy by now so we wouldn't be havin' this convahsation."

Davidson sneered and gritted his teeth. "Yeah, well you were supposed to toss the knife where she would find it but not suspect you. But you brought Cujo with you and walked around in the mud. You might as well have left your business card. The knife will put Hanlon away; I've got his DNA on it. But I had to warn you about the tracks Livingston found."

"So what're we gonna' do about the cawp lady?" Donnelly asked.

"I said I'd look into it. I'll give it a day and then tell 'er I interviewed you and you have an alibi for the time of the murder. Hopefully that'll shut her up."

Donnelly squinted menacingly at Davidson, "I don't like loose ends."

"Neither do I, that's why I'll handle it," Davidson said, putting his Ray Ban's back on. He rolled up the window, started his car and drove off, leaving Donnelly fuming.

⎯⎯⎯◆⎯⎯⎯

After the meeting with Davidson, Donnelly parked and took his dog into the dog park. He had a meeting with one of his clients. It was still early afternoon and most dog owners were not off work yet, so the place was almost empty except for a young woman staring at her cell phone while her designer dog sniffed the bushes. Donnelly took a seat at the bench at the far end of the park and waited while Daisy walked the fenceline. Half an hour later, a young man walked in, looked around, spotted Donnelly and made a beeline for him.

The kid was tall and gangly, had a pockmarked face and wore his Nike ball cap sideways, the way rap stars wore theirs. He had on a shiny coat over baggy pants, which made him stand out like a sore thumb in Montrose.

Donnelly winced when he saw him walking toward him. The kid sat down on the bench next to him. "I thought I told you idiots to lay low, blend in and not call attention to yourselves?" Donnelly scolded.

The kid shrugged and smirked as he said, "Whaddaya want me to wear slacks and a tie?"

"Anything but that," Donnelly nodded toward his outfit. "Whadja ya wanna see me bout anyway?" Donnelly asked, getting to the point.

"Well, you know, I been thinking," the kid said. "I put a beatin' on that bum like you asked, and I never got remunerated properly." He looked pleased with himself after pronouncing the big word.

Donnelly threw his head back and laughed, then turned to the kid. "Where the hell did you get that three-dollah wahd, remunerated?"

"Maybe I only finished ninth grade," the kid said defiantly, "But I been readin' books Mr. Donnelly. I got plans, big plans. Someday I'm gonna be my own boss, like you. I need to understand things like proper remuneration."

"Listen, kid, you're on my payroll," Donnelly said, his tone suddenly becoming low and threatening. "I don't pay extra for doin' yau job. If I tell you to beat the shit outta some bum in the pawk, you do it, understood?"

The kid stood up, looking angry like he'd been cheated. "Well, maybe I'll just tell someone what you told me to do. Maybe they would give me some remuneration."

Donnelly shook his head. These hillbilly rookies were gonna kill him. He was far from his Boston clan. "OK, siddown, kid, befaw you make a scene," Donnelly said, patting the bench. The kid sat down reluctantly.

Donnelly reached into his coat and brought out a small baggie filled with a white powder and showed it to the kid.

"I already got more a that than I can sell right now, Mr. Donnelly. This ain't Denver, where I could stand on a street corner and dole it out. It's harder here," he explained.

"No, kid, this is for your personal use," Donnelly said, holding the bag closer so the kid could see how much was in it. "This is not for sale, it's extra special stuff, kid. This will give you the high of your life. Let's call this your proper *remuneration*."

"I been readin' bout negotiation too, Mr. Donnelly. This is negotiation we're doin'. I get somethin', you get somethin, this is good, right? " the kid asked rhetorically, reaching for the baggie and slipping it into his pocket.

"Yau gonna get somethin' alright," Donnelly said quietly to himself, sneering as he watched the kid walk out of the park, baggy pants drooping off his ass,

21

OCTOBER 2022, MONTROSE COLORADO

After the meeting with Davidson, Hannah went back to finish her shift. It had been a slow Friday afternoon, until dispatch directed her to respond to a report of a man acting strange in the alley behind the northern City Market grocers. A high school student had called it in, but wasn't comfortable getting any closer to the man.

Hannah pulled up behind the store where the loading bays were located, jumped out and started a search of the area. Piles of crushed cardboard boxes leaned against the chain link fence, along with stacks of pallets. It was approaching dusk and long, dark shadows were cast across the back alley like giant, black puzzle pieces. Hannah touched her holster for comfort and continued her search. The loading bays at the back of the store were locked and empty. She looked down to the southwest corner of the building and saw two large dumpsters. *That's where I would hide,* she thought. Approaching the dumpsters slowly, she peered into the six-foot gap between them and saw nothing. She was about to look beyond the second dumpster when she heard shuffling. With her hand on her holster, she peeked around the second dumpster and saw a teenage boy in a T-shirt and shoes slumped against the fence, his head hanging down. His ball cap was on sideways like rappers and gang members liked to wear them. She slowly approached.

"Hey, are you alright?" she asked. He tried to lift his head, then slumped to the ground and began to froth at the mouth.

Hannah clicked her radio push-to-talk button. "Dispatch, this is Unit 201. I have a male subject unresponsive behind the dumpster at City Market North. Request immediate medical response."

"Copy all, Unit 201, medical response on the way as well as back-up."

Hannah knelt next to the boy and checked his pulse; she couldn't feel anything. She put the back of her hand in front of his lips and felt no breath.

The kid needed CPR but had vomit on his face. She ripped a small CPR pocket mask from her belt pouch, inserted it into his mouth, gave him three quick breaths, then started chest compressions. She was giving the fourth set of breaths when she heard the sirens wailing around the corner. The ambulance turned behind the store, passed her unit and two EMTs jumped out with a medical bag and a stretcher. It took them a moment to find her behind the dumpsters.

"Whaddo we have?" the first EMT said calmly as she opened the medical bag.

"Young male approximately eighteen to twenty years old. He was leaning against the fence but unconscious, then fell to his side and started throwing up. He has no pulse or breath. I started CPR at 4:42."

"OK, we've got it from here," said the EMT, immediately deploying an AMBU bag over the boy's mouth and pumping air into his chest. The other EMT laid the stretcher next to the victim then pulled out a set of portable defibrillator paddles, set the appropriate voltage and began to give the boy shocks to get his heart going.

Hannah turned away and started a careful search behind the dumpsters. Her gut told her this was an OD case, but an OD on what? She saw some empty chip bags and soda cans but nothing else. She snapped on a pair of rubber gloves and turned over all the trash bags and debris on the ground—that's when she saw the small bag of white powder. She bent down to have a look at it when her supervisor, Sergeant Jenkins, turned the corner. His long legs and short torso made him look out of proportion, like someone had stretched his legs in one of those medieval torture racks.

"What'cha got there, Livingston?" he asked, walking up to her and bending down to have a look.

She held up the small white bag to show him. "I'll betcha I know what this is," she said.

"It's probably not powdered sugar," Jenkins agreed, taking the bag from Hannah and holding it up for a closer look. "I'll get this bagged and tagged into evidence. Good job, Livingston," he said, standing up. "You mighta saved the kid's life."

"I hope so," she said, turning toward the waning sun. Jenkins was silent. He'd seen a ton of ODs from his time in the LAPD, but this kind of stuff didn't happen very often in little Montrose.

"Do me a favor, will ya, Sarge?" she asked, turning to him.

"Sure, what is it?"

"Can you let me know if the kid makes it?" she asked.

"Not a problem, I'm just coming on shift. I'll check later and give you a call."

"Thanks, Sarge," Hannah nodded. "I'm off now unless you need anything?"

"Naw, you can write this up tomorrow, go get some rest. I'll call you later."

◆

Hannah drove home as darkness settled over Montrose. The sun set over the Uncompahgre Plateau to the west of town, leaving the deer, elk, bear, coyotes and mountain lions to conduct their nightly rituals. She unlocked her door and immediately missed Armando's floppy tail and wet nose. "What a day," she said aloud. It was going to be a long night, but she needed to see Jake, not for any personal reason she told herself, but to get to the bottom of the knife she'd found in the park. As much as she cared for Jake, she was not going to harbor a felon. She called the phone she'd given him and he picked up on the third ring.

"Hello?" he answered.

"Hey, I need to come see you tonight."

"OK, somethin' wrong?"

"I just need to talk to you about some stuff."

"OK," he said warily.

"Have you eaten yet?" she asked.

"No, I was about to open a can of stew in the cupboard."

"I'll bring some dinner," she said.

"Sounds like a better deal than Dinty Moore," he joked.

"I'll see you in about an hour," she said and ended the call.

She slammed a shower and washed her hair. After giving CPR to that poor kid, sorting through the trash and her earlier search in the woods, she felt grimy. She toweled off her shoulder-length hair as best she could and threw on jeans, a blouse and a fleece pullover. She stared at herself in the bathroom mirror. She knew she was beautiful: she'd been told enough times in her life, but now she saw small lines on her forehead and around her eyes. "It's the miles, not the years," Amber had once said when they were joking about Amber's first gray hair. Suddenly Hannah had a deep desire to see her old friend again. There was no one else she could talk with like Amber. *But you screwed that up royally, didn't you,* said that voice in her head that kept score. She yearned to talk to Amber about Jake and get her view and advice. *Maybe there was a way,* she mused.

Her phone rang and she saw it was from Sergeant Jenkins.

"What's the good news, Sarge?" she asked hopefully.

"No good news, I'm afraid, the kid died in the ER."

Hannah was still looking at herself in the bathroom mirror and she felt tears beginning to form. "That sucks, Sarge. Do they know what killed him?" she asked.

"They said he had fentanyl in his system. It matches that baggy you found, too."

"Geez, when did little Montrose start having big city drug problems?"

"I know, right?" Jenkins agreed. "That's why I left LA—too many zombies. Let's hope that shit doesn't get a foothold here."

"I hope it's not already here," she said softly.

"Hey, there was one other thing you might be interested in," Jenkins said.

"What's that?"

"You know those two punks who beat up that homeless guy, Hanlon, who Davidson's looking for?"

"Yeah," she said slowly, wondering where Jenkins was going.

"Well, turns out this kid and the dead guy with the neck tattoos were the two assailants."

Hannah's heart skipped a beat. "You're sayin' the OD tonight was the other guy who beat up Hanlon?" she asked incredulously.

"Yep, he matches the description given at the time of the assault: tall kid, white sneakers, zits on his face, ball cap."

"What's goin' on here, Sarge? That's pretty weird, don'tcha think?"

"Who knows?" Jenkins said. "You play stupid games, you win stupid prizes."

Hannah was hardened after all the loss of life and carnage she'd seen, but she refused to become callous about the death of any fellow human being. "I guess," she agreed hesitantly. "Anyway. thanks for the heads-up, Sarge." She was eager to end the call.

"No problem, you take care."

"Thanks, you too. See ya tomorrow, Sarge."

She studied herself in the mirror one more time. Something was different in her face. She realized it was her eyes. They were lifeless, missing their normal sparkle. *I hope this is just temporary,* she thought as she grabbed her keys and headed out.

She picked up a bag of tacos from a little Mexican hole in the wall restaurant and headed east out of Montrose on US highway 50, which led to Gunnison. A few miles out of town she took a left on a winding road that led to the entrance of the Black Canyon of the Gunnison National Park. Though one of the least visited National Parks, it was also one of the most breathtaking. For millions of years, the Gunnison River had carved a stunning canyon into the black and ochre rock mountains, producing a canyon that was nearly as deep as it was wide. The sheer rock walls with their incredible striations of black, red, gold, brown and gray looked like something from another planet to anyone who first gazed into the canyon's depths.

The hunting cabin was located down a dirt road a few miles before the entrance to the National Park. She met the owner while riding dirt bikes at Peach Valley two years ago. He was an older guy living in Austin who came up to Montrose a couple times a year to ride dirt bikes and hunt. The first time he came to Peach Valley he was staring at a map trying to figure out where the trails were. Hannah walked over and offered to take him on a ride and show him the best trails. They hit it off after that and the guy offered to let Hannah use his hunting cabin anytime he was in Texas. She turned right down the road and drove about two miles until she came to the old cabin partially hidden by large pine trees. It was one large room made of hand-cut logs with a small deck out front flanked by two windows. A short black pipe stuck out of the roof as a vent for the old wood-burning stove in the corner. Before she could knock, Jake opened the door and let Armando run out to greet her. He bolted out the door and jumped on her as she approached, letting out a joyous squeal and a happy bark.

"He misses you," Jake said, standing in the doorway in jeans and a flannel shirt.

Hannah bent over and rubbed Armando's ears then stood up and looked at Jake. *Is this a killer?* she asked herself. She feigned a smile and walked up the deck and into the house with the bag of tacos.

Jake set two placemats, forks, napkins and bottles of water on the small table under the window. Hannah plopped the bag of food on the table, "I hope you like tacos," she said.

"Are you kidding me, I was about to eat a can of stew," he said, taking a seat at the small, square table.

Hannah's need to talk to Jake about the day was overcome by her hunger. She pulled tacos from the bag and put them on each of the paper plates, then unwrapped her first one and tore into it. The woodburning stove roared in the corner, filling the room with a dry, smoky heat. They ate in silence until Hannah finished, wiped her mouth and sat back in the wooden chair.

She decided to just get it out there. "I found a knife today at the crime scene where that guy who beat you up was stabbed."

Jake appeared stunned, but didn't respond. "Davidson sent me out there to have another look," she said. "I found it at the edge of some brambles about fifteen yards from the site."

Jake shook his head in disbelief. "What kinda knife was it?"

"A long, skinny blade, like a stiletto knife," she said, leaning back in her chair. "Davidson's convinced it will have your DNA or fingerprints on it. He plans to charge you for two murders, Jake." She watched his reaction.

Jake stood up, walked over to a pile of pinon pine firewood stacked next to the wood-burning stove and carefully placed another log on the glowing fire. He turned and stood in front of the stove facing Hannah, "So you're here because you think I did it."

"No, that's not true," she protested. "If I thought you did it, I would arrest you myself. You're here because I don't believe you killed your mother and Davidson was gonna string you up for it."

"So then why did you need to come see me in person?"

"It's not something you talk about over the phone," she said, standing up and clearing the table. When she was finished, she sat on the small couch in front of the fireplace. "There's something else I wanted to tell you about," she said, reaching her hands toward the fire.

Jake remained standing by the woodstove. "What is it?"

"At the site where I found the knife, I saw fresh tracks. There were boot prints about size six or seven and dog tracks. The dog was clearly being led on a leash. The strange thing is the dog only had three legs."

Jake looked confused. "I'm missing something," he frowned.

"You don't remember the guy who called 911 when you were attacked in the park?" she asked.

"Not really, I had a concussion."

"The guy who called 911 was short, like five-five or five-six and he had a three- legged pitbull," she said.

Jake rubbed his chin in thought, then said, "Yeah but the guy obviously walks his dog in that park. He probably went near the crime scene out of curiosity."

"Maybe, but I saw the prints right next to where I found the knife. Doesn't that seem a little weird to you? I mean this guy calls 911 on two thugs that were beating you, then one of them is stabbed and this same guy ends up at the site near the murder weapon?"

"When you put it that way, I see your point," Jake said, looking perplexed. But then suddenly he remembered something he hadn't told Hannah. "Hang on. After I went to see my mother for the last time, I let Armando play in the dog park. In the back corner of the park I saw Davidson in what looked to me like a heated conversation with this shorter guy, and now I realize it was the same guy who called

911. He had a pitbull lying at his feet, so I couldn't tell if it had three legs, but it had to be the same dog."

"Wait, are you saying you saw Davidson with the guy who has the three-legged dog? The same guy whose tracks I found near the knife?" Hannah asked, dumbfounded.

"Yeah, I think so. I didn't recognize him from a distance, and I was more focused on Davidson, but I remember thinking, *"Why is that detective here and talking to that guy?"*

Hannah ran her hands through her long black hair. There were any number of reasons Davidson might know the guy—Montrose is a small town, after all. But it was still a big coincidence that the same guy had clearly been at the crime scene that Davidson sent her out to search. She let that thought go for now, because she had another big reveal for Jake. "Jake, this afternoon I found a kid OD'd on fentanyl behind City Market. He died at the ER. My sergeant told me he was the other guy who beat you up."

Jake stared at her, incredulous.

"Tall kid, shiny white shoes, baseball cap, zits."

Jake stood there, unsure how to respond.

"I gave him CPR, tried to save him..." Hannah added quietly, trying to keep her emotions in check. She didn't want to talk about another life lost on her watch.

Jake sat down on the couch and turned to her. "I'm sorry that happened to you, Hannah. I've been through it a few times myself and I know how tough it is. I know what it's like to try to save a life, then have it slip away."

Hannah stared into the fire and remembered the look in the kid's eyes when she was giving him CPR. It was like he knew he was a goner, like he knew it was futile. She reached up and wiped a tear from the corner of her eye.

Jake slid next to her and put his arm around her shoulder. Hannah was about to stand up and move away, but his strong arm on her shoulder melted something inside her. He reached up and wiped another tear away and she turned to face him.

"I'm gonna turn myself in," he said softly. "I can't let you ruin your career for me. My life has been total shit up to this point anyway. I don't have a family, a career or much to look forward to. I just caused the death of my mother. Even though she was a horrible human being, I crossed a line. It's probably best if they lock me up."

Hannah shook her head vehemently. "Jake, gimme 48 hours," she whispered as her heart beat faster. "After that, go ahead and turn yourself in."

Jake looked into her dark eyes, then nodded slowly. She stared back at him for a long time then leaned into him and kissed him softly on the lips.

He didn't kiss her back at first, but then she turned her whole body, took his head in her hands and pulled his face into hers. This time he kissed her back, deeply, passionately. Hannah's whole body began to tingle as she yearned for human touch. Jake began to kiss her neck and she slid back on to the couch and looked over at the glowing embers in the stove as Jake gently lay down next to her on the couch and buried his head in her neck. The incessant critic in her head fell silent and she felt, maybe for the first time, that life was something more than a daily beatdown, that maybe there was a way out of the dungeon of her past. The thought of that kid dying from the overdose crossed her mind like a deer darting across a dark road. She said a little prayer for him, looked off at Ursa Major sparkling through the window and fell asleep soundly for the first time in a long while.

22

OCTOBER 2022, MONTROSE COLORADO

Hannah awoke just before 5 a.m. and saw Armando lying on the rug in front of the stove that was glowing with dying red embers. He stood up when she stirred, walked over to the couch and licked her face. She was on the edge of the couch, with her arm hanging down to the floor and Jake was asleep next to her on his side. She gently rolled to the floor, careful not to awaken Jake, who was still asleep. She padded quietly to the door in her socks, opened it and let Armando out for a few minutes. She dared not let him go far, with coyotes, bobcats and mountain lions all around the area, so she stood on the porch shivering as he did his business in the last of the moonlight, then she whistled softly and he came running back in.

She found her shoes by the couch, grabbed her fleece and quietly left, shutting the door behind her. On the way back home in the peace of the early morning, she thought about last night. She had slept on the couch with Jake, and even though it was cramped, it had been one of the best night's sleep she could remember. She was about to chastise herself for letting her guard down with Jake, but another feeling quickly made its way into her consciousness—maybe she could be happy after all, and that she could trust Jake. They hadn't had sex, but lying there spooning with him in front of the dancing flames was the most peaceful she had felt in a long, long time.

She put the memory of the sweet night on a mental shelf and shifted focus to the day in front of her. If she couldn't prove Jake's innocence in two days, he would turn himself in. The thought of that made her stomach turn. Several images bounced around in her head like a slide show as she drove down the dark strip of road back into Montrose: Davidson, the 911 caller—she knew she'd recorded his name in her notebook after Jake was attacked, the prints in the park, the knife, the kid dying of fentanyl—she had a powerful feeling that they were all connected. It was Saturday and Hannah was off duty, but she had an idea of how to try to make sense of all these puzzle pieces.

She stopped for a cup of coffee and breakfast sandwich at the truck stop to the east of town. Back home she took a shower, changed clothes and pulled her small notebook from her duty belt to find the name of the guy who had called 911. There it was, Ardon Donnelly.

She was sitting at her kitchen table thinking about her next move when her phone rang. It was Davidson.

"Good morning, Detective," she greeted.

"Hey, Livingston, I know you're off today but I wanted to circle back with you on a coupla things," Davidson said.

"Sure, what's goin' on, LT?"

"Well, first, we got a preliminary result on that knife you found." He paused. "We've pulled a print that matches Hanlon's."

Hannah's heart began to pound, but she remained silent.

"I also checked into that guy you said might've left footprints near where you found the knife." Hannah held her breath. "It couldn'ta been him. Turns out he was outta town, so he has a solid alibi."

Hannah knew better than to push back. She couldn't afford to tip her hand. But she did want to test something. "OK. But hey, what was his name again? I'm sure it's in my report, but I can't remember."

Davidson was quiet for a moment, as if he was reluctant to remind her, but then said, "Donnelly, Ardon Donnelly."

"Weird name, huh," Hannah mused. Davidson didn't respond. "Anyway, thanks for letting me know, LT. I'll see you on Monday."

She sat there processing everything that had happened in the last 24 hours. Her gut told her Jake was not a murderer. He'd had some bad breaks and made some dumb decisions, but she didn't believe he was a killer. But then again, she had made some terrible choices with her past relationships. Was she being blind to serious faults... again?

And then there were the fingerprints Davidson had found. She could only square that one of two ways: either Davidson was lying or Jake was lying. She needed to consider both possibilities.

Hannah knew she was getting in deeper with Jake and couldn't afford to misread him or their relationship. There was only one person who could help her, she knew. Unfortunately, it was the person she'd betrayed, a betrayal that ate away at her every day. She picked up her phone and stared for a long time at the contact information for Amber, then dialed.

"Hello," Amber answered in a deadpan voice. She worked at the Grand Junction VA Medical Center and was off on Saturdays, so Hannah figured she would pick up.

"Amber, it's Hannah," she said tentatively, and waited anxiously for the reaction.

After a long pause, Amber said, "Wow, it's been a while." It was true, but it sounded like an accusation.

"I know... I'm sorry. But you know why. You said you forgave me, but the truth is, I haven't forgiven myself," she explained with more honesty than she'd planned.

Amber sighed audibly and said, "OK, so why call now? What can I do for you?" She sounded business-like.

Hannah understood Amber's coldness and decided just to take the leap and see what happened. "I was wondering if we could meet. I'm in a tough spot and don't have anyone I can talk to about it," she said, realizing she sounded needy and pathetic.

There was a momentary silence, then Amber said, "Whaddaya have in mind?"

"How about I buy you dinner," Hannah suggested. "The Stone House at six o'clock tonight?"

Another awkward pause, but then Amber said, "OK, Hannah. I'll meet you there."

"Great," Hannah said with relief. "I look forward to seeing you."

"I'll see ya then," Amber replied, ending the call abruptly.

Hannah punched the air in exhilaration. She had done it, finally reached out to Amber. She hoped that maybe this could be a first step in healing their relationship.

Since she had the day off, Hannah decided to drive to the station and use one of the patrol officer computers to search databases and files. The area where patrol officers wrote up their reports and took online classes was empty this Saturday morning, with a bank of computers sitting on a long table and a large printer in the corner against the wall.

Hannah logged into a computer and pulled up the National Crime Information Center database. The NCIC allowed local police, state and federal agencies to share information about crimes and criminals. She'd used it occasionally to enter information about cars that were stolen in Montrose and a few other random crimes of interest.

She punched in the name Ardon Donnelly and got nothing. She tried a couple different spellings in case she'd written it down wrong but still got nothing, not even a traffic ticket. Next she did an exhaustive Google search and came up with the same results—there was nothing on the guy. She tried social media sites, again nothing. Finally, she looked him up in the Montrose tax database. That yielded an address for a home he owned, a copy of his drivers license, vehicle registration, tax information and voter registration. She stared at the screen for several minutes before she noticed something strange—all of the records had been entered into the system two years ago, but within a few days of one another.

Hannah sat back in her chair, puzzled. She couldn't see how or why all this random information could be entered into the Montrose database within a period of five days. The chance that Donnelly had bought a house, obtained a driver's license, bought a car, registered the car, and registered to vote all at the same time was almost impossible. These things happened over months, or even years, as people relocated to Montrose and slowly built their new lives here. The only conclusion she could come up with was that someone else had done all this for him. Maybe he was rich, she thought, and paid someone to come out and set up everything for him. But she knew the neighborhood where his house was located and it was not an expensive area. In fact, it contained older homes that were below the average housing prices in Montrose.

Then she had another idea. When she was in Iraq, she worked with a fellow MP named Dinah Schofield. Hannah had been Dinah's squad leader in the security company, and they had worked together closely to secure the Green Zone against terrorists. Dinah had left the Army after Iraq and went to work for the DEA. Hannah hadn't spoken to her in over a year, but tried her old work number in DC. She picked up after three rings.

"Agent Schofield."

"Dinah, it's Hannah."

"Livingston, how the heck are you?"

"Hey, I'm good. How are you?"

"Can't complain. Hell, no one would listen if I did," she joked. "You? Still a cop in Montrose?"

"Yeah, actually that's kinda why I'm calling. I know it's been a while, but I have a big favor to ask."

"Aha, so you're not just callin' to shoot the breeze with your old war buddy?" Dinah teased, knowing Hannah was never much for small talk.

Hannah laughed. "Sorry, Dinah, you know I'm terrible at that kinda thing, right?" she said by way of apology. "But listen, I came across a strange case here in Montrose. There's a guy I'm trying to get a better picture of, but he has no digital footprint. It looks like he came to Montrose two years ago and everything was set up for him within one week. I'd love to hear your perspective on what could be going on."

Dinah was quiet for a moment, then asked, "Do you still have my personal cell number?"

Hannah checked her contacts, then said, "Yep."

"OK, text me the guy's name and I'll call you back as soon as I can."

"That's great, Dinah. Thank you so much. I appreciate whatever you can tell me. And I promise we'll have a real catch-up session soon, OK?"

"Yeah, yeah, whatever you say, Livingston," joked Dinah.

They hung up and Hannah texted Dinah the name Ardon Donnelly. While waiting for a response, she entered Jake Hanlon into the NCIC database and started to search. He didn't have a criminal record or any felony arrests—that much was a relief.

Her phone rang only a few minutes later. "Hey," she answered.

"Hannah, what are you getting yourself into out there in the boondocks?" Dinah asked.

"Whaddaya mean?" asked Hannah. "There's been a murder and a suspicious death. I'm just doing my homework," she said vaguely.

"OK, listen up, Hannah. I'm gonna tell you this off the record, understand? This didn't come from me, and we never had this conversation, right?"

Her nerves were rattled now, but she answered, "Sure, of course, Dinah."

Dinah took a breath, then spoke quietly. "Ardon Donnelly is the new name of a thug named Sean O'Neal. O'Neal was a member of the Irish mob in Boston and got pinched on a big drug bust by the DEA three years ago. They gave him a choice of twenty-five years at Devens or he could rat out his buddies. He took the deal and helped send five members of the Irish mob to prison. After the trial, he went into witness protection with that new identity. It looks like the Marshall Service or DEA planted him in your little town. That's typical

WITSEC protocol—hide the snitch in a small town where no one will be lookin' for 'im."

"You mean this guy was a drug dealer and mobster in Boston?" Hannah asked with undisguised alarm.

"It's even worse than that, Hannah. O'Neal was suspected of being involved in several murders of rival gang members, but they never went to trial. He's a very dangerous man. You need to stay away from this guy. The US Marshals will be up your ass if you so much as blink at him, and if you get too close, O'Neal will try to kill you—he's a bad guy, Hannah. I dunno what you've got yourself into, but my advice would be to forget about this guy and let someone else do the investigating."

Hannah's mind was racing. "Gotcha. Don't worry, Dinah, I'll watch my step. And listen, I can't thank you enough for this—"

Dinah cut her off. "I mean it, Hannah, we never spoke. You need to forget this guy, do you understand?"

"Yes, I get it. Thanks," she said, hanging up without a goodbye.

She stood and paced the room. If Davidson had been talking to O'Neal like Jake had seen, it's possible Davidson knew the guy's background. Why else would they be talking? O'Neal was supposed to be lying low in Montrose. Hanging out with a police detective would not make sense unless there was something going on. Maybe Davidson knew about the witness protection and kept an eye on him?

Hannah went back to the Montrose database site and printed the page with O'Neal's address, vehicle, driver's license, voting and tax information, then she went to the internal Montrose Police server site and finished her report on the kid who'd OD'd. She scanned it one more time, then hit send.

She left through the back door of the station and was heading for her beater car when Detective Davidson stepped out of his vehicle and started walking toward the station. There was nowhere for her to duck or hide so she just stood there waiting to see if he saw her. He spotted her, paused, then crossed the street in her direction.

"I thought you were off today," he said, stepping up onto the curb beside her.

"Yeah, but I needed to finish up my report on that OD case," she said half-truthfully.

"Jenkins told me about that one. Fentanyl, right?"

"I hate that we have to deal with that poison here in Montrose," Hannah said.

Davidson bit his lip, then spoke. "Unfortunately, we're not immune to big city problems here. We just get them in little doses."

"Well, I gotta run," Hannah said, wanting to get out of there before she had to lie any more to a detective.

Davidson nodded as Hannah got into her car and pulled out. In her rear view mirror, she noticed that he was still staring at her car as she drove away.

⸻ ❖ ⸻

Davidson came to work most Saturdays to get ahead and plan out the following week. On a hunch, he went to the police report portal and looked for Hannah's report on the OD death. Sure enough, she had just submitted it fifteen minutes ago. He was about to start his planning for the week when something else occurred to him. As a detective, he had administrator rights on the network, so he logged on to the printer downstairs where Hannah had been working and entered the command to view the last document that was printed. He stared at his screen and clenched his jaw when he saw the result. It was all the detailed information on Ardon Donnelly.

"So you were just working on your report, huh, Livingston?" he said aloud, slamming his laptop closed.

23

OCTOBER 2022, MONTROSE COLORADO

Hannah walked into The Stone House early to pick out the best seats. Amber was always accompanied by Nikita, her German Shepherd service dog and Hannah hoped to get a corner seat toward the back of the restaurant. Nikita was good around people but Amber didn't like people ogling her dog. Hannah sweet-talked the host at the entrance into a quiet booth in the back corner.

The Stone House was probably the closest thing to fine dining in Montrose. The family-owned restaurant on the south side of town had a great menu, excellent service and a homey western feel, with lots of polished wood and a big stone fireplace in the middle of the dining area. Hannah suggested it because she wanted to do everything she could to make up with Amber.

She ordered two glasses of Pinot and waited nervously in the booth. She'd put on very light makeup, slacks and a conservative blue blouse. At 6:05, Amber and Nikita passed the fireplace on their way to the table, guided by a hostess. Hannah's heart beat like it was her first job interview.

Nikita broke the ice. She instantly remembered Hannah and surged on the leash to bury her nose in Hannah's lap and lick her face. Humans may seem like the more advanced species, Hannah thought, but dogs don't hold grudges. Amber smiled at the happy reunion. Hannah scratched Nikita's ears and kissed her long, black nose. "I missed you, girl," she said to Nikita in her sweetest voice, realizing she also meant it for Amber.

"Hey," said Hannah, standing up and greeting Amber, "Thanks for coming."

"No problem," Amber said as she took a seat. Hannah sat down and Nikita crawled under the table and lay between their feet. Amber had been a US Army MP and military working dog handler in Iraq and had been captured for a time by an Al Qaeda terrorist after a mission that went sideways. She'd been rescued, obviously, but the trauma she'd experienced caused her serious PTSD issues until she got Nikita. On top of that, her fiance, Chris, also a soldier in Iraq and the guy Hannah had slept with, had committed suicide when he returned home after his deployment. Hannah tried not to think about him, because it was a black stain on her soul. It was also the invisible elephant in the middle of the table between them.

"You look good," Hannah smiled, noting that Amber's blonde hair was longer than it had been the last time she'd seen her. Amber had never been one to dress up, and today was simply wearing jeans and a plaid shirt, but anything looked good on her.

Amber returned a half smile, her deep blue eyes assessing Hannah. "You too."

The waiter appeared and took their orders, breaking up the uncomfortable silence between them. Sensing that Amber was not up for chit-chat, Hannah got to the point. She began at the beginning and told Amber everything about Jake, starting with how she'd found him in the park. She went through all the strange occurrences since then, the stabbing in the park, how she'd let Jake stay in her studio, the story of his tragic upbringing, his time in Iraq, the death of his mother and then how she'd aided and abetted him by hiding him at her friend's cabin when Davidson put out an arrest warrant for him.

Amber listened intently throughout the whole story, but her eyes grew wide when Hannah said she'd been hiding Jake from the police. "You know what kind of risk you're taking, Hannah?" she asked, shaking her head. "You could go to jail for harboring a fugitive!"

Hannah knew that, of course, but hearing it said with such passion from Amber made her decision seem foolish. "I just think he's getting railroaded by this detective for some reason. I couldn't just stand there while they sent him to jail." She paused, looking down at her hands. "He was in the battle of Fallujah and lost his best friend, his parents abused him, he's been homeless, but despite all that, he's a good guy. He even got me a dog, Amber! A rescue named Armando," she grinned. "I just couldn't turn my back on him..." Her voice trailed off, but her despair was obvious.

"Are you in love with him?" Amber asked suddenly. "Is that what this is about?" It sounded like an accusation.

Hannah looked away and stared off into the fireplace, searching her soul for the truth, a truth she hadn't admitted to herself yet. "Yeah, maybe a little bit," she said softly as she turned back to Amber.

"I don't know if you can be a little bit in love," Amber said, now with more compassion. "It's like having a little bit of cancer. You either have it or you don't."

In her gut, Hannah knew Amber was right. She had buried her feelings for Jake and denied them, but the hard truth was that she was in love with Jake Hanlon. And that realization made her feel even more vulnerable. She shook her head and a small tear formed in the corner of her eye. It should have been a tear of joy at the prospect of love, but instead it was a feeling of deep regret for everything screwed up in her life, including all the death and destruction she'd witnessed in Iraq, sleeping with Amber's fiance, his suicide, her last boyfriend, who'd been a raging narcissist, and the possibility that this newly acknowledged feeling for Jake could literally destroy her life.

The moment of tension was broken when the waiter arrived with their dinner. Hannah wiped her eye with the napkin. She felt like a weakling, crying in front of Amber, who'd been through so much more and had every right to hate Hannah. But then Amber did something unexpected—she reached her hand across the table and let it rest there like an unopened invitation. Hannah's hands were in her lap, but she looked across the table at Amber and the outstretched hand on her side of the table. She slowly raised her hand out of her lap, moved it onto the table and placed it next to Amber's without touching. She didn't want to be presumptuous. Amber lifted her hand and placed it gently on top of Hannah's. The unexpected touch was like a jolt through Hannah's body and mind. The best she had hoped for from seeing Amber again was for some advice and perspective from an old friend. She looked down at Amber's hand on top of hers and willed herself to look Amber in the face. What she saw was not the look of disdain she felt she deserved, but compassion. Hannah held her gaze for a moment, and was about to withdraw her hand when Amber leaned forward and spoke. "I'm here for you, Hannah, even in this total freaking mess, I'm here for you. Let's bury the past. I miss my best friend, too."

Hannah was momentarily speechless. She tried her best not to tear up again, but then it came. It was a bitter, uncontrollable cry, but wrapped in a ribbon of joy at the prospect of getting her best friend back, of real forgiveness, at the chance to start over. She wiped her eyes with the back of her other hand and croaked, "Thank you," She squeezed Amber's hand before slowly returning hers to her lap. After an awkward moment, she added, "We better eat before it gets cold."

Amber pulled her hand back and the two of them began to eat. Through the magic of forgiveness, they ate together as if it was old times at Fort Bragg or in the Baghdad dining facility. They talked about good times and bad, laughed at shared memories and retold old stories from the barracks. "Do you remember when Chavez crapped her pants on duty?" Hannah recalled the hilarious episode at one of the entry points into the Green Zone in Baghdad. They both had to control their howls for the sake of the guests around them.

"She didn't tell anyone for two hours!" Amber laughed. "I kept wondering where that smell was coming from. It was worse than the burn pit odors!" They laughed for another hour at the funny and tragic stories of life in the Army in Iraq and caught up on each other's lives.

"Listen, I'm gonna do something for you," Amber said, suddenly turning serious. Hannah frowned, wondering what she meant.

"I have access to personal VA files at the hospital. I'll be breaking every rule in the book, but I'm gonna look up Jake and see what it says about him. From what you've told me, he should be eligible for VA care and disability."

"I can't have you do that, Amber," Hannah protested. "I don't wanna drag you into my problems. But I appreciate the offer, I really do."

"Nope, I'm going to do it, girl, for my peace of mind and yours. I can't have you falling in love with the wrong guy," she said, draining her wine glass.

"Oh, that's the story of my life," Hannah smirked self-deprecatingly and they both laughed. "But I guess if I can't stop you, I'll thank you instead."

They hugged in the parking lot before parting ways. Hannah finally got the words out that she'd meant to say all night long. "I am so, so sorry, Amber!"

"It's done, it's past, it was another casualty of that stupid war. I don't wanna hear about it again from you," Amber said, pushing back from the embrace and looking Hannah in the eyes. "Never speak of it again," she said firmly, her eyes like a blue flint under the crackling street light.

Hannah nodded and smiled at her battle buddy, her only real confidant in this world.

24

OCTOBER 2022, MONTROSE COLORADO

When she left Amber, Hannah pulled an address off her phone and drove back into town. She took a left down a side street off Townsend Avenue into an older neighborhood just east of Cerise Park. She saw the address she was looking for, passed by the house, drove to the end of the cul-de-sac, turned around and parked across the street from Ardon Donnelly's home... or rather Sean O'Neal's. It was dark outside, but she could see it was a small ranch style home with a two car garage. A dim light glowed near the front door, casting lined shadows off the front porch rails, behind which sat a single rocking chair. There was a small driveway to the right leading to the back of the house but a tall wooden gate blocked her view of the back yard. All three windows in the front of the house had their curtains drawn. Light seeped around the edges of the curtains, though, suggesting someone was home.

"What are you doing here in little Montrose?" she said quietly to herself, staring at the house. She thought of Dinah's warning: "Stay away from this guy, he's a bad man." Hannah knew it was good advice, but she felt sure Donnelly had something to do with Jake and the two deaths. She couldn't just let that go. She slumped down in her seat

216

and watched the house for half an hour. She looked at her watch and saw it was 9 p.m. She had one more day to sort things out before Jake turned himself in. This guy Donnelly or O'Neal might be innocently living a new life here in Montrose, but how likely was that for this kind of man? She was sure he and his dog had been at the crime scene where she'd found the knife. But he'd also been the one who'd called 911 when Jake was attacked—those were coincidences she didn't like. She just couldn't see the connections...yet.

Nothing appeared to be happening here so she headed home. She dialed the cell phone she'd given to Jake and he picked up on the third ring.

"Hello," he answered. Her heart skipped a beat at the sound of his voice. Tonight, under Amber's prodding, she had acknowledged her hidden feelings for Jake. She wanted to be there with him tonight, but it was a long, dark drive up a winding road to the mountain cabin and she had work to do tomorrow. "Hey, how are you and Armando getting along up there?" she asked.

"We've been walking every square inch of this property," he said, "It turns out Armando is a hunter. He caught a rabbit and he's been chasing everything that moves."

She laughed. "Well, I guess that's natural for a dog coming off the reservation," she said. "He probably had to catch his own meals."

"Yeah, you're probably right," he agreed. He was quiet for a moment, then said, "Listen, Hannah, I've been thinking about it and I can't have you sacrifice your career for me. I need to turn myself in. I can request the same lawyer. I'm sure she'll be able to help me."

Hannah knew he was right, but her gut turned over at the thought of Jake being locked up when he was innocent. "I understand," she said, not realizing that she sounded like she was pleading. "But please, Jake, just give me until eight o'clock tomorrow night. If I haven't come up with anything, you can come to town and turn yourself in. I'll call you at eight sharp and let you know either way, deal?"

After a moment of silence that made Hannah anxious, Jake finally sighed and said, "Alright, Hannah. But take care of yourself, OK? I don't want anything happening to you."

It had been a long time since any man had really cared about what happened to her. Several had come and gone in her life, but none really cared about her. They pretended they did, of course, but over time she realized they were all just using her for one reason or another. She had just about given up on men until Jake came into her life. "I miss you," she said quietly. It was another truth she let slip past her impenetrable armor.

Jake was silent again for a moment, then said, "I miss you too, Hannah. I'll talk to you tomorrow at eight."

"Good night," she breathed, wishing now that she had sucked up the long drive and slept in his arms on that couch again with the fire roaring and Armando lying on the floor next to them.

⸺ ◆ ⸺

Davidson sat on the couch with his wife as she watched a nature show on NETFLIX. He pretended to be interested as he sipped his bourbon, but his mind was elsewhere. He realized he couldn't wait any longer. "I've gotta make a call, don't stop the show for me," he said. He went into his home office, shut the door, took a deep breath and dialed a number on his cell phone.

"Whatcha calling me for this hour?" Donnelly snarled into the phone.

"Remember that problem I told you about?" Davidson asked, ignoring Donnelly's rudeness.

"Yeah, what about it?"

"I told that officer that you had an alibi, that it couldn't have been you in the park, that it must've been a mistake or someone else."

"Yeah, so? That was our plan," Donnelly confirmed.

"Well, it seems she's been doin' some digging on you. She found all your personal information on the Montrose tax portal."

"You've gotta be shittin me!" Donnelly yelled into the phone. "I told you that bitch was trouble. Who knows what else she'll dig up."

"There's nothing else to dig up on you, Sean, you know that and I know that," Davidson reassured him. "She has your address and registration, so big deal. She knows nothing because there is nothing to know."

"I don't like this," Donnelly said, raising his voice again. "I'm not having this fucking cop all over my ass. You need to do something more than give her an alibi or I'll take things into my own hands."

Davidson was quiet. He didn't like the veiled threat from O'Neal. "I agree, Sean, I agree, we need another plan. Lemme do some thinking."

"You better do more than think, Davidson, and stop calling me Sean. Sean O'Neal is dead," he snarled. "And why isn't Hanlon locked up already?" he asked. "That was our deal."

"I'm working on that, too," Davidson said and hung up.

Davidson tapped the password onto his computer and opened up a spreadsheet that showed all the people he owed money to for his gambling debts. Most of them would be patient, but that one SOB from Bulgaria worried him—the guy was crazy and mean as hell. *Why did I ever borrow from that nut job?* He did a quick tally in his head, *I'll never pay this off. This gig with Donnelly better work out, or I'm out of options.*

25

OCTOBER 2022, MONTROSE COLORADO

Hannah was back on patrol for a day shift. Her day was pretty routine until a call went out for any available officers to respond to a major accident south of town. She flipped on her lights and sped south. Three miles out of town, the traffic came to a halt both ways on the two lane highway. She moved right onto the shoulder, passing the stopped traffic, and made her way to the scene of the accident. A Colorado Highway Patrol officer was on the scene, but Hannah was the next law enforcement officer to arrive. Scanning the wreckage, she guessed what had happened. A small Toyota heading southbound had swerved into oncoming northbound traffic and hit an F350 Dually head-on. The scene looked like a bomb had gone off. One of the passengers in the Toyota had been flung through the windshield and flown over the pickup truck. The highway patrol officer, a large man with a crew cut and a football player build, had placed a white blanket over the deceased passenger and was now trying to extricate the second victim from the crushed Toyota.

Hannah parked and ran out of her unit to assist him. The trapped driver, who appeared to be a middle-aged male, was unconscious behind the wheel. The front end of the little truck had been completely

221

smashed and the driver was partly crushed by the crumpled dashboard and trapped by the steel, plastic and glass in his lap.

The CHP officer had a three-foot crowbar and was trying to crack open the door, but it wouldn't budge. "I can't get it open!" he yelled at Hannah as she arrived at his side of the vehicle. Hannah immediately stripped off her duty belt and bullet-proof vest and tossed them to the ground. The passenger side window was gone and with her slight frame, she was able to wiggle into the vehicle. "Hey, get outta there!" the CHP officer yelled at her. "This thing could go up in flames any minute!"

Hannah smelled the gasoline spilling out of the vehicle, but she ignored the CHP officer and crawled over the debris in the passenger seat next to the driver. Suddenly she was back in Iraq guarding the Green Zone. A civilian passenger vehicle had hit a landmine that had been placed by insurgents the night before just outside the southern gate for vendors. Hannah ran to the stricken vehicle from her guard post and saw a family of four inside. The mine had taken out the front of the car but the passengers were stuck inside. She was trying to pull them out when the vehicle caught fire. She held onto the hands of a young girl in the back seat, but couldn't pull her out. As the flames roared and hissed, Hannah dove away and the vehicle exploded in a ball of fire.

Hannah put a hand on the Toyota driver's neck and felt a pulse. "He's alive!" she yelled to the CHP officer still struggling with the crushed door. Sitting in the ruined passenger seat, she performed a quick assessment on the victim. Everything looked OK, but then she noticed his right leg was spewing blood onto the floor of the vehicle. She tore off the belt on her waist and wrapped it around the man's thigh, then twisted it using a broken piece of the dashboard, turning it into an impromptu tourniquet. Just then, the EMTs and a fire truck arrived on scene. In no time, they had the doors ripped open with the jaws of life. Other firefighters stood by with a hose, ready to douse any flames. Two EMTs reached into the remains of the driver's side door and carefully extracted the driver. Another pulled open the passenger door and helped Hannah out.

Hannah walked over to where they were loading the patient into the ambulance. "Is he gonna make it?" she breathlessly asked the female EMT who she recognized.

"I don't know," said the EMT, "But that tourniquet might have saved his life. His entire lower leg was severed when we pulled him out. You saved 'im from bleeding out. If he makes it, I'd say it was because of that tourniquet." The EMT turned and jumped into the back of the ambulance before it sped off to the hospital in Montrose.

Hannah walked over to the wreck, retrieved her duty belt and body armor and put them slowly back on her body. It was 38 degrees out and she started to shiver. She walked back to her unit and grabbed a coat from the back seat and threw it on.

"That was pretty fucking stupid," said a voice behind her. She turned around to see the big CHP officer. "You could've burned up in there before the fire truck arrived."

Hannah looked into his eyes, but all she saw was the face of the girl in the back of the car on fire outside the Green Zone after she'd let go of her hands and dove for safety.

"Hey, did you hear me?" asked the big man, raising his voice. Hannah ignored him, walked over to the side of the road and started helping other officers with traffic control.

Later that afternoon, Amber called.

"Hey," said Amber, by way of greeting.

"Hey... I had a great time last night," Hannah blurted out before Amber could speak.

"Yeah, me too. Listen, can we get together for dinner or drinks tonight? I've got some information for you."

Hannah's heartbeat picked up, but she decided not to ask any more about whatever Amber had to tell her. If Amber wanted to talk about it over the phone, she would've already done it. "Yeah, of course. I'm off early today, how about we meet at Colorado Boy Pizza at 5:30?"

"Perfect," answered Amber, "See ya there."

Hannah finished her shift and drove home. She'd hoped she would have time to do some more searching on the computers at work, but she was out of time. Even if she did have time before meeting Amber, she didn't really know what to search for next. It looked like she would be calling Jake tonight to tell him she didn't have anything new and that he should probably turn himself in.

She went into the bathroom to shower and that's when she noticed the cut on her chin. The blood had dried, leaving a red and brown slash below her mouth. She rubbed a cotton ball with hydrogen peroxide and did the best she could to clean it up. Luckily, it wasn't deep and had stopped bleeding. "Don't I look like a mess," she grumbled. She took a quick shower and put on jeans and a pullover, checking her face one more time before heading out.

Colorado Boy was the best pizza in Montrose. The long, narrow restaurant situated on historic Main Street between other shops was a local favorite. Hannah arrived first and found a table in the back near the large brick pizza oven, with enough room for Nikita to lay down in the corner. The rich aroma of baking pizza dough filled the restaurant. There was a quiet hum in the place, as customers talked and enjoyed a good meal. On the right side of the dining area was a full-service bar with bar stools about half full of patrons having a drink after work. Hannah poured herself a glass of water from the decanter and looked around to see if she recognized anyone. A younger man of Latin descent wearing a Carhart jacket walked in and sat at the bar in front of her. Amber strolled in with Nikita shortly afterwards.

Hannah stood and hugged Amber in greeting. After their long estrangement, she wasn't going to miss another opportunity to show affection for her closest friend. "What happened to your chin?" Amber asked with some alarm, stepping back from the hug. They both sat and Nikita scooted under the table.

"Big wreck south of town today. I got cut on the broken glass." She didn't want to talk about the accident, though. She was more interested in the information Amber had for her.

The waiter arrived and took their order for a pizza and a large salad to share. Amber ordered a glass of Pinot and Hannah stuck with water.

Amber looked around nervously, as if making sure no one was listening, then spoke. "I've got some information about Jake."

Hannah figured that was the topic, but was a little thrown off by Amber lowering her voice.

"I looked him up in the VA database," she said, scanning the room again. "His name pops up as a veteran, but the file is completely empty, nothing in it. I've never seen anything like it. Everyone has something in their VA file, even if it's just copies of letters the VA sent to the member, dates of service, shot records or other medical notes, but this file was empty, gone, wiped clean or something."

Hannah's heart began to beat a little faster and her breath quickened. *Where was Amber going with this?*

"After my captivity in Iraq," said Amber, "I was interrogated by this Army Intel officer. He gave me his card at the end of the debrief and said to give him a call if I ever needed anything. I've never seen a completely empty VA file, so I figured it must be something sensitive and I wanted to see if he knew what was going on. He's a full bird Colonel now working out of the Pentagon."

Hannah nodded, but let Amber continue without interrupting her.

"I gave him Jake's name and he said he'd get back to me. He called me this afternoon," she said, leaning forward conspiratorially. "First off, he told me he could only give me certain information over the phone, and even that was breaking a lot of rules. He swore me to secrecy on this."

Hannah shifted in her seat. *What the heck is going on?* she wondered, her anxiety growing with every minute.

"It turns out Jake enlisted as a Navy corpsman working with the Marines but later went through training to become a US Navy SEAL. He served in Iraq and Afghanistan and was highly decorated. Five years ago, he and some other select SEALs were recruited into a secret unit that worked for the DEA. The DEA was short on highly-trained operators and they turned to DoD and eventually the SEALs. It was some super secret unit—he wouldn't tell me more. He said Jake and the other SEALs had been used to take out several leaders of a cartel in Central America. On the last mission, something went wrong. Either the Colonel didn't know what happened or wouldn't tell me, but the gist is that Jake was the only one in his unit to survive. He walked outta the jungle and some fishermen brought him to the US Embassy, badly injured and barely alive."

Hannah's face went white. "Oh my God," she whispered, putting her hand over her mouth.

Amber paused as the server set the pizza and salad in front of them and walked away. Hannah had lost her appetite and found herself sweating, even though it was cool in the restaurant.

"They put him on a MEDEVAC flight to a military hospital in San Diego and the doctors discovered he had severe traumatic brain injury," Amber explained, looking at the growing fear and angst on her friend's face.

"But here's the strange part," Amber continued, lowering her voice to nearly a whisper. "He had no memory of the incident in Central America, or any of the missions against the cartels or even his time as a SEAL. When they recruited him into the unit, the DEA handler gave him a detailed cover story that he was a Navy corpsman again, doing humanitarian work in Central America, that he had never been a Navy SEAL. He was required to live that cover story and to memorize missions, dates, names, battles, everything to make the story plausible."

Hannah picked up a napkin, dunked it in the ice water decanter and held it against her neck. She was feeling hot. It had less to do with their proximity to the pizza oven and more about hearing the shocking information about Jake.

"The upshot is that his TBI combined with childhood trauma resulted in a mental state where he now believes he was a US Navy corpsman working with the Marines for his entire career in the military. His time as a corpsman and that DEA cover story became reality for him, and his time as a Navy SEAL and his work with the DEA was lost or buried in his mind. He was in the hospital for six months and they couldn't get him to recall his actual identity as a SEAL or as a member of this DEA unit. Oddly enough, he remembered his life before the military, including his abusive parents, but they think that somehow the TBI blocked the memory of his life as a SEAL."

Amber stopped to give Hannah a moment to process it all, seeing that her mouth was agape in astonishment. Slowly, she continued. "Someone high up in the DEA tried to get Jake involuntarily committed to a mental health institution. The Colonel thought that the DEA didn't want him to ever talk about those cartel missions, but the DoD doctors said Jake wasn't a threat to himself or others and they couldn't allow a highly decorated veteran to be institutionalized just for memory problems, so they released him."

"Jake told me he has these 'episodes' every once in a while," Hannah said, her voice cracking. "He didn't explain them and I didn't pry."

"Yeah, the Colonel said he occasionally blacks out and seems to have vivid dreams or visions of his cover story," Amber explained. "Everyone reacts differently to traumatic brain injury—I see it every day at the VA hospital."

Hannah sat back and put her hands over her eyes to hide the tears that were about to come for the second night in a row. "So I finally fall in love with a man who cares for me, and I find out he's bat-shit crazy," Hannah said a little too loud. The older couple seated next to them glanced over at the intense conversation.

"Hey, hey," Amber whispered, reaching up and pulling Hannah's hand back to the table. "Look at me," she said forcefully.

Hannah wiped her eyes and looked into Amber's eyes. "Jake has hidden wounds from those fucking wars, just like you, just like me," Amber said, gritting her teeth. "We both know soldiers, friends, fellow MP's who lost a leg, or an eye or are in a wheelchair, right?" Hannah nodded. "Jake just has wounds we can't see, that's all. He's not crazy, Hannah, he's just had an injury to his brain."

Amber's eyes were aflame with passion. "The military hospital let him go because he wasn't a danger to anyone. If you love him, I'm sure he's a great guy. This doesn't change that."

Hannah wiped her eyes again and looked up at her friend. She felt selfish and foolish for crying about lost love. What she was really feeling was sorrow for the shitty deal that Jake had to endure. This new information about Jake was the tipping point for her emotions. The terrible car wreck today, her memory of the little girl in Iraq she couldn't save and the knowledge that Jake was turning himself in and may not have the ability to mount a defense all filled her with gut-wrenching angst at the unfairness of life. It all spilled over into hot tears.

But after a moment of anguish, she pulled herself together, took a deep breath and nibbled at her pizza, but her mind was elsewhere. After dinner, they stood outside on the sidewalk under the green glow of the neon sign in the window. "I'm sorry about all this," Amber said with genuine warmth and concern. "I wanted you to know what you're dealing with."

Hannah put on a fake smile. "I appreciate it, Amber. It's a lot to digest, but at least I know the truth now."

They hugged one more time, and Hannah had the feeling that she might have been better off not knowing all this about Jake.

The parking on Main Street had been full when Hannah pulled into Colorado Boy, so she'd parked on a side street. She walked down the sidewalk in the dark toward her car and glanced at her watch. It was seven o'clock, an hour before she was supposed to call Jake. As she passed a dark van, a man stepped out of a narrow alley between buildings and came up behind her, putting a rag soaked in ether over her nose and mouth. She fought for a moment, then passed out as he quickly stuffed her into the side door of the van and sped off.

26

OCTOBER 2022, MONTROSE COLORADO

Jake paced around the small cabin holding the phone and looking at the screen periodically. He and Armando had just finished playing fetch with a small stuffed bear for nearly half an hour while waiting for the call from Hannah. Armando stood at Jake's feet with the tattered bear in his mouth trying to keep the game going. Jake looked at his watch. It was 8:15. Hannah had said she would call at eight. He waited another ten minutes then dialed her number. There was no answer and he didn't leave a voicemail.

He took Armando outside one last time to do his business. It was one of those incredibly clear nights when the band of the Milky Way looked like someone had spread small diamonds across the sky with a large paint brush. Jake looked at his watch again—it was now nine o'clock. Even if Hannah was caught up in an emergency at work, she would have texted or called by now. In his heart he knew something was wrong—it was not like her to break a promise. Jake stared out into the vast canvas of past and future light above and made a decision.

He packed up his clothes, grabbed Armando's food, bowl and toys and they jumped into the truck. He would go to Hannah's and wait for her there. She must've been caught up in something big on duty, maybe a large accident or something. He would see her one more time tonight before turning himself in.

On the way down the mountain, he tried to call Hannah two more times but only got voicemail. He began to feel more and more anxious. He couldn't understand why she hadn't called... unless something had happened to her. That's what tied his stomach in a knot—that somehow he was responsible for whatever was happening.

He pulled into the cul-de-sac and his anxiety spiked when he saw that her police cruiser was parked in front of the garage. *If she isn't at work, where is she?* he thought.

She had shown him where she kept a hidden key in case he ever needed to get in to let Armando out or get more of his food or snacks. He found the fake rock near the door in the gravel, pulled the key out from the bottom and opened the door. Armando shot through the doorway past Jake, running around the place looking for Hannah. Together they checked each room. Jake opened the door to the garage and saw that her Toyota beater car was missing. If she was off-duty, where could she have gone without calling him as she had promised? Even as a child, perhaps because he had abusive parents, Jake had developed almost a sixth sense of impending doom. He almost always knew when things were about to go sideways. It had helped him escape a few beatings as a kid, when he sensed the mood had changed in the home. And now he felt something was very wrong again.

Jake sat down at the small table in Hannah's kitchen and thought about his next move. That's when he noticed a folded piece of paper underneath the salt shaker. He pulled it out, unfolded it and read the report Hannah had printed out at the station that had local information on Ardon Donnelly. There was a tiny copy of his driver's license at the bottom. The name meant nothing to him, but Jake stared at the photo-copied image and it hit him: this was the guy who had called 911 when he was attacked. It was also the same man Jake had seen in the dog park talking to Detective Davidson. Why was Hannah interested in him? She'd told Jake she'd been trying to find out what was going on and wanted to dig up something that might exonerate him. Jake held up the picture and stared at it. "Why were you interested in this guy?" he said aloud, wondering what Hannah had been trying to prove. No answer came, but it was the only lead he had right now.

As Jake thought about Donnelly, he started to feel a menacing calm. It was a deeply hidden feeling that he hadn't felt in ages. He'd been angry a lot, sad, depressed, confused, all the human emotions, but this menacing calm, this feeling like a broadaxe being sharpened before a fight was something he hadn't felt for a long time. He stood up, went to Hannah's bedroom and searched her closets and under her bed, locating what he expected to find. Under the bed she kept a Remington 870 12-gauge shotgun. The home defense scattergun had the extra magazine extension and held seven rounds and one in the chamber. He ejected one of the rounds, noted it was 00 buck and smiled. *Hannah was not messing around with any intruders.*

He also found a loaded Sig Sauer P226 in her nightstand. The Sig had been the standard issue sidearm for US Navy SEALs for over a decade. He slipped it into his hand and found his fingers involuntarily jacking the slide back, locking the slide, ejecting a magazine and pushing the slide release button, as if he had done it a thousand times. The rapid, expertly smooth movement in Jake's hands caused him to stop and stare at the pistol. *How do I know this weapon so well?* he wondered.

It felt like an extension of his arm. He closed his eyes and repeated all the movements again, this time field stripping the pistol with his eyes closed. He opened his eyes and stared at the parts laying on Hannah's bed. With hardly a conscious thought, he began to expertly assemble the weapon. As he put it back together, thoughts and images popped into his head, passing through some temporary, permeable barrier in his mind. He saw a group of hard men in jungle fatigues standing together, loaded to the gills with weapons, bandoliers of ammunition and rockets. It looked like they were gathered for a group photo.

He closed his eyes again and suddenly saw a tall man with a beard at the edge of the photo, black smudges under his eyes that looked like facepaint. The man stared back at Jake with familiar eyes and instantly Jake knew that *he* was that man. He didn't know what the vision meant, and couldn't remember the scene or the other men. *Or could he?* In the memory, there was a man standing beside him in his photo vision. He closed his eyes and tried to recall the picture again. "Eric," he whispered. He tried to bring the picture into focus again but it faded like an early morning cloud.

In the garage, Jake found a pistol belt with a holster that Hannah used when she went hunting. On the left side of the holster was a scabbard holding a long hunting knife with a serrated edge on the backside of the blade. He adjusted the belt for his waist and slipped it on.

He walked back into the house, slid the pistol into the holster, grabbed the shotgun and caught a glimpse of himself in the mirror in Hannah's living room. He stopped and stared at the man looking back at him. It was his face, but his eyes were different. He moved closer to the mirror, staring hard at himself. The eyes drew him in like dark tunnels to another world, a world that was both foreign and familiar. He drew back and saw that his eyes were narrow and almost black now. He heard a voice in his head say, "The only easy day was yesterday, strap it on motherfucker."

Jake drew the hunting knife from the scabbard, ran it across the back of his hand until a thin red line of blood dripped down his thumb. He put his fingers in the pool of blood and painted a deep red slash under each of his eyes. He jacked a round into the chamber of the shotgun, producing an ominous sound that strikes fear into the heart of anyone on the wrong end of that weapon. "Let's go, Armando," he said quietly, then stepped outside into the dark, starry night.

27

December 2018, Guatemala City

Jake and his team sat on flimsy folding chairs inside a gray metal warehouse that the DEA owned on the outskirts of Guatemala City. The room they were in served as their briefing and planning room for each mission. An overhead projector sat in the back and a pull-down screen hung on one wall. It was the same room that Agent Hymie Flores had used to brief the team for their previous missions. Those missions had been fairly straightforward and easy, considering what kind of operations the SEALs on the team had conducted in Iraq and Afghanistan. The DEA stuff was mostly what the SEALs called capture or kill missions. They were inserted by vehicle into the jungle near a specific location and the team would lay up at a hide site, wait for the target to appear and then capture them preferably, or kill them as a last resort.

The missions so far had gone OK, but privately the SEALs on the team complained to one another and to Jake, who was their team leader, that there was a lack of robust planning and attention to detail that SEALs were accustomed to. The men were used to detailed contingency plans, air cover, a quick reaction force on standby to support them if they got into a mess, redundant communications and

MEDEVAC ready to go. These DEA guys definitely flew by the seat of their pants from the team's perspective and experience. But the extra pay was good, the missions had all gone to plan and the team had bundled up a string of low and mid-level leaders in the gang or cartel; Jake could never tell the difference between the two.

Flores entered through a door in the back of the room and walked around the SEAL operators seated in folding chairs, then continued to the small podium next to the screen in the front. The boys joked among themselves that Flores was a white Mexican. In fact, he had fled Venezuela as a young man, emigrated to the US, studied international finance in Florida and been recruited by the DEA. His thick, dark hair tied in a ponytail and his wire-rimmed glasses made him look like a hippie college professor. He was the only DEA agent that the team knew or worked with at the warehouse. Either the other agents worked out of a separate location or they vacated the building while the SEALs were living there.

Flores stepped up to the podium and scanned the SEALs in front of him. Including Jake, five SEALs had been selected to work with the DEA in Guatemala. Jake knew two of the men very well, Eric and Geoff, having been at the same SEAL Team with them and deployed together. The other two he knew by reputation as skilled operators. They had all been recruited individually by Flores after extensive interviews, then flown to a training camp in Puerto Rico where they practiced as a team and learned DEA protocol before being sent on to Guatemala City.

Flores adjusted his glasses and looked up at the SEALs, "Gentlemen, the mission tonight will be your last mission here in Guatemala. It will also be the most important one you have conducted so far."

He scanned their faces as he continued, "Tonight we will take out the leader of the cartel here in Guatemala. You've eliminated all his lieutenants and now we take the leader off the board. We have intelligence that he's planning to fly the coop now that so many of his subordinates are in our custody."

Flores pushed a button on the remote and a picture of a man flashed on the screen. To Jake he looked like a typical drug dealer with a pugnacious face, huge golden rings on his fat hands, slicked back hair and beady eyes. "This is our man, Javier Galindo, or The Gallo as the locals call him." Jake and the other SEALs knew that Gallo meant Rooster in Spanish. The guy certainly looked the part.

"Sometime tonight between the hours of midnight and 4 a.m., Galindo will meet a group of smugglers who will ferry him out of the country by boat, probably to southern Mexico, we think. He has connections and family there. Your mission is to interdict Galindo at the meeting site, capture him and bring him to justice. This thug is responsible for hundreds of murders, tons of poisonous drugs shipped to the United States resulting in countless deaths and ruined lives."

Jake shifted in his seat and asked the first of dozens of questions he knew the boys wanted answers to. "What's our infiltration platform?"

"I'll get to all those details," Flores said, almost dismissively, "But to answer your question, you'll be inserted by helicopter. There's a clearing in the jungle near the meeting site. The helo will insert you well before Galindo arrives and you'll have time to set up and wait for him." He briefed the rest of the mission parameters without any more interruptions. At the end of the brief, the operators asked several more questions. Finally, Jake spoke, "OK, Flores, we'll do some unit level tactical planning and get back to you."

Flores smiled at Jake and nodded. "I'll be in my office if you have any more questions." And with that, he left the SEALs to plan in private.

Eric, who had deployed twice to Iraq with Jake, spoke for the group. "This seems poorly planned," he began, looking around at the other guys for confirmation, seeing heads nod in agreement. "The QRF is supposedly some DEA agents on standby at another station, MEDE-VAC is the same helo that inserts us, but what happens if that helo has problems? This is starting to look like a clusterfuck. I'm guessing this Galindo guy is heavily guarded, so we may be in for a solid firefight and there's no QRF."

Jake stood up and looked at his men. "Gents, I agree with every-thing Eric has said. We all volunteered for this assignment and we can all un-volunteer right now and tell Flores that this mission is not ready for prime time." He gazed around the room; the guys had not expected that from him. He went on. "Or we can spend the rest of today doing our best planning and preparation to take one more bad actor off the table. I'm gonna leave it to you guys. I'll step out, you discuss it and vote amongst yourselves. Come get me when you have a decision." With that, Jake poured a cup of coffee from the lukewarm pot in the back corner of the room and stepped outside into the humid morning.

Twenty minutes later, Eric opened the door, spotted Jake watching a monkey in a tree and yelled for his friend and teammate across the field, "We're ready Jake!"

Jake strode back into the room and stood at the front of the room beside the podium. "OK, what's the plan, guys?" he asked. The SEALs all looked at Eric, who spoke for the group, "We're all in. This is our last mission, we'll go out on a high note and crush it one more time."

Jake looked at the faces of his men, his eyes aglow with a menacing calm. "Alright, the only easy day was yesterday, let's get after it." And with that, the men moved to the front of the room, gathered around the large topographic map of their target area and started brainstorming ideas and asking tactical questions of one another.

At 2100, a blacked-out Huey helicopter landed in the DEA compound and shut down its engine. The pilot, co-pilot and the single crewmember strode into the briefing room. Flores greeted the air crew in Spanish and pointed them to Jake. Jake had the impression that these guys were not DEA. They hardly spoke English. He figured they must be some contracted pilots. Like all the DEA missions Jake had been on, everyone kept their units, names and personal information to themselves.

The whole team gathered around the map and the lead pilot briefed the SEALs on their ingress and egress routes. They would head due south, leaving the high plains of Guatemala City at nearly 5,000 feet and descend westward towards the coast, flying over the jungle, avoiding towns and cities enroute. They would pass over the El Imposible National Park and insert the SEALs near the coast on the north side of the El Rosario River. From there the SEALs would move two kilometers to their planned ambush site and await the arrival of the drug lord and his entourage.

After a few more questions, the team put on their vests laden with ammunition, grenades, radios and escape and evasion kits, or E&E kits, slung their weapons over their shoulders and walked out to the Huey on the tarmac.

The air crewman gave Jake a helmet with a microphone and earpiece embedded so he could communicate with the pilots. It was dark and the stars were hidden by clouds as the air crewman shut the side door. Jake saw a bunch of bats fly overhead before the door closed; it seemed like a bad omen.

The pilot throttled up the helo and the Huey lifted off the ground, turned southwest and rose above the jungle tops. Jake looked out the side window and saw a sliver of moon peak out from behind the dark clouds. He was happy that this was the last mission. It had been exhausting living the cover story of being a Navy corpsman again. He had memorized pages of detail, some of it true, parts of it made up, to support his cover story and became very convincing when asked about his career and some of the humanitarian missions he had supported in Central America. Plus he'd had enough of this hot and bug-infested jungle for a while. It would be good to get back to the moderate weather of San Diego and to another SEAL Team.

The pilot came up on the radio periodically to inform Jake of the turns he was making at the designated way points. Jake followed along on the laminated map in his lap, keeping track of their location with a red lens flashlight.

A little less than an hour from take off, the pilot came over the radio to Jake in a thick Spanish accent, "Ten minutes until the LZ." Jake gave his men the hand signal for ten minutes out and each man checked his gear one more time and loaded a round into the chamber of their weapons.

Jake felt the Huey slowly decelerate as the pilot began to skim above the top of the jungle enroute to the landing zone in an open field along the river. He could just make out gray cliffs and large waterfalls as the helo dropped down a narrow canyon into the open plain of the coast. At one minute out from the landing zone, the aircrewman opened the side door and Jake saw a ribbon of dark blue river below him sandwiched on either side by thick jungle. In a few moments, the jungle gave way, the land below them opened up and the helo banked and began a slow descent to the open field at the bank of the river. Suddenly, Jake saw a swarm of muzzle flashes open up around the LZ.

The Huey was riddled with machine gun fire ripping through its aluminum skin, injuring or killing everyone inside and tearing through hydraulic lines and electrical boxes. Jake saw the pilot slumped over the controls, and the co-pilot trying to fly the damaged aircraft but Jake felt the helo descending rapidly toward the ground. He looked around at his men and saw all three of them had been shot. By some miracle, he had escaped the bullets, but as the helicopter fell toward the jungle below, he realized the impact would probably kill them all, and if they survived a crash landing, the flames of the fuel-fed fire would probably burn them to bits. The helo was spinning now in circles as Jake tried to get to his men to help them, but the centrifugal force of the spinning Huey kept him slammed into the seat behind the co-pilot. Suddenly, he heard the terrible crunch of the rotors hitting the tops of jungle trees, then the helo turned slightly on its side, making a terrifying screech as the rotors were ripped off the machine and the remains of the fuselage crashed onto the jungle floor.

The cabin of the Huey landed with a thud under a canopy of tall trees. The tail and rotors had been sheared off, but the trees had slowed down the falling fuselage, protecting it from total devastation. The helo landed on its left side with the open door on the right now pointing up into the dark night sky.

Jake had been thrown against the lower left side of the helo as it crashed. The bodies of his men and the aircrewman had provided a cushion for him as his body was smashed into the downward side of the airframe as it crash-landed. His head hurt like it had been hit with a hammer. He felt the top of his head and blood came oozing out of a deep wound. He stood up, felt woozy, but still checked on each of his men—they were all dead. Suddenly, he heard voices coming out of the jungle surrounding the downed bird.

Jake grabbed his rifle and peered over the edge of the side door, which was now facing up toward the sky. He saw lights in the jungle and heard men shouting in Spanish. Blood began pouring down his face from the wound on his head and he felt sick and dizzy. On pure instinct and adrenaline, he jumped out of the side door and ran to the opposite side of the jungle from where he saw the lights.

He crept back fifteen feet into the jungle and lay down in a patch of thick underbrush that still gave him a view of the helicopter. Ten minutes later, a group of armed men emerged from the jungle on the other side of the wreckage. Jake counted five men but then a sixth appeared. Even from twenty-five yards away in the pale moonlight, Jake recognized Flores, the DEA agent. He was taller than the others and his ponytail and glasses were visible in the scant moonlight beaming through the opening in the jungle canopy.

As Jake watched in horror, the men walked up to the helo and blasted machine guns inside to ensure no one survived. Flores yelled at them to stop then climbed into the Huey. He crawled out the side door a few moments later. "One of them is missing," he said in Spanish to the men crowded around him. "Andele, andele!" he yelled as the men immediately fanned out searching for Jake.

Jake lay there even after the men started looking for him, his brain not fully recognizing what had happened. His head felt like it was going to explode. For a moment, he forgot where he was and imagined that he was in a secret garden. But then something snapped in his brain and he knew that he had to get out of there, that those men were looking for him, that Flores, whom they'd trusted, was involved in the death of his men.

Slowly, ever so slowly, Jake crawled away from the downed helicopter toward the river. As a Navy SEAL, water was his friend, his escape. Most people were afraid of deep, rushing water, but not Jake. Suddenly, he heard noises near him. Then he saw the flashlights scanning the jungle like white lightsabers.

He crawled backwards on his stomach then began to move toward the river, which he could hear somewhere ahead of him. Behind him, the voices were getting louder. He stood up slowly. They were getting close, they might stumble on him. He began to move quickly toward the sound of the river, moving as fast as he could without making too much noise, until he tripped over a vine and fell to the ground with a thud and crash. The men began shouting and running through the jungle in his direction. He fired off a magazine of suppressive fire in their direction just to make them think twice about coming after him. He then stood up and sprinted toward the river. Rounds whizzed past him, slashing bushes and leaves, causing the bullets to spin like small saw blades. He ran for twenty more yards then came to a rock cliff above the river that flowed fifty feet below. He checked for an easier way down, but there was none and there was no time to search. He couldn't see any big rocks, but the dark torrent below was angry and violent.

Bullets ripped out of the jungle behind him as he leapt off the cliff, trying to clear the rock face below and land near the middle of the river.

He felt himself hang in the air for what seemed a long time, then he hit the water with a massive splash and found himself hitting the bottom of the river bed before he could push off and find the surface. His vest full of equipment and ammunition was pulling him down, so he held his breath, unclipped the buckles and let it fall to the river bed. That gave him enough buoyancy to swim upward and keep his head above the roiling water. He looked down stream and it seemed like the whole river was dropping away... but no, it was a waterfall. He tried to swim to the bank, but the current was too strong, so he took in a large gulp of air before he was washed over the violent falls. In the dark, hydraulic surge, he smashed his head on the bottom before he was shot out by an eddy from under the falls. The river was calm below the falls and the mild current floated him to a muddy embankment.

Jake lay on his back, coming in and out of consciousness. Time passed, but he had no sense of how long he was there in the sandy mud. Finally, he opened his eyes, lifted his head and looked around. For a few moments, he had no memory of how he'd been spit onto this muddy sandbar. His head felt like a bear was trying to clamp its jaws around his temples. What he didn't know was that pressure was building up inside his skull where his brain had been severely bruised. He had a momentary recollection of the helicopter crash, the men chasing him and Flores directing the cartel thugs to finish off everyone in the helo.

He sat up and felt that his left arm was either broken or dislocated at the shoulder. He tried to rotate it back into place, but a sharp knifing pain stopped him. He looked around and saw in the starlight that he was surrounded by towering cliffs. He was not going to be able to climb out of there with his bad arm. Slowly, like a water lizard, he slid back into the inky river and let the gentle current carry him towards the coast with just his eyes and mouth held above the brown, murky water.

Several hours later, he'd been carried to the coast. The narrow river widened and opened into a marshy bay surrounded by small sand dunes before spilling into the Pacific Ocean. Jake climbed out on the northern bank and rested in the sand. A pink slash of light to the east over the cliffs revealed that sunrise was coming. He got to his feet and began to stumble north along the coast, staying a quarter mile inland in case anyone on the beach was looking for him. Two miles into the trek, he came across a wide bay that looked like it had been carved into the sandy coast. He made his way above the bay, scrambling over rocks until he came to an overlook point. He peered around a large rock and looked down into the bay, where he saw a small jetty protruding from the beach.

Two vessels were tied up to either side of the jetty, with men moving back and forth from them to the shore. Jake ducked behind two big rocks that gave him a better view of the scene below. One of the vessels was clearly a semi-submersible craft. The cartels used these to move drugs into the US on one-way trips. They would load the long, narrow submarine-like boat with tons of drugs, then with a skeleton crew, transit north with only a small snorkel above the waterline to bring in air for the diesel engine to propel them forward. The tiny black snorkel above the waterline was almost impossible to spot. Jake watched as men loaded huge bundles of drugs into the hatch.

On the other side of the jetty was a large speedboat with four giant outboard motors. It resembled the massive offshore race boats that could fly across the ocean, skipping across the waves.

Jake watched the men load the last bundle into the submersible. Three men then climbed into the hatch while a crew member on the pier untied docking lines and the vessel began to slowly motor out of the small, protected harbor and into the ocean.

A jeep pulled up at the head of the pier and Jake saw Agent Flores exit the passenger side and walk down the jetty, then toss a bag into the speedboat and climb aboard. Two men already in the boat helped him board, then they started the rumbling motors, tossed off lines and headed out to sea behind the semi-submersible.

Jake tried to think about what it all meant, but his mind was fuzzy, and there was a terrible thronging between his ears. He only knew that he had to find help. He moved cautiously around the harbor and headed north again, staying inland from the beach. Two hours later, he came across three small huts on the coast underneath a stand of palm trees, next to a small creek that fed into the vast, blue ocean. He hid behind a small dune and studied the site. Eventually he saw some villagers working around the huts, tending fishing nets and keeping a small fire alive. The throbbing pain in his head was practically unbearable and he was sure he would soon lose consciousness. He knew he had to take his chances here.

He rose up and stumbled from the small dunes into the village. A woman in a colorful dress tending the fire saw him and called out to the others. Three men ran quickly out of the huts and stood together facing Jake. With his muddy jungle camouflage uniform, beard and boots, he looked like either a drug runner or some Marxist terrorist from hell.

The men remained calm once they realized he had no weapons, and simply waited for this stranger to enter their fishing camp. Jake tread across the waist deep creek, approached the men and stopped. In Spanish, and with concerned raised voices, they asked questions. Jake blinked slowly at the faces of the men, noticed a seagull floating lazily overhead, then fell to his knees and was engulfed by darkness and oblivion.

The next thing he remembered was waking up in a bare hospital room with two bulging Marines from the US Embassy in Guatemala City standing next to a cracked window while a small doctor with a nose like a beak stood over him. The doctor had performed emergency surgery to relieve pressure on Jake's brain eight hours earlier and wasn't sure his patient would ever wake up. But Jake beat the odds, opened his eyes and one of the Marines moved to his bedside. "Who are you?" he asked, to the irritation of the doctor, who waved his tiny hands to shoo the Marine away.

"I-I'm a US Navy Corpsman," Jake answered in a weak, cracked voice. "I'm part of the Marines...I'm on a humanitarian mission."

The big Marine nodded to the sergeant in the corner, who pulled out his phone and called the Embassy.

28

OCTOBER 2022, MONTROSE COLORADO

Jake drove Hannah's pickup truck slowly through town toward the address on the paper he'd found on her table. It was 11 p.m. and there were few cars on the road in the small town. He took a right off Townsend Avenue, turned west down a side street, drove a quarter of a mile, and clicked off his lights as he glided to the curb two houses away from the address he was looking for.

The low slung house was dark, but there was a faint light coming from behind the closed curtains. Jake grabbed the shotgun off the floor, racked a round into the chamber and turned to Armando, "You wait here, boy, I'll be back." With that, he stepped quietly out of the truck, gently closed the door and walked slowly to the house belonging to Ardon Donnelly. To the right was a tall vehicle gate leading to parking in the rear. Jake passed that gate, glanced at the front door as he passed it on the sidewalk on the other side of the street, then crossed the street and came to the front of the neighbor's house on the left side of Donnelly's. The moon had been hidden by clouds, so it was pitch black on the tree lined street. A small driveway at the neighbor's house was bounded by a fence between the parking area and Donnelly's home. Jake walked down the neighbor's driveway and stopped at the fence, listening for any noise. A few stars were now peeking out from the tree-lined street, but there was still no moon. When he'd heard nothing for over a minute, Jake reached up and pulled himself over the six foot wooden fence, holding the shotgun in one hand and landing on soft bark on the other side. Again he stood quietly for several minutes, letting his eyes adjust to the night and scouting the home in front of him.

Jake noticed two windows on the west side of the house but saw no doors. A heat pump sat on a small pad and hummed away. He crept up to the first window and peered inside. He was looking down a hallway and saw the kitchen at the other end lit by overhead lighting, but no people. He crept to his left and looked through the next window. Curtains were drawn but in the corner he could see that someone had been living in the small bedroom. It was clearly not the main bedroom, so he figured there were at least two people living in the house.

He turned a corner and crept around the back of the house, ducked under the kitchen window and came to a set of sliding glass doors. The place smelled like cigarette smoke, he looked down and saw cigarette butts scattered on the brick pavers at his feet. Vertical blinds covered the doors, but Jake peered through the cracks in the blinds into the small living room at the front of the house. Ardon Donnelly and another big man sat on a couch watching television. There was a pitbull lying asleep at Donnelly's feet, but there was no sign of Hannah. Jake studied the scene for a moment, with one eye peering from the dark night into the dim room. He made a promise to himself that he would not kill the dog—it was innocent enough.

He reached for the handle on the sliding glass door, knowing intuitively that it would be unlocked because one or both of these guys would be coming outside to smoke again before turning in for the night. Sure enough, the door began to slide as he pushed it slowly while peering through the cracks at the men on the couch. The door hit a snag, Jake pushed a little harder and the door slid open, but not without making a scratching mechanical noise. Immediately, the dog began to growl and the two men glanced at her and stood up. In the back of his mind, Jake sensed that he had stepped through doors like this into a gunfight many times in his life.

He slid the door quickly open, then stepped into the room as the two men yelled, pulled out pistols and fired at him. Jake jumped behind the kitchen island, slid to his stomach, rolled over, poked the shotgun around the corner and aimed at the big man who was shooting into the kitchen. Jake fired the shotgun and eight .33-inch steel pellets hit the man in the chest, blowing a hole in him the size of a bowling ball. He flew back against the wall in the living room, dead even before he slumped to the carpeted floor. The dog stayed in place, barking menacingly at Jake. Donnelly fired two more shots at him with his revolver then stopped to reload. Jake reached around the kitchen island again, aimed low, fired and hit Donnelly somewhere below the shin, knocking him over like he'd just stepped into a hole. As Donnelly fell, he dropped the pistol onto the blood-stained carpet.

Jake stood up from behind the counter with the shotgun aimed at Donnelly and calmly walked over to him. The dog came at Jake, but with only three legs, he wasn't very fast. Jake tapped the dog on the nose with the butt of the shotgun and it yelped and whimpered over into the corner. Jake stood over Donnelly. "We've got a few things to talk about, you and me," he said, looking down at the little man with the sharp features.

"Fuck you!" sneered Donnelly, gritting his teeth and yelling against the pain. Keeping his shotgun on Donnelly, Jake pulled his knife out and cut away the lower half of Donnelly's jeans so he could inspect the wound. He couldn't have Donnelly passing out or dying before he got the information he needed. Most of the pellets had missed but three or four had ripped through his shin and ankle. Jake cut off the piece of loose blue jeans and wrapped it tightly around the wound, stemming the blood flow.

Jake reached down, grabbed Donnelly by the back of his collar, hoisted him to his feet and dragged him to the kitchen. He sat him on one of the barstools at the island, then moved around to the other side, set his shotgun on the counter out of Donnelly's reach and pulled out Hannah's hunting knife, gently placing it on the counter between them.

"OK, Donnelly, I'm gonna start asking you questions. If you don't answer or you lie to me, I'm gonna start taking pieces off of you. Do you understand?"

"Fuck you!" Donnelly roared again.

Jake nodded calmly and asked, "Where is Hannah?"

Donnelly shook his head in defiance and spat on the floor.

Jake reached across the narrow kitchen counter, pulled Donnelly's arm and hand onto the table and before Donnelly could react, Jake cut off the tip of one of his fingers. The blood pooled onto the white linoleum like melted lipstick as Jake flicked the piece of finger into the sink with his knife. Donnelly screamed, dropped his head and threw up in his own lap while Jake held his arm tight across the counter.

"I'm gonna ask you again. Where is Hannah?" Jake asked slowly in a deep but calm threatening tone. Donnelly looked up, searing pain in his eyes, a beaten man.

"Davidson has 'er," he croaked, hyperventilating against the pain.

"I asked where she is," Jake said, moving the knife above Donnelly's next finger.

"I sweah I don't know!" he spat out in his thick Boston accent. "He has a traila up on the plateau off Divide Road. He's a huntah and goes up there this time of yeeah and hunts elk. He might have 'er there."

"I need more information than that," Jake said matter-of-factly, placing the blade on Donnelly's thumb.

"Uhhh," Donnelly moaned, "OK, OK, you go up Dave Wood Road, take a right awn Divide, go about three miles and go to the first open area on the left. He has a big gray traila, an ATV and a red Dawdge Dually pickup. Ya can't miss it," Donnelly whimpered through short breaths.

Jake nodded, sensing this was the best direction he would get from Donnelly. "And why does he have her?" he asked, pressing the blade to touch Donnelly's thumb again.

"He wants you, not her. She just gawt a little too smawt, stuck her nose into things she shouldn't've. She's just bait fau you now."

"OK. Why does Davidson want me?" Jake asked, letting Donnelly feel the blade pressing on his thumb.

"Cause I'm fawking paying him to!" Donnelly yelled, sounding more panicked than anything. "The son of a bitch is ova his head in gamblin' debts. A little birdie told me he needed the money pretty bad."

"OK, you better explain that. If you lie to me, I'll know, and I'll take both your thumbs off and run them down the garbage disposal. Are we clear?"

With a look of dread, Donnelly took a deep, ragged breath. "OK, I'll tell ya everything. Just please put the knife away."

Jake pulled the knife back, intentionally cutting Donnelly's skin just enough to make it bleed. "I'm listening."

"I need some whiskey," Donnelly pleaded. "It's unda the countah below you." Keeping his eye on Donnelly, Jake reached below, opened the cabinet door and pulled up a bottle of Tullamore Dew Irish Whiskey. He reached for a dirty coffee cup in the island sink and poured Donnelly a healthy dose of the whiskey.

Donnelly took two large swigs, then looked up at Jake. "It all stauted back in Boston."

"I've got nothin' but time, Donnelly," Jake said casually, wiping the blood off Hannah's knife and setting it on the counter in front of Donnelly.

"I was a drug runna for a gang in Boston. I got pinched by the DEA durin' a big drug bust, but then this DEA agent pulls me aside and makes me an offa. If I worked for him, he'd put me in witness protection. That's how I ended up in this shithole of a podunk town." Donnelly drained his whiskey and held the empty cup up to Jake.

Jake poured him a smaller splash and asked, "Why here?"

"The DEA guy was looking for *you*," Donnelly explained. "He sent me heeah to wait and wauch. You wau like homeless or some shit and he couldn't find you, but figured eventually you'd come to see yau ma, so he planted me heeah to sit on my ass and wait fa you to show."

Jake was dumbfounded. "So that meeting in the park wasn't accidental?" he asked, beginning to see the connections.

Donnelly shook his head as he tried to breath through the pain before continuing. "Naw, I hired those punks to give you a rattlin', put you in the hawspital for a day or two so I could follow you from there."

"What about one of 'em getting stabbed?" Jake asked angrily. "I was held overnight for that."

"The guy was playin' me fau a fool. I started dealing here and he tried to cheat me. But Davidson said he could pin the mauder on you and get you put in the pen. Only problem was you slipped outta da noose," Donnelly jeered, shaking his head.

"What about the other kid who OD'd on fentanyl earlier this week? Are you dealing that shit?" Jake asked.

Donnelly was quiet for a moment, but knew if Jake sensed he was lying he'd be down a major digit. He looked at Jake defiantly and confessed, "Yeah, he was sellin' some of the Apache fau me—guess he wanted to try it himself."

"What the fuck is Apache?"

"Street name for fentanyl," Donnelly clarified, draining his whiskey.

Jake's head began to hurt and sweat started to bead on his forehead, "So why does this DEA agent want me?" he asked, but in the deepest part of his mind, he already knew the answer.

"Some fawking DEA mission in Central America went south. You know too much and the guy wants you in jail or dead. If he gawt you in jail, he could pay some prison gang to get ridda ya."

"So what's this DEA agent's name?" Jake asked slowly and deliberately.

Donnelly shook his head, as if that was the one secret he couldn't reveal, the one that would get him killed.

Jake picked up the knife and placed it on Donnelly's thumb again. "What is the DEA agent's name?" Jake asked again, softer this time, but with even more menace behind his words.

"I can't, he'll kill me," Donnelly pleaded, dropping his head.

"Look at me," said Jake. "It is Flores?" he asked, staring into Donnelly's eyes for confirmation. Jake didn't know where that name had come from, but it had bubbled into his mind like a long lost memory suddenly recovered. Donnelly said nothing, but his eyes said everything.

"Tell me what he looks like," Jake said, now in a voice that scared Donnelly, as if Jake had become another person.

"Tawl, pale, pony tail, dauk hair, wire-rimmed glasses," Donnelly spit out, watching the knife poised on his thumb. Jake nodded as the image of Flores flashed through his mind like an out of control slide show.

Images started to flood through some barrier in his mind of men he had fought alongside, SEALs he had known, SEALs he had deployed with, missions he had been on, commands he had served at. He began to feel light-headed; an episode was coming on, his brain was working overtime.

Sensing that something was wrong, Donnelly waited until Jake closed his eyes and looked down at the floor. With his good hand, Donnelly reached across the counter to grab the shotgun. Jake saw the move out of the corner of his eye and slammed the blade down through the back of Donnelly's hand, piercing flesh and bone and sticking it to the countertop.

Donnelly wailed, then begged, "Take it out!! Take it out, please!"

Jake stepped back, picked up the shotgun, walked out the back door and left Donnelly to unstick his hand from the countertop.

29

OCTOBER 2022, MONTROSE COLORADO

Hannah sat up on the bed and heard an elk bugling a long, sad tone. That told her she was probably somewhere in the forest. She was locked in the front of a large toy hauler RV in what appeared to be the master bedroom. There was a small bathroom in the bedroom and a door between her and the rest of the RV. On the other side of the door was a tiny kitchen across from a dinette table, and in the back was an open garage area where an ATV had been unloaded through a large ramp door. Two chairs sat in the garage area, and hunting rifles and packs sat in the corner. There was one outside access door that led into the kitchen and dinette area and a separate access door in the side of the garage area. She knew she'd been knocked out by ether and shoved in a van after leaving the pizza place, but had no idea how she got here or who had taken her prisoner. She sat on the edge of the queen bed with her arms tied behind her back, but her feet were free. It was dark outside; she could tell from looking up at the small skylight over the bed. She felt like crap from inhaling ether.

She stood up, turned around and backed up to the door that led to the rest of the RV. She felt for the doorknob with her tied hands, and turned it slowly, discovering that it was locked as expected. There were small windows on either side of the bedroom, but the blinds were pulled so she couldn't see outside. She sat down on the bed and cursed under her breath, "I gotta get out of this place." She had no idea who put her in this trailer, but she knew for sure that it wasn't going to end well unless she could escape.

A generator kicked off and a few seconds later she heard what sounded like a microwave oven being opened and closed. Someone was heating up food. She stood up and moved to put her ear to the door. Two distinct voices were talking in hushed tones, but she couldn't make out the words or identify the voices.

She tried to move her arms to her side so she could see her watch, but someone had taken her watch along with her cell phone. She plunked down on the bed, dejected. *This is how Amber must have felt when she was captured in Iraq,* Hannah thought. *All my bad decisions have led to this moment,* she realized in despair. But then, just as quickly, she knew in her heart that she had done some good in this world, that she was not the same person she had been in Iraq, that she was moving forward in life and that she cared deeply for Jake. Ironically, this captivity caused her to realize that fully. Her feelings were in opposition to the rules, the norms, the advice of everyone, but she couldn't help them anymore than she could help loving sunsets, the color blue or Armando.

She couldn't explain it to herself, but she felt safe with Jake, loved and respected. With all the veneer of her freedom stripped away, she knew now what was important in her life, and it was Jake. Nothing else mattered, not even the job she loved. She needed to build a life with Jake. Even with his episodes and the traumatic brain injury Amber told her about, Hannah was undeterred. *So he's got buried memories of being a Navy SEAL, so what? He's not a bad man. I don't care,* she thought. *"I don't care,"* she whispered.

Jake followed the directions that Donnelly had given him up the dusty Dave Wood Road and turned right on Divide, another dirt road which ran north along the Uncompahgre Plateau, a large mountainous escarpment west of the Montrose Valley. There was a dusting of snow on the road and Jake saw at least a foot of snow under the pine and aspen trees, which seemed to fight each other for dominance in the quiet forest. Jake drove slowly, keeping an eye out for the first opening to the left that had the RV Donnelly had described as Davidson's hunting campsite. He looked down at the odometer—he'd come two and a half miles down Divide Road. He should be coming across the RV soon. At three miles, he saw only the dim forest at the edge of the road, but at 3.3 miles, the forest gave way to a clearing about half the size of a football field. Jake slowed and stared as he passed the site. There was a large toy hauler trailer with a big Dodge Dually pickup next to it. He couldn't make out the truck color in the dark, but it could have been red. He continued driving for a quarter mile until he came to a small dirt road to the right, where he could pull off and park the truck.

Armando stared out into the dense forest, aware that he was in a strange place surrounded by large animals. "You stay here, boy," Jake ordered, patting Armando on the head. Then he stepped out of the truck, grabbed the shotgun from the truck floor and closed the door. Armando lay down on the bench seat and put his head between his paws, but kept his ears up, primed to the sounds of all the animal noises in the dark forest.

Jake walked south along the edge of the road back toward the campsite. His instincts were to move into the concealment of the forest, but he knew it would slow him way down, since he'd have to step over deadfall and work his way across creeks, tree branches and rocks. He decided to move quickly along the side of the road until he came to the edge of the clearing where the RV and truck were parked. Once he was there, he crept along the treeline surrounding the clearing to get a better picture of the whole site while staying hidden in the forest. He could see dim lights on in the RV and noted that the trailer had two entry doors on the passenger side as well as the big ramp door in the back. His father used to have an old toy hauler RV, so Jake had an idea of the general layout—bedroom up front, kitchen and dining midships and a garage in the back. There wasn't really any other way to lay out these big toy haulers.

The moon couldn't pierce the deep cloud cover up in the dark mountain forest, making for an inky night. Jake's eyes had adjusted to the darkness during his walk to the site and he used his night vision to creep quietly up to the RV. The trailer was sitting on big tires, creating lots of ground clearance for the rig so Jake slid underneath on his back and lay there. He wanted to listen to the sounds and voices in the RV and see if he could tell where people were located and how many there were. The snow on the ground started to melt into his Carhart jacket, but he felt no cold.

A moment later, the generator for the RV kicked on, making a loud rumbling sound. Jake had an idea. Using the cover of the generator sound, he slid out from under the trailer and moved to the front of the

RV. He guessed that if Hannah was in there, they might have put her in the front bedroom. He moved slowly along the outside of the RV, came to one of the side windows up front and raised his head slowly to peek inside. The blinds were closed as he expected, but through a small gap under the blinds, he saw Hannah sitting on the bed. His heart almost leaped out of his chest—she was alive! He felt an anger rising up in his gut now—he would get her out of this mess and make those who took her pay a high price.

He tapped lightly on the window as the generator continued to rumble and Hannah got up from the bed and came to the window. She couldn't see out into the pitch black night, but moving her back to the window she pulled the shades up, turned around and put her face to the window to see Jake's face looking back at her. He motioned with his hands for her to unlock the window. She backed up to the window and tried to unlock the latch with her hands tied, but someone had wrapped wire around the latch, making it impossible for her to untwist it and open the window.

Jake saw that she couldn't get it open and motioned for her to lie down on the floor and cover her head. He tried to pantomime lying down in a ball. Now that he knew she was up front, he could focus on taking out whoever was in the back.

He could storm in and try to catch them by surprise, but there was a chance Hannah would get hit with a stray bullet. Suddenly, he had a better idea. He bent over to keep his body below the level of the RV windows, and walked to the back of the RV where the generator was rumbling in a rear compartment. The big pickup truck was only parked a short distance from the rear of the rig. Jake opened the compartment and turned the generator off then moved silent-ly behind the truck.

A few moments later, a man stepped out the rear entrance, went to the generator compartment and opened it up. He bent down and twisted off the gas cap, shining a small flashlight into the fuel tank—that's when Jake made his move. The man had no night vision, having come from inside the lighted RV and didn't see Jake moving like a cat behind him. In one swift move, Jake whacked him on the back of the head with the butt of his shotgun and knocked him out cleanly. The man let out a loud groan as he fell to the earth like a sack of potatoes. Jake reached down and turned the man's head and saw that it was some big guy with a red beard, not Davidson. He must still be inside.

Jake started to move back to the RV when he heard Hannah yell out. It was muffled, but he thought she'd shouted his name. Davidson must have heard the man groan and grabbed her. Jake ran to the rear door, set his shotgun down and slid the Sig Sauer pistol out of the holster. The shotgun would do too much damage in the confined space of the RV and he might accidentally hit Hannah. Instinctively, he pulled the hammer back on the pistol to the single action position so the trigger was ready to fire at the slightest pull of his finger.

He moved to the front door of the rig, hoping to create some confusion inside. The door opened outward, so he couldn't smash it and jump in. Suddenly the back door opened and Jake turned.

Davidson held a pistol to the side of Hannah's head as he stepped down the two RV steps to the ground and faced Jake, who was standing fifteen feet away by the front door.

Jake kept his pistol in front of him, but low at his waist, not in the firing position. Davidson was completely covered by Hannah as he bent down behind her, affording Jake no clean shot.

Jake waited but didn't respond. He would happily trade his life for Hannah's but he knew Davidson couldn't let either of them live now. "How did you find me?" Davidson yelled in a muffled voice behind Hannah.

"I visited your little buddy Donnelly," Jake said calmly. "He wasn't much of a talker at first, but he came around," he said with a venomous smile. "He told me all about your little arrangement," he said, leaving the details vague about how he'd left Donnelly.

"All I want is you, Jake," Davidson yelled. "Put your gun down and I'll let 'er go."

Jake didn't answer. Suddenly, thoughts and memories crashed through the thick barrier again that had been hanging in his mind like an old drape and his head felt like it was on fire. It was like his brain had lifted the veil on his deepest and truest identity in the face of the life or death situation in front of him. In an instant, he knew who he was—a United States Navy SEAL. The pistol he held now felt like an extension of his hand. He knew, without a doubt, that he had put tens of thousands of rounds through this weapon and could fire it with extreme precision.

"I'll tell you what, *Detective*," he spat, "I'll let you live if you let her go," he said in a frighteningly calm voice, slowly raising his pistol to aim at Davidson.

"I'll take my chances against a crazy, alcoholic bum," Davidson sneered. "You can go to hell, Hanlon."

Jake smiled. "Guess what, Davidson, your chances are zero—I'm a Navy SEAL, asshole." As Jake spoke, Hannah's eyes widened and she bent her head away from Davidson's pistol, creating just the slightest space between her head and the man holding her.

Jake saw the shot in his mind before he took any action. The tritium sites on his Sig glowed in the dark and danced in a tiny circle on Davidson's head as Jake's muscle memory and vision took over. He pulled the trigger softly like he was tickling a baby's chin. The shot rang out and hit Davidson just above the nose. He fell backwards, instantly dead as the bullet pierced his brain and shut down the rest of his body for good.

Jake lowered the pistol, de-cocked the hammer by instinct and set it back into the holster. Hannah ran up to him, tears in her eyes. "Lemme cut you loose," Jake said, pulling a Leatherman from his belt, moving behind her and cutting the zip tie. She wrapped her freed arms around his neck and kissed him long and hard. "You saved my life," she cried, tears welling up in her eyes.

"That's what I'm trained to do," he said softly into her ear.

Hannah pulled back and looked him in the face, "You mean as a Navy corpsman?" she asked, to see how he would respond.

"No, as a Navy SEAL, of course," he said, looking at her quizzically.

She closed her eyes and buried her face in his neck, tears of joy streaming down her face.

After calling 911 and describing the scene at the campsite, they went to her truck and let Armando out. His tail took on a life of its own as he smelled Hannah and ran circles around her, jumping and trying to lick her face.

Hannah grinned and bent down to give him a big hug and a good rubbing. "I missed you, boy."

They loaded up the truck and drove back to the campsite, parking fifty yards down the road so they wouldn't contaminate the crime scene.

The Cricket showed up with another police car behind him and parked on the dark dirt road, leaving his lights flashing. "What the hell happened here?" he asked Hannah, eyeing Jake suspiciously. Hannah gave him an abbreviated story of being grabbed outside the pizza joint and brought here by Davidson or his accomplice and then explained that Jake had rescued her. The Cricket looked dumbfounded as Jake continued the story of Donnelly and how Jake had left him knifed to the countertop with the other dead guy at the house in Montrose.

After an hour of questioning, Jenkins got permission to let Hannah and Jake go home, but he kept their weapons for evidence and forensics testing. The police had Davidson's accomplice with the beard in the back of a cruiser with an icepack on his head. It was 4:30 in the morning and everyone was exhausted. Hannah and Jake agreed to come to the station in the morning for interviews and to give more detailed statements.

30

OCTOBER 2022, MONTROSE COLORADO

Jake opened the passenger door of the truck for Hannah, and Armando jumped in ahead of her and took up a spot in the middle of the cracked vinyl bench seat. Jake walked around to the driver's side as Hannah climbed in. "Sorry, buddy," Hannah said as she picked up Armando, slid him to the passenger side window and scooted next to Jake. Jake turned his head, smiled and put his arm around Hannah as he started the truck and drove carefully down the dark mountainous roads.

"How did you find out about Donnelly?" Hannah asked as they drove through the dark forest.

"I drove to your place when I didn't hear from you," Jake replied, turning to look at her for a moment. "I went in and found the document on the table with Donnelly's information and figured you must have suspected him of something. I took a chance and it paid off."

"His real name is Sean O'Neal," Hannah said. "My friend in the DEA did some digging and found out he was a drug dealer in Boston and was placed here in the witness protection program after naming names."

Jake nodded but decided not to tell her yet that Donnelly was sent here because of him. He was still processing his new memories of being a SEAL and having worked for the DEA in Central America. He just needed time to let all that sink in and make sense before he tried to tell Hannah the whole story.

They made it home before the sun came up over the Cimarron peaks, with a hint of light in the eastern sky. Jake parked in the driveway, Armando shot out and Hannah walked around the truck, took Jake's hand and led him to her front door. "Come with me," she said softly, turning to Jake at the doorway.

"Are you sure?" Jake asked, holding both her hands. She pulled her hands away, reached around his neck and gave him a deep, passionate kiss.

"I'm sure," she whispered. She took his hand, and started to unlock the door with the spare key when Armando started to growl. "What is it, buddy?" she asked. She'd never heard him growl before. Suddenly the door to the condo swung open and a man stood in the doorway with a silenced pistol aimed directly at them.

"Well, come on in, lovebirds," the man said sarcastically. "Leave Cujo outside or I'll shoot 'im.'"

Armando was about to rush at the man in the doorway when Jake reached down, grabbed his collar and pushed him back as he and Hannah stepped into the entryway and closed the door.

It took Jake a moment but then he recognized DEA Agent Hymie Flores. The pony tail was gone and he was wearing a ball cap, but it was him.

"Long time no see," Flores said, looking at Jake. "Or do you even remember me? I heard you lost your mind or some shit. Is that true?"

"I know who you are, Flores," Jake said.

"Well, that's what I was afraid of," Flores said with a nasty smile. "You're the last loose end to my new life, Hanlon, and I don't like loose ends."

Flores was six feet away from them and began to step back to create more space when Hannah dove for his legs in a Jiu Jitsu style take down. Flores pointed the pistol downward and shot Hannah in the back as she dove toward his knees, but she knocked him to his back before she fell to the floor on her face. When Hannah dove, Jake's instincts took over and he rushed Flores like a linebacker. He went straight for Flores' right wrist to prevent him from getting off another shot. Flores tried to raise the gun, but Jake was on him in a second. Flores was strong and wiry, but Jake was bigger and fought like a lion. He grabbed Flores' wrist, pulled it to his mouth and bit deep into his arm, causing Flores to scream and drop the pistol. Flores was on his back now with Jake on top. They both reached for the pistol behind Flores on the floor, but Jake smashed his elbow into Flores' face, crunching his nose and grabbed the pistol before Flores could get it.

The long silencer on the barrel of the pistol made it unwieldy and Flores was able to reach up, grab the silencer and shove it toward the wall while trying to wrestle the pistol out of Jake's hands. They both fought for control of the gun, swinging it back and forth. Jake glanced over and saw Hannah's back covered in blood and a new strength surged through him, knowing he had to get her help and couldn't waste any more precious time fighting with Flores. Pulling his head way back, he slammed it into Flores' nose, causing Flores to momentarily let go of the silencer as blood gushed from his face. Jake wrenched the pistol free, jammed it under Flores's chin and pulled the trigger twice, killing Flores instantly.

Jake tossed the pistol to the ground, jumped next to Hannah and put his hand over the hole in her back, blood oozing between his fingers. He tore off his own shirt and stuffed a portion of it into the bleeding wound. They were less than five minutes from the hospital so he picked her up, raced her into the cab of the truck and sped like an Indy driver to the ER. He pulled up to the curb, ran around to the passenger side, pulled her limp body out and ran straight into the ER. He didn't stop at the check-in desk, but ran straight back to the first nurse he came to. "I've got a gunshot victim!" The startled nurse pointed him to the first open bed in the ER as several other nurses and a doctor appeared when they heard the commotion.

An older nurse who had seen her share of trauma stepped in front of Jake, who was shirtless, bloody and still trying to help Hannah. "Hey, let us take it from here," she said calmly, putting her hands gently on Jake's shoulders and directing him away from the bedside. Jake moved to the corner, but refused to leave the room.

"I need you to step out of the room, sir," she said to Jake with more force, pointing to the door. Jake ignored her and stared at the two nurses and the doctor working on Hannah. They had IV's in her and were hitting her with paddles.

"You have to leave," the nurse said in a more demanding voice. Jake gave the nurse a look that clearly communicated that they would have to drag him out of the room. She shook her head, sighed resignedly and stepped outside.

31

OCTOBER 2022, MONTROSE COLORADO

Jake sat in a chair beside Hannah's bed. She was in the ICU ward with a host of wires and tubes sticking out of her. He hadn't left her side except to call Amber. He didn't know her number but was able to contact the VA hospital in Grand Junction and track her down. Amber swung by Hannah's place to take care of Armando before she drove to the hospital. Nikita and Armando sniffed each other in greeting but otherwise ignored each other. Amber fed Armando and put him in her truck with Nikita. It was just getting dark as she pulled into the hospital parking lot.

Two police officers stood guard outside Hannah's ICU room. It was a show of respect and protection. One of the officers was from the Montrose PD and the other was from the Montrose County Sheriff's Department. They were there to support one of their own. Sergeant Jenkins had made up the watchbill and nearly every police officer on the force had volunteered to stand guard in their off-duty time. Even the Chief of Police had put himself on duty for the midnight shift. The senior police officer on duty checked Amber's ID, made a call to get the all clear from the officer on duty at the station and let her enter Hannah's room.

When Amber walked in, Jake was seated next to Hannah, his head down on the bed, holding one of her hands as the machines blinked and beeped above her. Amber pulled up a chair next to him. "Jake, I'm Amber," she whispered. "Hannah told me all about you," she said with a sad smile. "I was her best friend until she met you," she joked, trying to bring a little humor to the situation. Jake looked over and saw a beautiful blonde woman who was clearly in pain, just as he was.

"Hannah told me about you, too," he said, rubbing Hannah's hand, though getting no response.

"What's the latest?" Amber asked.

"Her heart stopped in the ER, but they brought her back to life. She's been unconscious since then," Jake said, shaking his head at the thought of losing her.

"Have they given a prognosis?"

Jake turned to look at Amber and tears rolled down his face. "She was shot in the spine, so even if she lives, they don't know if she'll ever walk again," he said, choking up.

Amber's mouth dropped open at the news. She looked like she wanted to say something to Jake, but nothing came out. The thought of her friend potentially paralyzed was too much. "My God," she breathed with shock.

At that moment, Susan walked into the room. She'd heard about the shooting from her friends on the police force. "I heard the word God," she said, standing behind Jake and Amber and putting her hands on both of their shoulders. "That's who we need right now. You don't have to do anything, but I'm gonna pray," she said.

Jake remained motionless with his head down. Amber looked over her shoulder and gave Susan a small nod of acknowledgement. Susan closed her eyes, paused for a moment, then spoke in a soft voice, "Almighty God, we ask for your blessing upon your daughter Hannah, a defender and protector of the citizens of this community. We know that you are working in her life and we ask you to be with her now in this time of great need, amen."

"She saved my life," Jake said, speaking to no one and to everyone with his head down. "She saved me in the park, gave me a place to live, saw past the beaten down homeless vet and never gave up on me." He paused, then spoke quietly, as if to himself. "She saved me again last night, diving at Flores. He wanted me, not her. She saved my life... again," he said, his words trailing off into a whisper as Amber and Susan both put their arms around him.

The police chief walked up to the lectern in a small conference room at the Montrose PD headquarters. The room was buzzing as the national news crews set up their cameras and jostled for position towards the front of the room. The two local reporters stood towards the back, muscled out by the big networks who had arrived several hours earlier with entire teams.

The chief checked his talking points. As a small town police chief he didn't have a dedicated press officer, so he'd written up his own notes. He looked at his watch, it was time. "Ladies and gentlemen," he said in a loud voice over the din of the reporters. He waited for them to quiet down, big cameras on tri-pods began rolling, and the room became quiet. "I'd like to make a statement, then answer a few questions."

Someone with a microphone on a pole, stuck it even closer to the chief, like some long tree branch wavering in the wind.

"On the evening of October 28, two suspects were killed, a third was injured and a Montrose Police Officer was critically wounded in what we are looking at as a conspiracy, possibly related to drug smuggling. The names of the four individuals are being withheld at this time pending further investigation. We are working alongside the FBI and the DEA to get to the bottom of this horrible incident. I'll now take a few questions," the chief pronounced, setting down his notes and staring at the lights and cameras.

A national reporter in the front row stood up and yelled out, "I have information that one of the suspects was a detective with the Montrose Police Department, can you confirm this and if so, what is being done to ensure any other corrupt officers are being rooted out?"

The chief shuffled his papers then looked up, "I cannot confirm the identity of any of these persons until we complete our investigation."

"I'm not asking you to identify the person, I'm asking if he was a detective with Montrose PD," the same young reporter shouted above the voices of other reporters. The chief looked like he was going to ignore her, then said, "This is an ongoing investigation, and further details will be released as soon as possible."

A young man from a Denver news station yelled out, "We understand another man was involved in the shootings, a veteran, possibly a Navy SEAL, can you comment on that?"

The chief looked over his shoulder at the FBI agent in a dark suit who stood against the wall stonefaced. The chief turned back to the crowd, "Another person was involved with these shootings, but we have not yet determined his role."

"That sounds like a yes," yelled the young man from Denver. The room then turned into a melee with multiple reporters shouting over each other to get the chief's attention.

The chief looked to the back of the room beyond the fracas and saw one of the local Montrose Press reporters with a raised hand. The chief pointed to the back of the room, to recognize him, "Jerry, go ahead."

"Chief, is it true that the recent stabbing in Cerise Park and the overdose death near City Market are related to this case?" The local news had been following those deaths and connected the dots to the current case while the big city news crews had just arrived in town.

The chief nodded, "Yes, Jerry, at this time we think those two deaths may be related."

"Does that mean that fentanyl is now being distributed in our town?" Jerry responded.

This time the chief looked at the DEA rep to his left who stepped up to the podium, "The DEA has been tracking the expansion of the sales and distribution of fentanyl closely throughout the country. Our experience is that criminal organizations start distributing fentanyl in big cities, but eventually they network out to smaller towns and rural areas more slowly; but yes I can confirm that it has been found here in Montrose."

The other local reporter from the Montrose Mirror had her hand raised and the chief pointed to her while standing next to the DEA agent. "Can you tell us the extent of the injuries to the Montrose police officer in the hospital and is she being looked at as a suspect in these crimes?"

The DEA agent deferred to the chief and stepped back. The police chief was getting tired of being circumspect, "I will not be discussing the injuries to our police officer, however I can tell you that she is not a suspect, but a hero who saved lives; and I hope I can trust you all to give her some privacy," He said, letting a flash of anger cross his face. "That will be all the questions for now."

32

December 2022, Montrose Colorado

Jake stood on the porch of the cabin near the Black Canyon and tossed the ball to Armando. The dog bounded through powdery drifts of snow, unbothered by the chilly December temperatures, retrieved the ball and brought it back to Jake on the porch, dropping it with a look of profound expectation. Jake reached for the ball again, but heard a stir inside the cabin. He tossed the ball far, then went inside.

Hannah had finished her nap and was sitting up in the small bed, sipping a bottle of water. Jake walked straight to her and kissed her on the forehead. "Are you ready to get up?" he asked.

Hannah nodded with grim determination and Jake reached one hand under her legs and one behind her back, lifted her gently and set her in the wheelchair next to the bed then placed a blanket over her legs. The wood burning stove was glowing red in the corner, but the thin insulation in the cabin couldn't keep the heat from escaping quickly.

"Let's go outside," Hannah said, looking up at Jake. He nodded, helped her put on her down jacket, then layered her with two more blankets and pushed the wheelchair out onto the small porch. Armando ran up the steps and dropped the ball at Hannah's feet. She smiled at him, but couldn't reach the ball. Jake picked it up and tossed it deep into a snowbank.

"Sit next to me," Hannah said, pointing to the small hand-carved bench on the porch next to her wheelchair. Jake sat down and said, "Hey, I was thinking tomorrow after physical therapy we can have lunch with Susan at Horsefly, whaddaya think? Then we can go by the condo and see how the construction is coming." Hannah had hired a contractor to make her condo wheelchair accessible, lower the cabinets and counters and make the bathroom work for a wheelchair. Her fellow officers at the Montrose Police Department had all chipped in and paid for the renovations and donated their own labor. Hannah had tried to argue with them, but it was useless. Jenkins had set up the construction watchbill and every officer came on their day off and worked on Hannah's condo under the supervision of a general contractor.

Hannah breathed in deeply then spoke, "Jake, I need to tell you something."

"Sure honey, what is it? What can I do for you?" Jake said, reaching over and patting her hand that was resting on the wheelchair armrest.

"I need to be by myself for a while." Even as she said it, she knew Jake wouldn't understand. He had been by her side 24/7 since the shooting and she would never have made it this far without him. He carried her when needed, did everything around the cabin and was her rock. She loved him more than she had loved anyone in her life. Despite her injury, the last two months since she'd left the hospital had been among the happiest in her life, with Jake at her side day and night. But she realized, after fighting it for weeks, that he had to go away.

"Baby, come 'ere," she said, turning her head and reaching out her arms to Jake. He slid off the bench and kneeled next to her on the porch. She stroked his hair, kissed him on the forehead, then said, "Look at me."

Jake raised his head and looked up at her. "You've been my savior and the best thing that has ever happened to me, Jake. I love you with all my heart." She let that sink in as Jake bowed his head. She ran her fingers through his thick, dark hair.

"The thing is, baby, I need to learn to live on my own," she said, knowing it would hurt him, but needing to say it anyway. "Not permanent, nothing like that. I just have to learn to live with my new life. You've done everything for me, my love," she said, leaning over and giving him a kiss on the top of his head. "But now it's time for me to learn how to live like this," she said, gesturing to the wheelchair. "I can't do it while you're doing everything for me." She knew it sounded like an accusation, but it was just a hard truth she'd come to accept.

"But what about us, what am I gonna do, where should I go?" Jake asked, truly blindsided by her words. He'd fallen so deeply in love with Hannah that he didn't even notice her disability. She had saved him twice and now he felt saved a third time by just being at her side these last few weeks. It had given him the purpose that he so desperately needed. "Do you think you're ready to take care of yourself?" he asked, knowing in his gut she could do anything she put her mind to.

"Come closer, Jake," she said. He bent over and put his face in her neck. She kissed him all over his face then spoke. "My condo will be ready next week and my car will be set up for driving with my hands. I'm gonna be OK. I want you to go back to San Diego, find a place to live near the SEAL Teams and go be with your brothers." Jake shook his head. "I'm serious, Jake—you need this, too. I want you to reconnect with all your brothers in arms, go for long ocean swims, run on those sandy beaches and scope out the beautiful women in bikinis." Jake pulled his head back and scowled at her, as if appalled at the suggestion. "I'm serious," she said, kissing him on his forehead.

"I need six months to adapt to my new life and become self-sufficient," she said, hoping she could finish the sentence without throwing her arms around him and telling him to forget everything she'd said. He looked up at her with tears in his eyes.

"You need to re-claim your place as one of the baddest motherfuckers on this planet, Jake," she said forcefully. "Six months from now, if you haven't shacked up with one of those beach bunnies and can pull yourself away from the brotherhood, I will be here waiting for you. Plus, you need to get treatment for your TBI now that your memories are coming back and the episodes have stopped. There aren't any experts here in Montrose. I've already researched it and contacted The Navy SEAL Foundation. They'll get you proper treatment and take care of you when you get to San Diego."

Jake stood up and walked out into the snow, not knowing how to handle his emotions. He paused to watch the sun throw a red glow on the peaks in front of him, and knew it was called an alpenglow. He stood there for nearly fifteen minutes until his feet began to freeze. Armando lay down next to him in the snow and Jake heard a voice in his head whispering a SEAL truth, "The only easy day was yesterday."

33

DECEMBER 2022, MONTROSE COLORADO TO SAN DIEGO CA

The following morning, Jake headed west out of Montrose on I-70 in the beater that Hannah had loaned him. The night before, Hannah had asked him to spend the night at the studio and leave the next morning because she didn't want to see him off. She couldn't trust herself not to change her mind and ask him to stay.

Jake drove up to Grand Junction and followed the 70 as it slowly bent west into Utah. The December morning was cool but sunny as he crept down the 80 mph highway in the far right lane doing 65 under a bluebird sky. Hannah's ole' beater was reliable, but not fast. The towering red rock formations of the San Rafael Swell dropped away into the high desert. South of Salt Lake City, he picked up Interstate 15, which would take him all the way into San Diego via Las Vegas.

Running on Red Bull, sunflower seeds and a nasty looking taquito off the roller at a Maverik's gas station, Jake made it to the outskirts of Las Vegas by dusk. He pulled into a rest stop north of town and parked as far away from the big diesel rigs as possible. The hum of their engines idling all night filled the air as he saw the glow on the horizon to the south of the most ostentatious city in America, as if it were its own sun. Jake leaned the seat back in the old Toyota and fell into a deep sleep.

He awoke from his death slumber as a pickup truck pulled next to him in the parking lot and the driver and passenger slammed their doors and laughed at something. Jake rubbed his eyes and checked the time - it was 5:30 a.m. He walked into the bathroom, splashed water on his face and noticed the bags under his eyes. Yesterday, while driving, he cried twice when thinking about Hannah. When pulling out of Montrose, he felt completely dead and empty inside, knowing he wouldn't be seeing her for a long time, and then somewhere in Utah he thought about her injury and the wheelchair, the unfairness of it all and he screamed and punched the window of the beater, adding another crack to the already splintered windshield.

He walked back to the car, jumped in and headed out of the rest area and back on to Interstate 15. He figured it would be good to get through Las Vegas in the wee hours before the traffic picked up anyway. He passed the gaudy casinos, parking lots full of gamblers at 6 a.m. and near infinite neon lights, punctuated by the sounds of police cars or ambulances responding to emergencies. He was glad to see the lights of the garish city in his rearview mirror.

It was only five hours from Vegas to San Diego and he made good time. The heat of the Nevada desert finally gave way to the coastal coolness of San Diego as he followed Interstate 15 to the highway 163 cutoff downtown. Rolling his window down, he passed palm trees, eucalyptus, lush flowers and smelled the salty ocean just a mile away. His senses came alive. Suddenly he felt what it must be like for a salmon to return to the small creek where it was hatched. Jake was born and raised in the San Diego area and the training he had endured as a Navy SEAL in San Diego had left an indelible mark on his psyche. Off to his left he saw the top of the Balboa Naval Hospital. With clarity now, he remembered being a patient there for many months as the Navy doctors attended to his brain injuries and tried to coax him out of his illusion, belief, chemical imbalance, whatever it was, that he had never been a Navy SEAL.

Highway 163 dumped into Interstate 5 and Jake immediately took the offramp to the Coronado Island Bay Bridge. Cresting the top of the bridge, he looked down at the tall sailboats and vessels plying the San Diego Bay. In the distance, he could see one of the aircraft carriers tied up at Naval Station North Island. Passing the peak of the bridge, Jake peered down at Coronado Island. Not a true island due to the strip of land that connected Coronado to Imperial Beach to the south, Coronado was nonetheless an island city unto itself. Called the Emerald Island, it was undoubtedly the most beautiful little city in the San Diego region. Immensely green, with golf courses, gorgeous parks and incredible mansions lining the winding streets, Coronado was like a little refuge from big city San Diego. It was also the home of the SEALs. Jake dropped off the bridge, took a left on Orange Avenue, passing all of the quaint shops and restaurants, then took a right at the Hotel Del Coronado and parked along the road near the beach north of the famed old wooden hotel.

It was 1:30 p.m. as Jake hid the keys to the beater under his seat and stepped out into the cool fall afternoon. He was wearing shorts, a T-shirt and sandals as he walked across the sandy beach toward the aqua-green ocean. Instinctively, he studied the shore and knew it was somewhere near high tide right now. He kicked off his sandals and shirt and stepped into the frothy green water swirling at his feet. He felt the cold stinging his ankles and remembered all the nights he'd spent on that beach or off the coast swimming, diving and freezing. Unlike the East Coast, the currents off the West Coast flow from north to south, carrying the icy waters off the coast of Alaska all the way to the California coast. Even at the height of summer, the ocean off San Diego rarely rose above sixty-eight degrees.

Jake stepped farther out into the cool ocean now, taking note of the waves. He used to have to report on the size and shape of the waves each morning as a periodic duty to help the Navy decide if they could practice amphibious landings that day. He now stared at moderate surf with waves coming in at 45-second intervals with faces of two to three feet. It was not big surf, but each wave still carried the power of a swell that started thousands of miles away.

He stepped out to waist deep water where the waves would roll in about head high and try to knock him down. He planted his feet deep into the sand and rooted himself to the bottom. The sun was shining above, casting diamond-like reflections on the foamy waves. Seagulls floated above him, circling in huge arcs as they searched for small bait fish, and a pod of dolphins swam parallel to the coast heading toward Mexico. His racing mind stopped. The bombardment of worries, fears, regrets, concerns, mistakes made, opportunities lost and an unknown future all faded away. All he felt was the cool ocean washing over him, his feet in the sand, the screeching of the gulls and the warmth of the sunbeams. For some period of time, his thoughts dissolved and all he became was consciousness. He was fully immersed in the aquatic world around him and nothing else.

And then, out of that completely relaxed state, came the thought of his mother. It was as if it was being plated up for him to digest. He felt the pain of his upbringing, the betrayal, the loss, hurt and anger. But then he remembered the picture of his mother holding his hand when he was little and he knew that was enough to let it all go. A wave hit him in the face with a slap. He deeply regretted his role in her death. It had been roiling below the surface of his consciousness. After a few more waves, the regrets and anger he harbored toward his mother and his role in her death were washed away, at least for now.

Thoughts of his friend Eric from the Teams, the madman Flores, the corrupt Detective Davidson, and the evil Sean O'Neal rose to the surface of his consciousness like rotten jellyfish. But again a wave rolled over him with bone-chilling crispness and began to wash those regrets and thoughts away, too. His body came alive, shivering and fighting the cold. As his thoughts receded, he became hyper-aware of the feel of the foamy water around him, the salty taste, the shivering in his chest. His regrets floated away like pieces of a broken raft drifting to shore.

The sun was now lower against the horizon, the heat of the day giving way to a winter chill. Jake had been in the water for nearly three hours. He knew the stages of hypothermia. He had passed through the stage where you feel warm and was now shivering uncontrollably, and yet he wasn't ready to get out of the cleansing, purifying ocean. Finally, he forced a thought of Hannah to the surface, like a dolphin breaching crystal blue waters. She was a thousand miles away and he knew he couldn't see her for at least six months. That seemed like an eternity of time and space. His heart broke as he thought of her alone, in her wheelchair, trying to make a new life without his help. Just then a wave smashed him in the chest, knocking him off his feet. He plunged to the bottom and came up just as another wave rolled over him. He dove again into the dark water and a feeling came to him, like a warm blanket against a cold surge, that he could just hold his breath and stay underwater until there was no more pain, no cold, no regret. His feet touched the bottom in the washing machine-like wave action and he knew he had work to do. He needed this separation, too. He had lost himself and now he was back in the world of reality, back to knowing who and what he was. He realized Hannah was right, he needed to learn to live again in his new skin before he could be good for anyone.

He pushed off the bottom and popped to the surface with a huge breath, turned and made his way back to the beach as the sun set against his back. A few beach fires were blazing in fire rings as Jake approached the shore in the dusk. He was beyond shivering, where hypothermia tried to trick him into feeling warm. His hands, feet and face were numb. He walked straight to the closest fire pit and stepped through the circle of people around it, stood next to the fire, and reached out his hands to the flames to get some feeling back. He felt his shivering slow down as he gazed at the six or seven young men around the fire pit in beach chairs with beer cans in their hands. He noticed each man had a buzz cut, a sunburnt face, rippling muscles and a look of determination on his face.

"What class are you guys in?" Jake asked, realizing they were BUD/s, or Basic Underwater Demolition students going through initial SEAL training.

"361," replied a tall one to his left.

"I was in 157," Jake said, turning back to face the fire.

The young men turned and looked at one another with wide eyes. Here was a gift in front of them from Neptune. A longtime Navy SEAL who could give them advice had just walked out of the ocean into their little campfire. The boys were desperate to make it through the hardest training in the US military and to know what they could expect if they were one of the few to make it to the SEAL Teams.

The tallest one stood up and moved closer to the fire next to Jake, then the rest stood and moved in around him, the flames dancing in their young faces as Jake looked at them across the blazing fire.

"What's the key to getting through training?" asked a short stocky young man on the other side of the fire. All eyes were glued on Jake.

"Gents," Jake began slowly, "The key to getting through training is to never quit."

He looked around at their astonished faces. "It's that simple. If you never quit, you'll make it," he said, gazing around the firepit at the best America had to offer, at the pure enthusiasm, drive and yes, patriotism of these young men.

Once the boys had pondered Jake's simple advice for a few minutes, one of them had the brass to ask, "Sir, can you tell us a story from your time in the SEAL Teams?"

The cold in Jake's heart and body had begun to melt away. He looked up at the ambitious young men and saw in their eager faces a little of himself and his SEAL teammates from so many years ago. "Lemme tell you about the time I landed a parachute on a high power line in the middle of the desert at night," he began.

The young men glanced at one another with awe in their eyes, crowded around the old Frogman and listened intently as Jake imparted his experiences to the next generation of American heroes. The fire dwindled, the stars shone brightly above and the waves rolled gently onto the shore, wiping clean the beach as it had done for millions of years, as Jake recalled everything from his life as a US Navy SEAL and did his best to impart nuggets of wisdom to these brave young men. It all came back to him now. It wasn't all good, but it was real and alive, a life, a series of experiences he could see, smell and taste in his mind, endless amazing people he had worked with. The veil finally lifted and he saw his whole life as a warrior in one beautiful arc.

"Sir, are you alright," one of the young men asked hesitantly, seeing Jake was staring off toward the ocean with tears in his eyes.

"'I'm good to go, guys. Let's go to Danny's and I'll buy you all a midnight hamburger," he said, turning to the young men with open arms and ushering them up the beach toward their destiny and his.

Epilogue

Jake parked the Beater under the shade of a row of tall palms in a neighborhood of mid-century homes near the beach in Oceanside. He glanced over at Daisy who was curled up in the front seat next to him like a big furry brown ball. Jake had adopted the three legged pittie after Donnelly went to prison. He'd worked with the local shelter in Montrose and paid to have her delivered to San Diego. Daisy sat up and looked out the windows, panting. Her huge mouth seemed like it was in a perpetual smile to Jake. Noticing that they were not at the dog park, she looked over at Jake as if to say, "Where are we?"

"You need to stay here girl." He reached over and scratched her little ears and rubbed her nose. "I'll be back in just a bit." He pulled a rawhide dog chew out of the glove box and gave it to her. She sniffed it then took it gently from his hand. These last few months with Daisy were as peaceful as Jake could remember. There was something in her slow gait that caused him to pay more attention to the world around him. Gaining his memory back with a full realization of who he really was and what he had experienced forced him to spend a lot of time thinking and tugging at his memories. He'd been seeing a specialist funded by the Navy SEAL Foundation twice a week, which had been super helpful.

He had found a studio apartment in Coronado, not much bigger that a walk-in closet really, but it was perfect for him, situated above a restaurant on Orange Avenue close to the beach. The Navy SEAL Foundation had also helped him obtain disability payments from the VA for his injuries. He took a short term job as a cook at the restaurant below his studio and the income from that along with his VA disability kept him and Daisy fed and out of the cold.

Like Hannah had suggested, he'd reconnected with the SEAL community. He looked up a couple of his old team mates, attended the UDT/SEAL reunion in San Diego and even went to the SEAL Training graduation for the new young SEALs he had met on the beach. He also reconnected with the Marines at Camp Pendleton. One of his friends who he went through corpsman school with was now the Command Master Chief at the hospital on Camp Pen. Jake had visited him a few times for coffee and they had enjoyed sharing recollections.

But most of Jake's time was spent thinking and reflecting, mostly on how he could be a better man. Anger and depression made up the two-headed hydra he fought every day. He had been trained to act with extreme violence, but he didn't want to let that genie out of the bottle anymore, except in the defense of the innocent. He wasn't sure of the cause of the depression: being away from Hannah, the loss of so many of his military brothers, some side effects of his brain injury or the lingering results of his abusive childhood. He scoured his mental landscape, looking for a path forward and that's when it came to him that he had to do something he dreaded, something he should have done a long time ago.

Jake stepped out of the car, closed the door gently and walked up the driveway towards a small single story home that was nearly hidden from the street by a massive hedge of red poinsettias. He walked slowly, deep in thought, rehearsing his words. He stopped at the door and ran his hands over his face. *I can do this.*

He pushed the doorbell and looked down at the figurine of a ceramic hula dancer standing in a patch of ice plant as if she was totally lost. The door opened and a large Hawaiian woman in a flowery muumuu looked at Jake, "How can I help you young man?" she said in a deep voice.

"Mrs. Luongo, I served with your son Tony."

"You...you must be Jake," she said, her voice cracking. "Tony told me all about you."

Jake nodded in acknowledgement and then bowed his head in shame. His best friend in the Marines, his running mate, the man who had traded his own life for Jake's, had asked him to do one important thing, and Jake had failed... but now he was here.

The woman's dark eyes narrowed for a moment, then she stepped forward and wrapped her large, soft arms around Jake and kissed him on his forehead. They both began to cry and Jake reached his arms up, returning the bear hug.

Acknowledgements

A famous author once wrote, "Editing is not rocket science, it's harder." I can attest to that based on the help I received from my editor Lisa Messinger. She caught every flaw and made the story so much clearer. We didn't agree on everything, but her advice has been invaluable.

My wife is a constant source of encouragement and drive. She kicks me in the tail when I need it and I can't thank her enough for the support and all the hard work she does behind the scenes to promote my books.

Lastly I want to recognize the law enforcement officers in our communities who put their lives on the line every day to keep us safe. I'm honored to call many of you my friends.

<u>*The Suicide Detective*</u>

Colorado Author's League Award winner for Amateur Sleuths 2025

A retired Navy SEAL haunted by survivor's guilt becomes an unlikely investigator into a string of veteran suicides. What begins as a personal mission turns into a deadly conspiracy no one saw coming. Gritty, emotional, unforgettable.

<u>**Black Dog Escape**</u>

Colorado Author's League Finalist for Thriller 2025

Navy SEAL Jack Thibideaux thought the enemy was behind him—until PTSD and betrayal threaten everything he has left. When a new mission offers a shot at redemption, Jack must fight through the darkness or be consumed by it.

Want more stories of courage, redemption, and the fight to come home?

Join WL Bach's reader community at wlbachauthor.comand be the first to hear about new releases, free giveaways, and behind-the-scenes stories from a Navy SEAL turned storyteller.

Scan or click on the QR code for a direct Amazon link to WL Bach's books or to leave a review.